THE
FORGOTTEN
WOMAN

Also by Angela Marsons

Detective Kim Stone series:

1. SILENT SCREAM
2. EVIL GAMES
3. LOST GIRLS
4. PLAY DEAD

Other books:

DEAR MOTHER
(originally self published as THE MIDDLE CHILD)

Angela MARSONS

THE FORGOTTEN WOMAN

bookouture

Published by Bookouture

An imprint of StoryFire Ltd.
23 Sussex Road, Ickenham, UB10 8PN
United Kingdom

www.bookouture.com

ISBN: 978-1-78681-044-1
eBook ISBN: 978-1-78681-043-4

This book is dedicated to my fantastic editor and treasured friend Keshini Naidoo who made sure that I did not become a forgotten woman.

CHAPTER 1

Kit

'Come on, girl, you can do this,' Kit chanted to herself as she attempted a shortcut around a backstreet to escape an icy wind. There's nothing to it, she told herself, I'll stand up, say my bit and that'll be it.

She felt no better and realised that a pep talk worked better if it included more than one person. Her jumping nerves were not soothed by the fact that she was not going to make her first meeting on time.

The shortcut led her to an alley where lurking fire escapes jumped out at her from the darkness. She was forced to retrace her steps to the main road. Great, that little caper had made her even later.

She pressed the button on a pedestrian crossing harshly, waiting for the red man to turn green. He wasn't quick enough so she darted across the road anyway. She was narrowly missed by a silver BMW that sped past, covering her back and legs in murky sludge left over from a brief snow storm.

'Bloody idiot!' she screamed, raising her middle finger. She chose to ignore the fact that she shouldn't have crossed.

The patchwork leather jacket prevented the cold water from seeping through into her T-shirt but the black canvas jeans absorbed it and clung damply to her legs. A furtive glance around told her that the embarrassment level was low: no one had seen.

The dark, open mouth of an underground passage loomed ahead. It didn't frighten her nearly as much as admitting her weaknesses to a group of fellow drinkers who would now think her incontinent as well. I know, she decided, I won't go. I'll walk around until the meeting has finished, go back to the hostel and tell Mark I'm cured. The thought appealed to her for little more than a second, until she realised that her action would mean that she was running away and lying to Mark. Her thoughts changed pace. Why the hell should it matter that he'd smile with understanding while trying to hide his disappointment? Why should she care that his earlier pride and encouragement had been a waste of time? He was nothing to her. It was his job anyway – he got paid to irritate her. The aggression faded as quickly as it had appeared. It did matter.

It wasn't exactly where she'd imagined herself at twenty-three; wading through used condoms and syringes in a subway, on her way to meet a group of strangers to bare her soul. There was just one problem; she'd sold it years ago to the devil himself.

The odour of stale urine invaded her nostrils as three youths came forward out of the darkness with cans of beer and lecherous expressions. Kit tensed slightly as she passed them. The crude catcalls started as she'd expected. They were unoriginal and nothing she hadn't heard before.

'Hello, darlin', come and put your mouth round this!' shouted a receding voice behind her.

If he'd been talking about the can of lager she might have considered it.

'Fire your bloody scriptwriter, you ignorant tosser!' she called back before picking up a speed that she maintained until she reached the safety of the street.

She shuddered with relief. At last a bit of life, a few crowds. Figures scurried hunched with heads down as protection against a wind that could freeze spit. Even at five minutes to seven the city centre was still buzzing with people leaving work.

A brightly lit wine bar mocked her from across the street. She closed down all of her senses; taste, smell, sight, she could even hear the brandy calling. She groaned audibly as she passed by with her head bent low.

Fifty yards before the entrance to the meeting place Kit spied a silver BMW parked beneath a street lamp. It looked suspiciously like the one that had almost reduced her to roadkill. A tiny red light flashed on the dashboard, which luckily she noticed just as she raised her foot in the direction of the driver's door. She peered inside, wondering what it was like to be in the front of one of those cars. She'd spent plenty of time in the back doing her job.

She took a deep breath before entering the building. The steep staircase, barely covered with a loose-fitting, threadbare carpet, did nothing to calm her churning stomach. She entered the smallest room on the top floor. The meeting had already begun and her attempt to join the sombre circle quietly was ruined by a loud screech as she pulled out a chair that had rubber missing from two legs.

Oh well, no chance of being teacher's pet now, she thought, sitting down as quietly as she could, just as the man beside her stood up.

'My name is Kevin and I've been sober for seven months.' Claps and cheers filled the room.

'My name is George and I've been sober for twelve months.' Enthusiastic claps, cheers and a lone whistle bounced back off the plasterboard walls.

This cannot be real, Kit grimaced as they worked around the ten people there. There were men in suits, men in casuals and suit men dressed in casuals. This has to be a low-budget movie, she thought as she realised it was her turn.

She stood abruptly. 'My name is Kit and I've been sober for…' she paused and checked her watch '…about thirty-five minutes.'

An unappreciative audience remained silent. 'Okay, okay, I'm sorry,' she apologised.

'Sit down, Kit,' Jack said, shaking his head. Kit sat and stopped listening. She hoped the humiliation was in her mind only.

Her long legs stretched lazily before her, crossed at the ankles in a position of forced nonchalance, bare arms folded across her breasts. The warm palms of her hands achieved little as they moved quickly over areas of goosebumps rising from her skin. Her body gave an involuntary shiver as a breeze of icy February air found its way through the wooden window frame and brushed past her bare neck. She wondered idly if she would receive another chastising glance from the group co-ordinator if she retrieved her jacket from the back of her chair to protect her from a room as warm as an Eskimo's attic. Nope, she was in enough trouble already.

When the pinstriped suit beside her clapped, she copied, throwing an occasional 'well done' in for good measure. Next came a cake complete with candles. Ooh, it's a birthday party. Yippee, jelly and ice cream all round, Kit cringed, until she realised it was for a middle-aged man with a ruddy expression who'd abstained for a year. Yeah, so what, she wondered, fighting back the envy. Dry for a year, if only.

She glanced at the redheaded woman opposite who even to her untrained eye was clad from head to toe in designer labels. The cream Armani jacket sat ramrod straight without touching the back of the chair as though supported by wooden stakes. Wouldn't want to get that nice, expensive jacket dirty, would we, Kit thought. Cold eyes stared right over Kit's head.

Her interest was piqued slightly as one man told how he'd been a doctor for twenty years after drinking continuously since medical school. It hadn't affected his work until he'd chosen to get help. Kit was surprised until she thought about it: alcohol had numbed the effects of her job too.

'Okay, that's enough for now. Refreshments over there,' Jack stated, motioning to an unvarnished table housing bottles of fruit juice and a stack of plastic cups. Kit didn't hesitate. Anxious to leave the orange plastic chair that had imprinted itself on her behind, she hated sitting for long periods. Her legs were long and demanded exercise.

She reached for the orange bottle – she could at least pretend there was gin in it. The telltale trembling returned as she tried to pour the juice into the feather-light cup that refused to stay upright against the force of the liquid.

'Shit,' she cursed as the table began to disappear beneath an orange blanket. She looked around for something to mop up the spillage as it seeped to the end of the table and trickled to the floor.

'Let me help,' murmured a strong female voice behind her. Kit's gaze met with the cool, slate grey eyes that belonged to the redhead.

'People have told me for years that I can't hold my drink. I guess I've just proved them right.'

A polite smile that held little warmth was the reply.

Kit sensed rather than heard a presence loom up behind her. Her heart jumped inside her chest. She didn't like anything behind her, it made her too vulnerable. She turned quickly, her body tense, but it was Jack, just Jack, the group co-ordinator. He registered her startled expression.

'Sorry if I made you jump. Just trying to help.'

Kit smiled shakily. She was being silly. She grabbed a cup of weak liquid from the table and stood against the metal radiator that kept her back safely against the wall.

She chastised the jumping nerves in her stomach, but it was too late. An unwanted vision of Banda charged into her mind.

His ebony face punctuated only by the absolute white of his eyes that held a manic glint that could travel the hundred miles that separated them and chill her blood to ice. Her memory filled in the detail of the shimmering blade in his hand. She shivered and forced the image away.

'Are you all right? You looked a little shaken.' Kit hadn't seen Jack approach from behind. 'I was only wondering why you were wet.'

She forced a smile, imprinting Jack's round, bearded face on top of Banda's. 'Some idiot in a flash car almost mowed me down and then attempted to drown me.'

'Which probably wouldn't happen if people used crossings properly,' said the redhead, who was standing four feet away. Kit wondered if she could taste the plums that lived in her mouth.

'Well, thanks for the shower and the heart condition,' Kit sniped, hardly able to believe that such a car had been carrying an alkie no better than her.

'Thank you for the hand gesture. Exactly what phrase would that be in sign language?'

'I was trying to tell you to fu—'

'Kit,' Jack warned, as the woman re-took her seat.

'What the hell is a woman like that doing here, and how many people did she sleep with to get that car?'

Jack shook his head.

'Inspiring surroundings, don't you think?' she remarked wryly at the drab paint that peeled in places from the wall. The stark emptiness punctuated only by an occasional suitably encouraging poster. The message was as outdated as the flared trousers and wide lapels of the individual smiling the heartening words. She'd been in rooms much like this one in London. The walls were the same, even the posters were similar, except those had warned against sexually transmitted diseases and encouraged contraception. She'd been escorted by Banda for her three-monthly check-ups to make sure she was clean. Even that indignity had to be observed by him after one of his girls had escaped by attacking the nurse and jumping from a second-floor window. Banda never made the same mistake twice.

'I bet he needed a stiff drink after seeing that haircut,' remarked Jack, following her eyes to the poster.

'Hmm, very *Saturday Night Feverish*,' she replied, pulling herself back from London. 'How the hell are we expected to bare our hearts and souls in a room that's like the inside of a fridge, but without the food?'

She wondered at the likely reaction of these people if she bared her soul. She could imagine the faint expressions of distaste if she revealed her hidden nightmares. Which would shock them most? The one that lived in a two-up, two-down terraced house in Liverpool, anonymous in a line that stretched for half a mile; or the terror in a London flat that she'd escaped less than three months ago.

Her hand softly touched the skin around her left eye. She had to remind herself that the bruises had gone but beneath the jeans a scar ran the entire width of her buttocks. It served as a permanent reminder. She would never forget.

Jack summoned them back to their seats. It was time for the twelve Twelve Steps to be repeated and discussed. As it was Kit's first night she was not expected to contribute too much, only observe. She noticed that Miss Fancy Pants said very little too. Kit listened while wondering idly if the AA principle was correct. Was alcoholism a disease of the spirit? And was spirit really a suitable word?

An audible sigh of relief filled the room as the words, 'See you at the next meeting,' left Jack's lips.

Kit was already reaching for the heavy jacket behind her. It would be some comfort during the walk back to the hostel in the cheek-numbing wind. She was out of the door and down the stairs while some of the others waited for a private word with Jack.

A coffee shop beckoned from across the road. She shrugged. Hell, why not make a night of it?

The cafe was spacious with American diner booths that aided privacy. Fifties music played quietly in the background. Waitresses tended tables dressed in rock'n'roll attire, down to the nylon scarves and thick belts.

Kit checked her back pocket. Three pounds was her total asset value yet she was about to blow two-thirds of that on a cappuccino. Sheer decadence.

'Let me get that for you,' said the news-reader voice of the redhead from across the road. Kit hadn't seen her approach.

'No thanks, I'm no charity case,' she snapped, handing over her money.

'I meant as an apology for our earlier altercation.'

Kit didn't even know what that was, but guessed she meant her attempt to get a breathing motif on the bonnet of her car.

'Nah, I'll just sue you instead,' she snapped, heading directly for a booth beneath a ceiling-mounted blow heater. She removed her coat and shuddered as the circulating warm air caressed her bare arms.

Shit, thought Kit as she saw the woman approaching her table. She wondered if the words 'misfit magnet' were stamped across her forehead.

'Mind if I join you?'

'Didn't realise I was coming apart,' Kit said.

'Frances, Frances Thornton,' the woman said, offering her hand.

'Kit Mason,' she replied, ignoring the outstretched hand, wishing this alcoholic would remain anonymous.

The woman removed her drink from the tray and returned it to its proper place. Kit's remained on the table. She sat at a perfect ninety-degree angle just as she had in the meeting. Christ, has she got a built-in spirit level or what? Kit wondered.

Frances leaned forward. 'That child by the counter is going to raise hell in a minute,' she stated confidently.

How utterly thrilling, Kit thought.

As if on cue, a huge shriek, followed by a loud sobbing tantrum, ensued. Frances looked satisfied.

'Got a crystal ball in there, have you?' asked Kit, nodding towards the Gucci handbag.

'I heard him wheedling and threatening for another piece of chocolate fudge cake. His dad was quietly telling him no as I walked past. It must be hard being a single parent.'

'You can't know that,' Kit snapped.

'How old do you think that little boy is?' Frances had to raise her voice over the increasingly dramatic squeals emanating from the small body.

Kit shrugged disinterestedly, wishing this stranger would just go. 'Dunno. Six or seven?'

'Exactly. No wedding ring. It's half term. It's nearly nine thirty and they're in an Americanised burger bar. He's with Daddy for the school holidays.'

'Well, I wish Daddy would shut him the hell up!' Kit exploded at the exact second the child ceased crying. She was rewarded with a chilly expression from the father as he led his son out of the door.

'Christ, there I go again! I only open my mouth to change feet. Thanks a lot, I'm thrilled you decided to sit by me,' Kit said, trying not to laugh.

The pursed lips turned slightly upwards into what Kit guessed must be a smile.

'You got any kids?' Kit asked, just for something to say.

The shutters on her face slammed shut. Kit decided there were two people in that body.

She shook her head. 'You?'

'I love kids but I'd struggle to eat a whole one,' Kit said with a straight face. 'Anyway, it's too many years until you can send 'em to the shop for fags.'

Kit had never really had a lot to do with children. She couldn't remember being one and they'd had no place in her life in London. She thought that maybe she would like to have a child one day but she had plenty of time. She wanted to become a whole person by then.

The muffled ringing of a mobile phone made them both jump. Frances scrambled in her bag. She pressed the answer button harshly. 'Hello,' she barked into the mouthpiece. Kit watched as her face closed up completely. 'No, Mother, I'm not at home… Yes, the case went well… Yes, Mother, we won… No, promotion hasn't been mentioned yet… I'm… s… so… ther… ad… li…' Frances said, waving the phone about. She switched it off and placed it back in her handbag.

'Nice trick,' Kit observed.

'Works every time. She keeps telling me to get a better phone.'

'You're a lawyer?' Kit asked suspiciously, eyeing the woman with bronze curls pulled so far back that her temples puckered with the strain.

Frances nodded confirmation. There was no pride in the movement. I should think not, thought Kit. The words 'scum of the earth' ran through her mind.

The hot liquid scalded Kit's mouth in her efforts to get out of the coffee shop. What the hell was she doing sitting here chewing the cud with a lawyer of all things? A tribe of people Kit would trust less than the Manson family. All lawyers were scum, feeding off other people's misery. As far as she was concerned they were no better than drug-pushers, and a lot less honest. Nope, you couldn't trust a lawyer as far as you could throw one.

The cup smashed back into the saucer as she grabbed her jacket and legged it.

The sight of the hostel loomed up ahead. She should have hated it but she didn't, purely because no strip search awaited her as she walked through the door. The anonymity of the busy road leading into the city centre thrilled her because no one knew her. Buses heaved and lorries trundled past, shaking the ground. She slowly walked the last fifty yards enjoying the sensation of cars speeding past her instead of drawing up alongside and winding down their windows.

The shrubbery and tall spindly trees that stood behind the knee-high wall welcomed her. Set amongst the numerous bed and breakfast establishments that lined either side of Hagley Road, it didn't look out of place.

A removal van thundered past. Kit looked at the retreating vehicle and found it strange that no matter how many possessions you accumulated during your life, it would always fit in one huge van. A whole life in a van. It occurred to her that the driver was probably on his way home to a wife who'd warmed a tin of tomato soup for him, like on the Heinz adverts. He'd walk in, hug his wife and peer around the bedroom door, checking that their two-point-four children were sleeping soundly. Someone, somewhere, was going to be pleased to see him once he'd parked his vehicle up for the night. Did those families really exist? Kit wondered. Or were they the fantasy of idealistic directors where immaculate, size 10 women washed, ironed, raised kids, worked and still had time to produce something home-made for tea. Who would direct a film of her childhood – Wes Craven perhaps?

She mounted two chipped stone steps that led to the front door and delved into her back pocket for the keys. The first door unlocked with the black-tabbed key. It closed behind her and locked automatically. She turned in the small foyer, causing the straw mat beneath her feet to swivel on the polished tiled floor. The second door also locked automatically with a reassuring click.

'Everything okay?' shouted Mark from the communal lounge that adjoined the hall.

She threw herself into a green easy chair opposite. 'Those people are so depressed.'

Mark raised his eyebrows.

'I haven't been drinking. Look…' She held out her hands. The trembling was obvious. 'See, I'd be steady as a rock if I had.'

'Any incidents on the way back?' he asked, folding his newspaper and removing his glasses.

She didn't like walking alone at night. He'd offered to meet her but she'd refused. These were her battles to fight.

'Yeah, three champion wrestlers threatened to rape and pillage me but I showed them a photo of you and they ran off screaming.'

Kit studied the telltale signs of the thirty-one years that lived around his eyes, adding a depth to his boyish face. He wasn't classically handsome but his features appeared to be set in deliberate concentration. His expression rarely relaxed but the azure eyes speared and rooted you to the spot. She had nearly laughed out loud when she'd first seen him. Her first thought had been, how in hell is this boy going to protect me? I have pimples older than him! That was before she'd sat and talked with him. He did protect her and made her feel safe. Even from that first night when they'd sat together in the kitchen, whispering, as he prepared a veritable feast of beans on toast.

'Well, do I have to forcibly extract an answer out of you – how was it?'

'It was nearly as exciting as Sunday school, but not quite,' she replied, looking away.

'Cut the act,' he ordered.

'It's bloody hard, okay! Is that what you want to hear? Sodding torture every single day that I can't have a goddamn drink.' Her eyes blazed at his probing. How much of her pain did he want? 'I go to sleep thinking about it. I wake up thinking about it. I dream of having a goddamn drink. Whisky, brandy, cough mixture, I don't give a shit what it is. Okay?'

'Incidentally, I'm opening up a swear box tomorrow. Why not give me all your money now?'

'Piss off!'

Mark laughed at the hostile tone.

'Are you ever off bloody duty?'

'Nope. What are the others like?'

Kit held her head in despair. 'Questions, questions, questions... For God's sake, can we talk about something other than me?'

'How about the weather?'

'How about *you*?'

Mark sat back in the chair, placing his feet on the teak coffee table. 'Ask away.'

'Why do you do this job?'

'Why not?' he shrugged.

'Do you ever get pissed off?'

'Should I?'

'Are you going to answer every question with a question?'

'Why, does it bother you?'

'Oh, get stuffed!' Kit laughed as the heat of the room permeated her body.

Mark puzzled her. As the 'house mother' she knew it was his job to remain perfectly balanced but the ease with which he related to her and the other four occupants surprised her. One thing she could never get from him was a reaction. Christ, she'd tried hard enough. Almost like a child tests its parents to see how far it can go. His permanent state of well-being convinced her he'd either had a full frontal lobotomy or he was on Valium.

'Mark, lift up your hair,' she asked.

'What?'

'Humour me.'

He lifted the untidy blond fringe, shaking his head.

'Okay, it's the Valium,' she stated raising herself from the seat. She bade him good night and climbed the stairs to the room that was similar in size and shape to the one in London. But this room was not threatening. Fear and humiliation didn't breathe inside the brickwork. This room had bright patterned wallpaper and curtains that didn't quite meet in the middle.

The bed was half of a bunk-bed set and suited Kit because it was small and nestled into the corner beneath the window. She always slept using only half of the undersize bed by lying on her right side, pushing her back and buttocks up against the coolness of the wall. Then she felt safe.

She sat at the dressing table and removed the harsh make-up that covered smooth white skin, and prepared to face the most torturous time of the day when the memories were harder to escape. During those dark hours when the whole world slept her mind would jump between Liverpool and London. Eventually she would fall asleep and dream. The two worlds would meet and become transposed. Banda's hate-formed features would vanish beneath the fleshy, slack chin of Bill. Then she would wake, crying and trembling and alone but for the occasional vehicle that rushed past, shining its headlights into her room. She would sit, afterwards, on the edge of her bed trying to force it all away but sometimes she tried to examine and understand the events that had conspired to bring her to her knees.

It was easier to keep the memories of Bill hidden. She'd had years of practice and the assistance of a mind-numbing, memory-reducing friend. Alcohol. She knew he was there, in her head, but for now he remained locked in a cell in the dungeons of her mind until it was safe to let him out, but Banda was another story. He would not rest until she was dead. She had committed the worst possible sin: she had escaped.

She quickly undressed and burrowed under the covers as though the fabric of the quilt would keep out the past. She wasn't there any more. Her hand reached under the pillow and felt the smooth hardness of her oldest possession, the flick-knife, which had accompanied her while she'd hitchhiked from Liverpool to London.

She instinctively reached for the reassuring coolness of the bottle. It wasn't there. It was in London with her money and eight years of her life. She craved the comfort it had given her nightly as she'd held it possessively close while the others had slept.

She remembered the feeling of well-being behind which she'd hidden. She could recall the spinning head and random thoughts that had been her friends. But then, unlike now, she had fallen into the spiralling depths of an alcohol-induced dreamless sleep. Now she had to wait for fatigue to come and claim her, guiding her into a hazy world where her legs were made of feathers and would not move fast enough when the ghosts chased her. She always woke just in time, unsure which one would have caught her first.

She lay with her eyes open wide, listening for unfamiliar sounds as the determination fought with despair. She seesawed between the aggressive conviction that she would have a better life where she wasn't controlled by fear or addiction and the tormenting, unrelenting terror that she would never be whole, that her past was so deeply ingrained into her skin, third-degree burns wouldn't cleanse her.

She quashed a rising swell of pride that was trying to take hold. She'd attended her first meeting and she wanted to be pleased. She wanted to feel good about her achievement but she couldn't. Pride always came before a fall.

So what, she told herself, you're still nothing more than an alcoholic with an attitude problem. That's what people see, and that's what you are. She was aware of her own aggression, knew it, protected it and honed it. Sometimes it tired her. Occasionally she would wish that she could drop her guard, just a little, to see who she was, but she couldn't. It was a wall built of bricks and mortar. The foundations were deep, supporting the first course that had been laid before she was ten years old…

CHAPTER 2

Kit

Katrina Mason sensed she was an unwelcome surprise to her devoutly Catholic mother, April, who had known from an early age what her life would be. She had expected nothing more than the two-bedroom terraced house that quickly filled with screaming babies. And she didn't complain when she got it. She was too tired to hug and kiss the dark-haired baby who was nothing like her three sisters either in looks or temperament, already anticipating the time when they would move on to their own lives, that would be just like hers.

Aware of her mother's lack of interest, her sisters' impatience and her father's fear, Kit continued to throw herself against the rocks that surrounded their emotions until a granite shell formed around her small body, signalling the acceptance of her exclusion.

As she grew older she spent less time inside the crowded house. Instead she chose to play with the other kids in the street, watched by some of the mothers who stood on the front steps of garden-less houses twittering like birds atop television aerials. The 'over the bridge' area of Vauxhall, separated by the Leeds and Liverpool canal, prided itself on its tight-knit community spirit but one by one apron-clad mothers whisked their dirty children inside as dusk fell. Kit hoped daily, as the long street darkened against night-time, that her mother would call her in. The other kids begged and pleaded with their mums, dads, older brothers for another five minutes while glaring enviously at Kit, whose curfew exceeded their own. One night, she sat on the stone step, entranced by the stars that winked at her from above. She didn't know what time it was that her father found her there as he returned from The Swan. She only knew that her mother hadn't called her in. Kit didn't really try to talk to her father. There was always something that needed his attention more urgently than her, like the daily paper or the racing results or a game of dominoes at the pub. She tried to understand why, on the rare occasions he looked at her, his eyes were almost wary.

On her ninth birthday, the family sat around the crowded kitchen table awaiting his return from the iron foundry, as they did every night. He would come in, place his dusty sandwich box on top of the fridge ready for April to prepare his sandwiches for the following day. Then he would sit down and inspect his dirt-filled fingernails as April placed a plate of food before him. Only when his blackened face had accepted the first mouthful were they allowed to start. No words passed between husband and wife. Kit thought it was like watching a mime show.

That night six o'clock came and went. Kit and her sisters continued to sit and stare at the empty place, then looked to each other for guidance. Kit knew it was Wednesday because the fried eggs were growing cold. She wanted him to hurry up home. She was eager to tell him about last night, about her dream where he'd come to her and whispered 'Get away from here' into her ear. She knew it must have been a dream because he never spoke directly to her in real life, but she wanted to ask if he'd dreamt it too.

Eventually they were told by their mother in a quiet voice to go to bed. Kit never saw her father again. She didn't really miss him. It was like being told you couldn't have chips for your tea – it was a shame, but no great loss.

Three weeks later, Kit watched her mother being led away to 'The Briars' after walking around the high street, shopping, in her dressing gown. Carol, at sixteen the eldest sister, looked after them, with regular visits from Mrs Jenkins from over the road. She cooked, cleaned, kept them clothed with the family allowance money and took them on two bus rides to see their mother.

The bus was hot and stuffy and Kit knew everyone was looking at them. She scrunched up her eyes and pursed her lips into what she thought was an intimidating stare back.

Carol called her father names and talked about poverty and starvation. Kit's fingers closed around her last humbug sweet, the one she'd been saving for the bus journey. She uncurled her fingers and left it, deep in her jacket pocket. They might need it later, she thought.

Kit entered The Briars with a handful of pictures produced at school, sure they would make her mum happy. The rolled-up paintings were carried with the protection reserved for a chocolate bar that was all her very own.

She didn't really understand what The Briars was – she only knew that she'd heard people in their street laugh about it. 'Stop acting like you've come from The Briars,' she'd heard Mrs O'Reilly say many times to her two noisy sons. The Briars had always been a place of ridicule and amusement in their street, and now her mum lived there.

The heavy, double doors were closed behind them. The turning of the locks made Kit want to run back outside into the sunshine. Were they locked in now? Did they have to stay? She'd ask Mum when they found her.

As they wandered further into the building Kit instinctively huddled behind her sisters, who began pointing and giggling at an old woman dancing alone in front of an unwatched television. Kit found that strange. If the television wasn't watched in their house it had to be turned off. Why didn't Mum tell them that?

Two men in pyjamas chased each other around a battered sofa with the middle cushion missing. There was laughter but it didn't sound like funny laughing and one of the men had something strange dangling out of a rip in his pyjamas. Frightened, Kit huddled closer as Carol spotted their mother. She too was wearing nightclothes and Kit wondered if it was nearly bedtime here. But it couldn't be, she'd only just had watery porridge.

She tried not to notice the smell that reminded her of Nanny Smith's outside toilet and wished that Carol hadn't worn a pair of Mum's high-heeled shoes. They echoed like thunder along the grey-walled corridors that had coloured lines painted on the floor.

Kit felt safer once she saw her mum sitting beside the window staring out. There was no need to be frightened now. She stood right in front of her and offered her the pictures. The hands that sat limply in her lap didn't move. Kit stared into her mum's eyes, which looked like her doll's at home.

She opened her mother's pliable fingers easily and put the pictures there. They slipped to the ground. Carol pushed her out of the way and stood on the discarded papers. Kit backed away and remained unnoticed.

The taunting at school started about her clothes. Having already been worn by three sisters plumper than her, they hung on her skinny body. The other kids made fun of the odd buttons and clumsy stitching borne of late-night repair work. Kit ached for a pair of trousers instead of the short skirts that she had to wear. She often she sat picking at the bobbles, caused by too many washes, in the hope that she could make the clothes look as new as Pamela Bate's. Kit sat behind her in class and stared longingly at the pretty slides and clips in her hair, which changed daily. She promised herself that she would have pretty things like that when she was older.

The insults grew worse when they were aimed at her mother. 'Yer mum's gone loopy,' they chanted at school. At first she was unsure what 'loopy' meant. Carol dismissed the trouble by telling her to ignore it, but once Kit realised they were calling her mum a crazy lady, she fought back.

The first fight she had, she got pounded. Her scalp stung where a handful of hair had been ripped from it. Her arms were scratched and covered with gravel holes where she'd been thrown to the ground. A graze covered half of her chin and a bruise circled her right eye. But she was determined not to cry. She walked home with trembling legs and a quivering lip. Carol would take care of her. Carol would wipe the blood that had dried between her nose and her mouth. Carol would tell her it wasn't true about their mum… Carol slapped her for fighting. Then Kit let the tears fall, but not before running upstairs to her bunk bed in the room that she shared with the others.

That night, amidst their chatting and laughing about things that did not concern her, Kit took the top blanket from her bed and tucked it under her sister's mattress above so that it fell down and enclosed her. She didn't want to listen even if they did speak to her.

Kit tried to remember which way she had faced the previous night. It mattered greatly. Mum coming back could depend on whether or not she slept with her head on the pillow or facing the wall, she was sure.

One night, three months later, she got it right. Mum did come home. And with her she brought a present: Uncle Bill.

Kit peered at him closely. She wasn't sure if it was the slightly stained shirt open to the waist exposing a flabby hairy stomach or his leg perched territorially over one side of the armchair or the tobacco stains evident on his teeth as he slowly and deliberately appraised and then grinned at her. She only knew that she didn't like him one little bit.

From what Kit saw he didn't do anything. He didn't work, he didn't cook and he didn't clean – he sat in the front room smoking cigarettes and drinking beer. Everything returned to normal, only now they said 'Bill' instead of 'Dad'. Her mother seemed pleased just to have a man in the house and remained as distant to Kit as ever.

By the time Kit moved to the 'big school' her sisters had all left home to marry at young ages with their mother's consent. On the first day of term Kit turned up for school in an ill-fitting 'free' school uniform and her fate was swiftly assured. Easily identified by the other girls, the teasing she'd hoped would stop ensured that within her first week she went home with torn clothes and a bloody nose. That was all the teachers needed to label her a troublemaker and ignore her presence in the classroom.

After obtaining a reputation for being tough, the only girls that came near her were the ones from the high-rise flats. Kit admired their school uniform of jeans and T-shirts. They chewed gum, smoked just outside the school playground and only went to lessons when they felt like it.

'Wanna go shopping tomorrow?' asked Tracey, a tall girl with cropped green hair.

'Sorry, money's tied up in trust funds,' she snapped with an attitude borne of loneliness.

Tracey nodded appreciatively. 'Yeah, mine too but what the fuck, we'll make our own fun,' she laughed, nudging one of the other girls.

Kit shrugged and agreed to meet them. What the hell, it was better than staying at home being ordered around by a lump of lard. And she liked the idea of walking around the shops with some friends. She liked the idea of having friends.

The high street heaved with people walking from shop to shop to get their weekly groceries. The girls barged and laughed their way into the one department store. Kit hid her surprise and wonder – that wouldn't be cool. She'd never set foot in it before. She'd had no need to and the pretty furnishings, clothes, shoes and jewellery excited her.

'Here we are,' said Tracey, pulling up alongside a selection of knives. Kit admired them. One in particular had a brown, oak handle with an Indian inscription running along it. 'Go on then,' Tracey whispered in her ear as the others milled around.

'Uh,' Kit mouthed, unsure what she was supposed to do.

'Emma's going to occupy that bloke so just put your hand in your pocket like this,' instructed Tracey, demonstrating how to position her hand so she could grab the item through the thin fabric of the jacket lining.

Kit looked around, sure that anyone watching them knew what was going on. It had never occurred to her that they were going to steal anything, but the more she looked at the knife the more she wanted it in her pocket. It was so pretty. Mixed with the fear was an undeniable excitement.

'Okay, now,' Tracey whispered urgently into her ear. Kit deftly retrieved the knife from the counter top and slid it beneath her jacket. She looked to Tracey for further instructions, feeling the need to run, and not stop.

Tracey turned around and sauntered towards the entrance. Kit followed. Each step nearer sent her heartbeat racing faster. Any second a security guard would tap her on the shoulder. One more step and she'd have to make the decision whether to run or be led away to jail. One more step and sirens would blare and bells would sound. One more step and she'd be outside.

The fresh air on her face felt like a release from prison. She'd done it and no matter how hard the guilt tried to take hold, the pure exhilaration beat it down.

'You did it, you're not a virgin any more!' cried Tracey, punching the air on Kit's behalf.

A shaky smile formed on her face. 'But what about—'

'If you're feeling bad, forget it. These places make more in a week than we'll see in our whole fucking lives. Anyway they expect theft. Keeps 'em on their toes and gives the plastic pigs a job.'

The following week Kit pinched a pair of jeans. It was the first item of clothing she'd ever had that her three sisters hadn't worn before her. She ran her hands across the rough denim and knew she'd never felt anything so good in her life.

The police visits that followed, a court appearance and an overnight stay in jail were met with the same response from April: a quiet shake of the head. Kit came to hate that weakness in her.

Two days before her fifteenth birthday she returned home from a day spent truanting to find a police car already outside her house.

Oh shit, she thought as she approached. What the fuck have I done now? She mentally checked the day's events. She and a few friends had headed to Stanley Docks. For a while they'd sat on the locks near to Howard Street Bridge sharing a couple of cigarettes. A bit later she'd won a competition to see who could throw stones and hit the most panes of glass in the fourteen-storey tobacco warehouse. As the bricks left her hand Kit vaguely remembered being told in class by an anal history teacher that when built in 1901 it had been the biggest building in the world. Personally, she was more proud of the fact that 2,000 of the 5,000 recorded deaths of cholera in 1849 had been in Vauxhall's Scotland Road area. Now that, she felt, was an achievement.

As soon as she opened the door she knew it wasn't her. There were two police officers and the female one smiled at her straight away. It was also strange that Bill was sitting at the kitchen table with his head bowed. How weird that he even knew where the kitchen was.

Kit didn't speak. She just looked from one to the other feeling the claustrophobia of so many people in the poky room.

'Sit down, dear,' the female police officer said, placing a reassuring hand on her shoulder. Kit shook it off.

The male constable cleared his throat. 'I'm afraid there's been an accident. It's your mother, she's…'

Dead. Her own mind finished the sentence as his words trailed away. She didn't move as they continued to wait for her response. She stared back. A quiet sobbing that came from Bill's lowered head was the only sound in the room. He continued to stare down at the table. Kit wanted to ask him if he was upset that he'd now have to fetch his own beer, but looking at the sympathetic eyes all fixed on her, she knew that was not the appropriate response. In fact, she didn't know what the appropriate response was. She merely nodded her understanding.

They both sighed and stole a quick glance at each other. Relieved, she guessed, that there'd been no hysterical crying, shouting or dramatic faints. Their expressions told her they thought she was in shock. Maybe she was because all the workings of her mind were not putting together the pieces of her mother's death – they were trying to remember the last conversation they'd had.

On the day of the funeral she didn't cry. She desperately wanted to, if only to ease the guilt, but it wasn't there. She glanced at her sisters, who grieved openly and comforted each other around their mother's casket. Back at the house she listened as they lamented the good times with their mother. Kit didn't remember any of it and wasn't totally convinced that the episodes they recalled had ever happened. At least not in the way they remembered.

She ate and drank nothing. Instead she sat in the corner and observed everything. She watched Bill's shaking hand reach for another glass of whisky. She saw each of her sisters ascribing sentimental value to anything worth more than a few pounds and she shook her head as she listened to the neighbours' talk about a woman she had never known. She wondered if the phrases 'salt of the earth' and 'good as gold' were wheeled out for every funeral they attended.

One by one her sisters left the house after the funeral, in the same order they had deserted her to start their own lives, muttering insincere platitudes as they went. 'You know where I am' had the undertone of 'But don't ever come there', while 'Take care' meant 'Do as you bloody well like'.

Kit knew that they had each left the house relieved. None of them had to take her with them. They had all agreed with the decision of the social worker who had visited the house to undertake an investigation as to her welfare. The woman conducted the in-depth examination over one cup of coffee, and decided that she should stay with Bill. She left without having once opened her genuine leather briefcase.

Mrs Jenkins was the last to go, taking the curled-up ham sandwiches with her, leaving Kit and Bill alone in the house they would now share. Kit only hoped that they could exist without meeting too often.

'Look, yer my kid now,' he grumbled, loosening a tie that was almost as wide as the Mersey.

'My dad will—'

'Ha, your dad's long gone so ya can forget that lark!'

Kit hadn't realised that she'd been secretly hoping for her father's return until the words left her mouth.

'So let's just try to get on, eh? It's what your ma would have wanted. I'll look after ya,' he said as his tie fell to the side, revealing buttons that strained under the pressure of his huge bulk. 'We've gotta get on, Kit, 'cos neither of us is going anywhere. What do you say?'

Kit was gobsmacked. Few direct addresses had ever come from Bill, she'd only felt his eyes follow her around the house. She nodded dumbly. He was right – she had nowhere else to go.

Shortly after he left for The Swan. Nothing interfered with his nightly visit, not even death, Kit thought and then stopped herself. Maybe she wasn't being fair. Maybe she should give him a chance. Neither of them had anyone any more and he'd lost someone who had actually shown him affection. She was judging him too soon. Perhaps she could treat this like a real home, somewhere she'd actually like to spend more than the eight hours she slept. They could eat their meals together and share the housework. He'd never actually done anything to harm her. Would he have been nicer if maybe she'd tried a little harder? She resolved that it was time to give him a chance.

Later, she was awoken by his cursing as he staggered in from The Swan. He knocked over a table and stumbled into furniture in his battle to find the temporarily absent light switch.

Kit snuggled further under the coarse blankets when she heard the familiar creaking of the ninth stair. She burrowed down and clenched her eyes shut tight. Even so she became aware of the shaft of light from the landing as her bedroom door opened. This had happened two nights earlier when he'd pulled her out of bed to fix him some supper.

It went dark again. She sighed with relief: her plan had worked. Then she heard his laboured breathing. She moved her head out slowly and opened her left eye. His huge frame blocked the light from the open doorway. Kit tried to keep her breathing even but she was sure her rapid heartbeat was lifting the covers. Something was different this time.

Unable to bear the pig-like grunting any longer she opened her eyes properly just in time to see the brightness behind him increase as his huge bulk came towards her. She pushed herself up into a sitting position, trying to read the expression in the yellowy whites of his eyes.

'Bill, wh—'

She was silenced. The breath was forced from her body as he launched himself on top of her. The sheer force of his weight threw her head back against the wall.

Her mind reeled against the rising nausea from the blow to her head. She began kicking and screaming as his intentions became obvious. He placed a coarse fleshy hand over her mouth as he undid his zip with his free hand.

His knee forced her legs apart. She gathered all the strength she could muster into her teeth and bit down on the flesh of his middle finger. He slapped her hard. Kit tried to position her left knee to ram him in the groin but he pre-empted it by placing himself right in between her legs as he prised them open. His fist was curled inside her mouth, forcing her jaws wide apart and preventing her from screaming. Her mouth filled with saliva that she couldn't swallow. Words and phrases thundered through her mind; words that had given her a small ounce of hope.

Let's just try to get on!

Her hands flailed wildly at his face, her eyes filled with murderous rage. He laughed out loud at her efforts before removing his fat middle finger from inside her to punch her left eye. The swelling was immediate and painful as the room spun around her.

Look, yer my kid now!

'Fucking bitch, keep still! You know you want it.' He breathed neat whisky fumes into her eyes, making them water.

I'll look after yer!

Sharp physical pain ripped her insides apart. She tried to move her head from side to side. The hot throbbing organ forcing her open wider.

It's what yer ma would have wanted!

She became still. Everything she'd done in her life so far was almost an acceptance of her present. The stealing, smoking, fighting, it was a way of survival in a place where she had no one. It was a way to get by until she could get out. This one thing, her virginity, had been held on to. It was a hope for the future, that some day she'd leave this place behind and take something of value with her to a new life. A gift. Almost a symbol of something inside her unhurt. And now it was gone.

She left her body and watched his obese behind thrusting in and out of her. Silently she observed as the movement intensified and then stopped completely. She watched as he lost control and urinated all over her. She didn't move. She didn't struggle. And she didn't cry.

The following evening she awaited Bill's return from the pub behind the front door, in the dark. As he entered the house she thrust a flick-knife at his balls. He froze in shock. Dressed from head to toe in black, only the whites of her eyes were visible.

'Empty your wallet,' she demanded without emotion.

'Fuck—'

'Without money I can't leave…' she stroked his fly with the sharp knife, totally in control '…and you'll have to sleep some time.'

His hands shook as he hurriedly extracted all the money from his wallet, which wasn't much.

She jabbed the knife once more before pushing past him out of the house.

That night Kit hitchhiked to London with a flick-knife in her pocket. Chester to Coventry tried it on. Coventry to Oxford didn't dare once he'd seen the manic expression in her eyes and Oxford to Soho left her alone.

Val spotted her in front of a hippy, tie-dyed clothes shop in Carnaby Street. She sat on the kerb, oblivious to the drug deals taking place behind her, of the group of youths, eager for a laugh, sizing her up from fifty feet away.

She wore black canvas jeans, T-shirt, patchwork leather jacket and looked right at home to the untrained eye. But Val's eye was trained – her life depended on it.

She could see the girl's uncertainty. She wasn't sure what to do next. It's so simple isn't it? Val thought, reading her mind. Go to London, get a job, find a place to live and leave the past behind. Forget all your problems.

So here she was in a city she didn't know, frightened by the noise and holding on tightly to something in her pocket. Val guessed it was a knife or weapon of some description.

She'd watched as the girl had walked for two hours in her efforts to find a quiet backstreet where she could sit and collect her random thoughts. Val had done that too. But each noisy street led on to another noisy street filled with grotesquely made-up men teetering along on absurdly high heels and wearing low-cut sequinned dresses.

Some of the shops started pulling down their shutters. Val wondered what she'd do now. Where would she sleep?

The girl stood and dusted the dirt from her behind and sent a withering glance in the direction of a youth moving towards her. Val guessed he was around eighteen. He continued to move in her direction. Val watched as her suspicions were confirmed and a knife appeared from inside her pocket. He retreated. Hmm nice, thought Val watching as the knife disappeared back into her jacket and her attention turned to the gold dust in her pocket. You'll need every penny of that, Val thought.

Val remained closely behind as she followed her to a chip shop, one of the few remaining shops with a light on. She bought the cheapest meal she could find and ate it greedily. There was nothing left inside the paper when she balled it up and placed it in a rubbish bin.

The crowds around Val were changing. There were still as many people but the female population had decreased. Gangs of men now littered the pavement, huddled. The occasional shout or laugh reached her as packets changed hands.

Val followed as she walked quickly through Regent Street, past the bright lights of the department stores. Her butt met concrete as she sat down in a doorway.

A police officer approached with a view to moving her along or taking her to the station as a runaway. It was time for Val to make her move.

'Oh Wendy, sorry I'm late. I missed my bus,' sighed Val breathlessly. She caught the girl's surprised expression, which she quickly hid from the police officer. 'Is there a problem here?' she asked, looking from one to the other.

'Do you know this girl?'

'Of course, she's a friend of mine. I told her to meet me here but I'm late,' she lied with ease.

He looked thoughtful for a moment. 'Don't I know you?'

'I don't think so,' Val said, shaking her head.

He looked her up and down, gave them both one more suspicious look and moved on.

'Who the fuck are you?' the girl exploded once the police officer was out of earshot.

'You're welcome,' Val replied, aware that the thin veil had slipped to reveal her own strong cockney accent.

'I didn't ask for your help.'

'I'll call him back then, shall I?'

A shake of the head. 'Does he know you?'

'Let's just say he would if I was wearing my work clothes.' She glanced at her watch. 'Which reminds me, I'd better be getting back. Got anywhere to stay?'

Another shake of the head but with more defiance, Val noticed.

'You can stay with me if you like,' she offered. 'By the way, I'm Val and if you're still suspicious I was just passing and thought you could do with a little help.'

'Thanks for that, but I'll manage on my own.'

'These streets aren't too friendly in the middle of the night,' she advised, giving her one more chance to accept the offer.

'I'll manage.'

'Suit yourself. See ya,' she said cheerfully as she walked away. Four strides later she turned. 'If you're gonna sleep rough, head for Cavendish Square. They haven't had a murder there for a couple of weeks now.'

Val was rewarded with an expression of horror on the girl's face accompanied by a few swift chews of her bottom lip before she continued to walk towards the corner of the street.

She waited for a few moments before taking a cursory glance back. The girl was looking at the street signs. Val nodded as the figure began walking in the direction of Cavendish Square.

It wasn't too busy at the moment, Val thought, following closely behind. She checked her watch, but in an hour's time, well…

One bench remained free and the girl approached it. Val shook her head, the kid had no idea. She spotted the owners of the bench before the girl did and moved closer, protected by the darkness.

'Move the fuck away, bitch!' the smaller one ordered.

'Huh…'

'That's ours,' said the first one, closely shadowed by another.

'What…'

'The bench, bitch. It's ours, so fuck off!'

'But I've got nowhere—'

He leaned in closer. Even Val could smell the stale urine and sweat. 'Do you want me to move ya?' he asked menacingly. 'Or you can stay if you'll suck…'

The girl jumped up from the bench and walked away quickly, checking behind her as she went. She stood beneath a lamp and pulled her jacket around her tighter.

A week, Val decided. The kid would need no longer than a week and then she'd be ready. The night was young yet. Everywhere the kid tried to settle she'd be threatened and assaulted. Later, the winos would be making their way back to their favourite haunts and others would turn up during the night. Even if she found a secure place, she would get no sleep for fear of having her clothes ripped from her body or her throat cut. The dealers would be around in roughly two hours plying their trade, first one free, second one cheap and before you knew it… Val shuddered. She knew exactly how that scene would play out – she herself had acted it out nine years earlier.

She slipped back into the shadows and made her way back to the flat to tell Banda there would soon be a new recruit.

For six days Kit managed to stay alive within the confines of Cavendish Square, the place to which she returned each night seeking small comfort in its familiarity. At least this set of drunks now knew her face and left her alone, and she also knew where to walk to avoid the discarded syringes and needles. The first night she'd been offered the stuff herself. She'd refused and edged away nervously, wishing she hadn't been too proud to accept the offer of help from the strange woman.

On the seventh day she was beaten and robbed. The last few coins in her pocket were taken by two men and one woman. It was unprovoked and it was unnecessary but it was tough shit – Kit knew that.

The frightening figure who had shoved her off the bench that first night watched as she was beaten and robbed and then offered his bottle to her. She took it gratefully and enjoyed the warmth both inside and out as the alcohol stole around her as comforting as a bear hug. He then cracked the empty bottle over her head, screaming maniacally that she'd stolen it. She began to run, drunk with dizziness caused by the blow to her head. He caught her easily in a side alley and beat her again. Finally, she heard his retreating footsteps fading along with his threats as he left her.

She didn't get up. She couldn't get up. It was safer to stay down and then maybe she'd just die. A comforting blackness was just descending when she heard an exclamation of horror. Hands clutched her arms as she was forced into a sitting position. Still she didn't open her eyes. If she opened them she'd be alive, and she didn't want to be.

An insistent voice kept asking if she could stand, but she ignored it. The presence was beside her now, on the uneven ground, still talking to her. Arms reached out and encased her. She didn't have the strength to pull away. She collapsed into what she thought must be a hug. Finally, she was being hugged.

She awoke in a bed looking into the face of the woman who had saved her from the police. She knew that her flesh was bruised, her skin had been torn in places and her joints felt like they'd been ripped from their sockets. But more importantly she was in a bed, in a room, and a friendly face was watching over her.

As she slept and healed she asked for only one thing, alcohol, which was brought to her by a man with a charcoal face that faded in and out of her dreams. Kit didn't know who he was and she didn't care.

They bathed her, dressed her, tended her, and fed her. It couldn't have been only a week that she'd spent on the streets. She felt like her whole life had happened in that time.

By the time she could walk her gratitude to these people was endless. She asked what she could do to repay their kindness and they told her. She'd been doing it ever since.

'Fifty quid, mate!' shouted Kit, leaning on the window glass, her black fishnet stockings more visible as she bent. Long shapely legs ended at a pert rounded bottom. As she leaned into the car the cherry red lace top fell away to reveal her cleavage.

'What are you… twenty-two… twenty-three?'

'Old enough for you, darlin',' she drawled, hardly able to remember her age, but he was close enough.

'Nah, you're about ten years too old for me, sweetheart!' He wound up the window, forcing Kit to stumble backwards.

'Sick bastard!' she shouted, walking back to where Val and Trish huddled for warmth. 'Pervert's into kids. Move over, Val.' Kit shoved Val from beneath the direct glare of the street lamp. At thirty-five it didn't do her any favours. She'd aged badly since the night nearly eight years earlier when she'd saved Kit's life.

'What you got?' Kit asked Val with a slight slur.

Val checked her pocket. 'Two hundred and thirty.'

Kit was confused: a trick was fifty quid.

'Last bastard said he only had thirty quid. So the wanker shafted me, then shafted me.'

'Come on, girls. The strip it is,' decided Kit, reaching into her tiny bag for the bell-shaped bottle of whisky. A top-up was needed. She was becoming lucid.

'Shit,' they said together.

'Got any better ideas? Val's seventy quid short. We can't go back with less than three hundred each. Banda will rip our fucking throats out, just for fun.'

They started walking. Val hardly ever made three hundred any more but Kit and Trish subsidised her to save them all from the beating they would get if she returned to the flat short.

They waited outside a particular strip club known for groups of teenagers on the piss. On cue three lads Kit guessed to be about seventeen staggered towards them, red-faced and unfocused.

'Fancy a blow job, lads?' offered Trish. They looked from one to the other as though they'd just seen Father Christmas.

'How much?' slurred the tallest.

'Tenner.'

Kit watched as they guffawed and nudged each other excitedly, pooling their money. They slid up an unlit alley. It was too dark to see anything but Kit performed mechanically with her eyes staring straight ahead. The smell of rotten food invaded her nostrils from the industrial waste bin her punter leaned against. He pulled roughly on her short hair, bringing tears to her eyes. She bit down on his penis. Recognising the signs Kit removed her mouth just in time. Val finished two seconds later.

'Come on, you fucking black bitch, do it!' screamed Trish's punter. His eyes darted between his friends. Kit could see his humiliation at being the last. His masculinity was offended. He slapped Trish hard. She fell sideways into a murky puddle.

Kit was on him in seconds, her flick-knife at his throat. 'Get out of here, you tosser, before I call your mummy!'

Val tended to Trish while Kit stood against the wall. She sighed and shook her head. It was time to do it all again.

'Good night, girls?' asked Banda as they walked into the flat. 'How about you, Val? Did you make it?'

'Yes… here,' she said shakily, handing over the creased notes. The others did the same. Banda looked from Trish to Kit, amusement dancing behind his soulless eyes. 'I knew you would,' he said, leaving Kit in no doubt that he knew what they'd done. 'Three-fifty from now on.'

'But—'

'But what, Val?' Banda turned on her. The amusement had left the eyes that speared her and dared her to argue. The black skin, like hardening tar, tensed slightly where it covered his jawbone.

'Umm… nothing,' Val stammered as Kit closed her eyes. She knew what was coming.

'Okay, girls, strip.'

They all began to slowly peel off their clothes. Down to the bare skin. Not for sex, Banda wasn't interested in sex with his girls, only control. The nightly ritual was to ensure that no money had been kept back. Kit's hand went instinctively to her watch strap as Banda came up behind her and poked a finger into every orifice in her body.

The grotesque masks that littered the room stared back at her. When she'd first seen them she'd assumed they were from some sort of carnival and they had looked quite harmless. That was before the night she came downstairs in the early hours to retrieve another bottle of vodka. He hadn't seen her standing in the doorway.

His back faced her in a room lit only by candles. The masks which normally hung from hooks around the room now sat on a table that she could see served as a type of altar. Their gaze held hers transfixed for a moment as the eyeless holes stared eerily at her. In front of the masks were three wax effigies that lay in tiny handcrafted coffins. She was frightened to breathe but she had to watch. Never in her life had she seen anything like it. An eerie presence filled the room. A presence that he welcomed and that she felt, and feared.

He held a piece of black cord about three feet in length, which he passed through the heat of a candle and the fragrance of an incense burner several times as he whispered words that she couldn't hear.

She watched transfixed as he began to tie knots at regular intervals in the cord and after each one he chanted in a voice that she didn't recognise. It was soft, but no less menacing. She listened carefully.

By the knot of one, the spell's begun.

He tied a knot in one end of the cord.

By the knot of two, it cometh true.

He tied a knot in the other end.

By the knot of three, thus it shall be.

He tied a knot in the middle.

By the knot of four, it's strengthened more.

Another knot.

By the knot of five, the spell shall thrive.

Another.

By the knot of six, this spell I fix.

Another.

By the knot of seven, the stars of heaven.

Another.

By the knot of eight, the hand of fate.

Another.

By the knot of nine, what's done is mine.

She watched as he tied one last knot and then once more passed the cord through the fragrance of the incense. Kit couldn't move as she watched him almost tenderly pick up one of the wax dolls. He retrieved a long dressmaker's pin from the altar and thrust it into the stomach of the doll.

Kit had to cover her mouth to stop the terror forming a scream. Unnoticed, she edged out of the door and trembled all the way back to her room, reliving what she had just seen. The effects of the alcohol had worn off completely; the fear inside caused her to stare unblinking at her bedroom door, holding her stomach protectively. Sleep did not come that night. Every minute that took her closer to daylight was a triumph.

Before six she was startled by moans that turned to screams. She ran into Val's room to find her clutching her abdomen, her face as white as the wax effigy still imprinted on Kit's brain. Banda materialised beside her and only Kit noticed the expression of triumph that curled up his fleshy, pink lips. From that day on Kit's fear of the man that didn't sleep had taken on a very real, sinister element.

'Okay, you're clean,' said Banda, disturbing her thoughts.

A quick wave of the hand signalled satisfaction with the results of the body search and that he was in control. They were dismissed. 'Wait, Kit,' he ordered.

He waited for the others to leave the room. 'On your knees, in repentance for Val,' he ordered while undoing his trouser zip. Kit knew what was coming, or rather who. She knelt down and performed as she always had to when Val stepped out of line. His eyes stared straight ahead and she knew he'd had enough only when he pushed her roughly away from him. 'Now apologise,' he said.

'Wh... what?'

'Apologise for being such a whore. Apologise for getting to your knees so easily. Apologise for what you are.'

Kit bowed her head. When did it stop? When did the humiliation end? How much more could she take?

'I'm sorry,' she murmured because she knew what would happen if she didn't. It would be Val's turn as it had been four years earlier when Kit ran away. She was gone for almost a month but he'd found her, working part-time stacking shelves in a supermarket and sharing digs with five other girls. He'd waited for her one night after work and a single blow to the head had rendered her unconscious.

Kit had braced herself for the beating that was about to come. And it did. A broken nose, two black eyes, a fractured cheekbone, cut ear, split lip and two broken ribs, only they weren't hers. They were Val's and she had to sit and watch every punch and kick, knowing it was her fault.

Val had never made a sound as the blows landed one after another. When it was over, it had been Kit's job to clean her up.

That was how Banda ran things. If they stepped out of line it was one of the others who got it. Banda knew everything. He understood that even though Val had brought her into this life they all had to make friends with someone. And inevitably, night after night, out on the street, it was with each other. Then came the loyalty. For yourself you could take the beating but if you ran away it was one of your friends who got it. It held them closer to Banda than glue.

'You're not working tomorrow night,' he stated as she waited to be dismissed.

Her breath caught and she felt the nausea begin to rise. There was only one reason why they didn't work.

'You're going scouting. I want fresh blood. Val's an old slag now and while you're wasting time down the strip subsidising her, you could be earning real money.'

Kit tensed. She'd always managed to avoid scouting. The thought of bringing a young girl into this sickened her – it was part of the punishment to keep her in line, she knew that.

'Some of my contacts are after young blood. And I mean young. Do you understand?'

Kit nodded and quickly left the room. She needed to vomit.

Banda's laughter followed her up the stairs.

Kit crawled into bed, wide awake. Just a little longer, just a little. If she could carry on just a little longer she might be able to get away. She listened carefully. No sound. She quickly removed her watch, revealing an indentation that circled her wrist where it had been pulled so tightly that the carefully folded notes beneath wouldn't be detected.

Feelings she'd never had before began darting around in her head. She knew she was nearly there. She had nearly enough money to get away. A few more weeks and she'd have enough to take Val. Soon, her life would begin. She would be able to go where no one knew her, start again. Every punter was taking her a little closer to freedom. She thought of the money rolled up, hidden painstakingly inside unused tampon applicators. It warmed her. She reached for the bottle that lived beside her bed – that warmed her too. She swigged greedily; she needed the comfort before she lay down to sleep. Without it the events of the day would run around like a virus in her blood. The drink helped her separate herself from the whore she had become.

She clutched the bottle possessively, drank it like orange juice and waited for the feeling of well-being, which she knew would inevitably be followed by sleep. Her spinning head and random thoughts were old friends.

A soft tapping at the door told Kit it was Val. She closed the door quietly behind her and sat next to Kit on the bed. Her eyes stared straight ahead.

'I was listening, you going scouting tomorrow?'

Kit tried to focus and reached for the light switch.

'No,' Val ordered. 'Leave it off.'

Kit pushed herself up in bed, the effects of the alcohol subsiding. Something was wrong.

'You have to leave,' Val told her quietly. 'Tonight.'

'I can't,' replied Kit. They both knew why.

Val turned to face her in the darkness.

'If you do what he asks tomorrow it will be the last step. Once you've scouted and secured your own fate for another, you'll never go back. The hatred inside will eat away at you. It's an act that will confirm to you that your soul is gone and every day you'll watch that girl and know she's here because of you. Trust me, Kit, I know.'

'But I can't leave yet,' she protested.

'Why, because of me?' Val spat. 'You're staying because of what he'll do to me. After it was me that brought you into this?'

'But I remember the last time—'

'That's not important now. The fact that you're willing to stay means there's hope for you, can't you see that?'

'But you're so close now to being retired. That's why I'm recruiting tomorrow.'

Val moved closer. 'What the fuck do you think retirement is, Kit? A two-bedroom flat and a pension? I'll be lucky to make it out of here alive and even if I do, where the hell am I going?'

'You could get a job, a place to live…' Kit tried to stop the emotion gathering in her throat.

'I'm a thirty-five-year-old drug addict with no money, no family and no skills. Where exactly am I going, Kit?'

The tears were falling openly down her face now. 'But he'll—'

'Let me worry about that. I'll be okay, but you have to go tonight. You *have* to.'

Kit nodded, her tears glistening from the street lamp that shone in from the pavement.

Val moved forward and pulled her close. Kit hugged her tightly, trying to push the sobs down.

'Look after yourself, kid, I'm sorry.' And then she was gone.

Kit dressed quickly. The drawer made the familiar grinding noise as it slid open. She felt inside for the box but it was gone. She searched again, urgently, the smile frozen on her terrified features. Beads of perspiration began forming on her forehead, the effects of the drink way behind her now. She was stone cold sober and no matter how hard she looked, the box wasn't there. Maniacally she pulled the few clothes out of the drawer. A slight noise in the dark caused her to glance behind, just in time to see the sharp, unforgiving piece of metal that came towards her, attached to Banda's hand.

Three days later she regained consciousness in a hospital bed and remembered. She had staggered on to the pavement, where a passing businessman had used his mobile phone to call an ambulance before he disappeared. Banda had watched from the window above as she bled from stab wounds on to the pavement.

As she was placed on a stretcher and carried into the ambulance her eyes travelled upwards and met those of Banda. He blew her a kiss: it was the kiss of death.

She wasn't expected to survive. Apart from the cuts and bruises that mottled her welted, swollen body, the two causes for concern were the amount of blood she'd lost from a deep cut that ran across her buttocks and a blow to the head which had cracked her skull in two places.

Social services were informed by a junior doctor pulling a forty-hour shift, who still believed in the system. He knew what she was and guessed it was the work of her pimp. Punters didn't go to this much trouble.

The first day she couldn't move and had no choice but to sit motionless and listen to a man in his early forties tell her he knew what she was going through. She stared at the ceiling and let him think what the hell he wanted just so long as he could get her away from here. He promised a rehab programme in Birmingham and so she said nothing.

On the third day when she could finally sit up he showed her a small item in the newspaper. It told the story of a blonde prostitute found dead near King's Cross. The report stated the cause as multiple stab wounds inflicted by a punter.

Val had known what Banda would do to her, Kit realised, as her heart wept. She wished her friend peace and knew, without question, that it wasn't over.

CHAPTER 3

Fran

Fran pulled away from the kerb slowly. A quick glance in the rear-view mirror told her that the insufferable woman, who bore a macabre resemblance to Morticia, had just faded into the darkness, where she belonged, judging by her appearance.

When the woman had first entered the meeting Fran had felt a little sorry for her obvious embarrassment. And although intrigued by the black-haired woman, the aggressive appearance had deterred her from making contact.

She was like an exotic puma, Fran thought. Dark and mysterious with limbs that moved effortlessly and carried her elegantly but with a demeanour poised for attack at the earliest opportunity. Like a shaken bottle of pop she was ready to explode if anyone was brave enough to open the top.

Fran was mortified when she realised she'd been driving the car that had almost run the woman over. That lasted for at least two seconds, or rather as long as it had taken for the awful woman to open her mouth, revealing a tongue sharper than secateurs. Fran had even, through a sense of decency, tried to make her peace at the coffee shop but bad manners and delinquent responses had been her reward. Hmm, civilised conversation indeed. Bad mistake, she'd realised before her first sip of espresso. Maybe I should have knocked her down when I had the opportunity. At least I'd have been doing the other members of the meeting a favour. Who on earth did the woman think she was to treat the whole subject as a joke? There was no room for humour in that place.

It was with a clear conscience that Fran put any feeling of culpability out of her mind and focused her thoughts on the meeting.

She recalled the words of Step One that she'd spoken with the others and yes she admitted she had been powerless over alcohol and that her life had become unmanageable. : 'She was sure that the judge, who had watched her pass out while defending an important case, would agree. The memory of the events that had followed, the total betrayal by her mother, had caused her to stumble over the words of Step Two.

She wouldn't, couldn't think about that now, not while she was driving – she made a conscious effort not to take her mother to the meetings. Her memories in that department were sure to send her crying and screaming to the nearest bar. She focused on a military cannon, loaded the cannonball and lit the fuse, blowing away the image of her mother.

As she entered the apartment building through the freshly painted plaster pillars that supported a deep green canopy she nodded curtly at the doorman. The pillars were painted every eight weeks which kept them up to standard but Fran felt the canopy was a little pretentious and the doorman's uniform a little too British. She often saw residents chatting with the portly chap and wondered what on earth they'd have to say to him. At Christmas she put twenty pounds into his collection but for her that was it.

From outside it probably looked like a community. Two residences only on each of the eight floors should have encouraged a cosy atmosphere. As far as she was aware none of the professional people living in the building knew each other. It was no more than a collection of dwellings but it had the right postcode.

The only evidence that the lift was moving came from the wrought-iron dial that turned like the hand of a clock against the arc of roman numerals. As she stepped from the carriage the keys were already in her trembling hand and the buttons of her ankle-length raincoat undone. She pulled across the two brass bolts and secured the deadlock behind her before placing the car keys on the grey marble fireplace as she did every night. She hated it when people complained about losing things. It was unnecessary.

Immediately she headed for the bathroom. Fran didn't use public bathrooms if she could possibly avoid it. The rule her mother had imposed when she was seven had been good training: no visits to the bathroom during the night. Her mother had called it an exercise in self-control and discipline and, although Fran had to admit it had caused her tears of discomfort as a child, the training served her well now. As usual she tore off the first two squares of velvet toilet tissue. Another habit formed from her younger years – 'One never knew whose hands had touched those two squares'. Although she was in her own home and knew who'd used the bathroom last, it was still an automatic response.

The frosted glass doors in her bedroom slid soundlessly along their runners to reveal a walk-in closet six-foot square. Her jacket was hung straight on to a blue satin hanger, the shirt on to the pink and the cream trouser suit on to the white. The high-heeled court shoes, which emphasised her five foot ten height, were placed in the vacant spot of the shoe rack that ran the entire length of the closet in the same colour-coded system as the clothes. That way she didn't need to search for matching outfits. The underwear was removed and placed immediately in the laundry basket.

White silk pyjamas were taken from a drawer that housed more than twenty pairs. Some had not been removed from the tissue wrapping. Once she'd found the item of nightwear that fitted her perfectly she bought numerous pairs in case they stopped manufacturing them, just to be safe.

The favourite part of her nightly ritual was saved until last. She released the wild curls that reached halfway down her back from the restrictive clips, grips and slides that held it in place throughout the day. Then she shook her head, allowing the hair to break free and breathe. Her long fingers massaged her scalp.

She removed her make-up expertly and without the aid of a mirror, choosing not to look at her reflection unless necessary. She couldn't see the beauty that other people referred to. She only saw extraordinarily high cheekbones and arched eyebrows that received no help from her. The eyes she thought passable and that was about it.

The perfect end to the day would have been a couple of glasses of Chardonnay, she thought wistfully as she filled the percolator jug. Although it had been quite some time since she'd been able to drink only two glasses. When did I cross the line? Fran asked herself for the hundredth time. When did a relaxing drink after work develop into an unbreakable habit? she wondered.

It hadn't just changed, she knew that. Each night it had just taken a few more sips to dull the craving emptiness in her stomach, head, heart. She wasn't even sure which void she'd been trying to fill now and even when breakfast had consisted of three glasses of vodka, convenient because of its lack of smell, she'd convinced herself this was normal behaviour.

Her first ever taste had been during a school trip to the Loire Valley. She and her school friends had listened with ill-concealed boredom as their teacher, a woman in her early thirties who taught French and thought herself French, had explained the process of fermentation. The fourteen-year-old girls had been uninterested in whether the soil, climate and weather had affected the grapes. They had rolled their eyes while observing the grapes being pressed gently so the juice was clear. They chuckled at words like 'cat's pee', 'quaffing' and 'dirty socks', deciding that the vocabulary for the trade was disgusting. And after hearing words like 'malolactic fermentation' they turned their attention to more important things, like French boys.

The wine tasting had come a little later as they'd watched experts tip the half-filled glasses towards a white background to determine colour, then swirl the liquid around before placing their noses in the tops of the glasses to take deep breaths. Only then would they take a sip, swishing it gently around their mouths while trying to suck in air, and then depositing the contents in a metal dish.

The girls had been instructed to follow suit but while Miss Parry had stood talking quite animatedly with one of the vineyard workers, they forgot the last step and it was seven drunken teenage girls being tucked up in bed that evening.

Fran had never felt anything like it. The joy that invaded every inch of her body surprised her. The other girls were suddenly her best ever friends, her soul mates. She could trust them with her life. But more than that, if she tried hard enough she knew she could fly. Nothing mattered. Her parents faded from her mind. There were no horrible questions like, why has she never held me? Why can't I remember one hug, one kiss? Why is every case they take more important than me?

Her heart, which growled like an empty tummy, was quiet for once and it felt good. The nausea and the headache the following morning had been worth it for the way she'd felt.

That was when it started, Fran knew. But she'd had a drink problem since she was sixteen, when she'd thought that maybe, at last, she would be given the opportunity to love someone. Someone of her very own. But God had taken that option from her when her baby's life was lost.

The clatter of glass against metal woke Fran from the memory as the coffee jug loosened itself from her fingers and slid into the sink. She fought the pain back into its cage like a quarrelsome tiger – it was easier to handle when it was behind bars but something still wanted to escape. A feeling, a tear. That was it, she wanted to cry, to grieve. She would not. It wouldn't bring him back. Nothing would change. Tears solved nothing. She'd still have papers in her briefcase to look over, she'd still have to meet her mother for dinner tomorrow and she'd still go to bed alone tonight. No, definitely no crying.

She decided against coffee and switched the kettle on. A cup of herbal tea might be more suitable. No caffeine if these were the thoughts terrorising her mind. The last thing she wanted was to lie in bed chewing on old bones. Her hand hesitated as she pondered the numerous sachets. She had camomile for relaxing the mind and body, valerian which reduced anxiety, peppermint for mental clarity, borage for depression and lime flowers for insomnia. Briefly she considered throwing in the whole lot.

The shower relaxed her while *La Bohème* played on the stereo. The cool fabric of the pyjamas soothed her scalded skin as she sipped on the camomile tea that was no substitute for a proper drink. She settled against monogrammed cushions with her legs folded beneath her and began to read. A droplet of water landed on the notes of a case she was currently building for a man charged with the physical abuse of his wife and child. The drips from her hair became more frequent. When Fran realised she was paying far too much attention to the pattern the drips formed on her notes she knew she wasn't in the mood.

After putting the papers aside she cupped her hands around the glass of hot tea, trying to remember her first case. She was defending a businessman whose conifer trees had grown so out of control that they obstructed the light of the old lady next door. Her kitchen was forced into total darkness at three in the afternoon. The frail woman was suing her client for mental anguish.

During the woman's testimony she complained that the co-
nifers did not obstruct his light at all. After forcing her to admit
that she'd been into his garden to have a look, Fran made it clear
she was uninvited and got the case thrown out for trespass. Her
earlier cases when she'd first left law school had not challenged
her but allowed her to earn her wings for the company where
she still worked. Gradually the cases had become harder, the clients wealthier and the fee higher. And still she hadn't lost a case.

The inside of a courtroom had not seen her for a while, the
partners choosing to keep her desk-bound until the gossip died
down. But soon, with the case she was now working on, she'd be
back and ready for a fight.

Once tucked under satin sheets Fran took out her faithful
diary. She entered the details of the day which when read back
appeared in bullet-point form, following the tidy, staccato tone
of her thoughts. She tried to force herself not to turn back the
pages, but it was useless. The impending monthly meeting, as
she referred to the dinner with her mother, forced her once more
to examine the woman's actions. As if by divine intervention she
turned right to the page.

Dear Diary,

I think this is my fifth day without a drink. It is also the day I found out
that I am not here by my own consent, and that I cannot leave until
SHE says so. I can barely remember the courtroom or the judge or
even the man I was defending against what charge. It's gone. Probably
a good thing. I can't remember how I got here but I know that it was
through HER.

A doctor with no emotion tells me that I am a danger to myself. I am
being encouraged to explore the person inside me. My biggest fear
remains; what if there's no one there?

Fran's eyes misted over. The fear and loneliness of that time stole around her like a shroud of choking grey fog. Those words she had written three months ago after being forcibly signed into the most exclusive rehabilitation clinic in London by her mother.

She'd read the words deliberately to bring back the events, searching for a missed memory that would convince her that her mother had done it with her best interests at heart. There were none. How she must have hated that I was drunk two days after leaving the clinic, Fran thought. Yet how pleased that I have otherwise become exactly what she designed – a cold, hard duplicate of herself.

She shook herself mentally and locked the diary away in the top drawer of her bedside cabinet, unsure exactly who it was being hidden from. Her parents never came here. No one ever came here. Yet still she locked the diary away.

She settled down to sleep and imagined countless sheep jumping fences in an effort to tire her lively mind. She finally realised it was fruitless when the same sheep began to reappear.

As usual, the night before the monthly meeting with her mother, she would not sleep.

Fran saw her mother's straight back in the customary navy blazer. The simple cut belied the expensive price tag that emphasised shoulders strong enough to take on the world, if necessary. The raven-black hair that never changed in length, colour or style, tucked under the strong determined chin. Fran didn't need her mother to turn around to know that the square features that termed her handsome rather than beautiful would be perfectly displayed. The cheekbones, ever high and haughty, would hold just the right shade of colour. Sharp features held just the right amount of hauteur to assure anyone who saw her that she was a formidable force. Fran secretly thought her mother embraced middle age, glorying in the respect she now commanded.

No cosmetic surgery for Alicia, unlike many of her friends who had been nipped and tucked so many times they wore expressions of eternal surprise. No jewellery was used to soften her image except the plain gold band on the left hand that now tapped impatiently beside a half measure of brandy. Fran silently congratulated Alicia on her tact.

'Mother,' she said more as a statement of fact than a greeting.

Alicia almost imperceptibly swept her gaze over Fran's slender figure as she always did, ensuring there was no weight gain. 'You're looking well, Frances.' She kissed the air to the side of Fran's cheek but skin did not meet skin at all. 'Your father wanted to come but he's working on an important case at the moment.'

The words were delivered matter-of-factly and brooked no argument. Fran had always known that work came first. She'd discovered that as a child when days or even weeks would pass without a glimpse of her parents as they worked jointly on their current caseload. She had invented stories that they were off saving rainforests in the Amazon or exploring uncharted territory in Africa – it was easier than believing they were in an office twenty miles away, making arguments for their clients.

Fran only wished her mother wouldn't always make it sound quite so acceptable. All her life these words had haunted her and she had been expected to accept without question the priorities of their lives. And she had. She recalled other absences – 'We can't attend the school play, dear, we're defending someone important.' It wasn't until Fran was older that she realised that these important people were drug importers, fraudsters and occasionally murderers.

As a couple they were very powerful people. They associated with high-ranking government officials, judges and diplomats, most of whom had required their services at some time or might do in the future.

'Frances, are you listening?'

'Umm, yes, of course,' replied Fran, feeling like a five-year-old all over again as she allowed the waiter to seat her.

'So, how is he?' her mother repeated with an edge to her voice. Alicia didn't expect to have to say anything twice.

Fran hadn't been listening but she knew to whom her mother referred. 'We're not together any more.' She wondered why a note of apology had crept into her voice.

'Oh, why not, what did you do?' Her voice echoed with the assumption that Tim had ended it.

'I broke it off.'

'Yes…?' Alicia wanted more information.

Fran realised she'd had opposing lawyers friendlier than her mother. 'That's it, it's just over,' she replied wearily.

'Why for goodness sake…' she paused to dismiss the waiter with a flick of the hand, '…he was a lovely boy. Good job, good prospects. What's wrong with you?'

'At thirty-one he was hardly a boy and there's nothing wrong with me.' Her foot began to twitch beneath the table, irritated by Alicia's words. 'I didn't love him,' she added as though further explanation was necessary.

Fran saw the dismissive look in her mind before it formed on her mother's face.

'Still a hopeless romantic at twenty-four.'

From anyone else the words could have been said with motherly indulgence but as the maternal instinct had been surgically removed from Alicia, they were a definite criticism.

'You may as well face it, Frances, you're not getting any younger. You need to settle down and have children.'

Again her mother's lack of tact amazed her. Her expression never changed. She'd just shot an Exocet missile at her daughter's heart and not a shadow crossed her face. Could she really have forgotten? Fran wondered. A lonely candle burned in her bedroom every year on his birthday. The eyes of her mother were blank, hard and cold. The memory wasn't there.

How could she have forgotten? Fran wondered as Alicia picked up the menu and perused the seafood section. She almost found the courage to ask but the waiter who had been dismissed earlier arrived at their table at the perfect moment.

The tightening jawbone of her mother caused Fran to shudder. Oh no, here we go, she thought, wondering if anyone would notice if she disappeared beneath the table with her mother's glass of brandy.

'Young man, did you see my hand raise to summon you or indicate in any way, shape or form that we were ready to order?'

Fran watched the poor waiter's fair hair produce a red curtain that fell, covering his whole face.

'I'm sorry, Madam, I—'

'If you feel the need to rush us out of here then I will insist on speaking to the manager to explain your conduct.'

'I'm… s… s…'

Fran closed her eyes. Stammering, stuttering and any other speech impediment irritated her mother to the point of paranoia.

'Don't make excuses! When I require your services you will be summoned to the table. Do I make myself clear?'

Afraid to speak, he nodded.

'You may go,' she dismissed him.

He went, quickly.

It occurred to Fran that her mother had been born much too late and in the wrong country. She should have been a southern matriarch before the American Civil War.

'Mother, was that really necessary?' asked Fran bravely.

'Don't be such a child, Frances. You were taught years ago how to treat service people.'

After talking about a recent case for a couple of moments and having made her point, the waiter was summoned by a slight nod.

Fran noticed how his hand shook slightly as he took their order of steamed clams. He narrowly missed another tongue-lashing through his hesitation when Alicia demanded confirmation that the house white was chilled to ten degrees.

Little conversation took place during the consumption of the perfectly cooked clams. Only when the steaming Turkish coffee arrived did Alicia speak again, disturbing Fran from the engaging aroma of the herbs mixed with dark, strong coffee.

'How are things at the office?'

What else could she have asked? As far as Alicia was concerned, if work was okay then life was perfect. Fran almost expected to receive an agenda the night before they were due to meet.

'It's fine, Mother,' she replied, aware that a headache was forming over her eyes. Eighteen-hour days, legal papers, appeals, twelve cases at once, the pressure of winning, no problem. One dinner with her mother and her head pounded like a jungle drum.

Fran checked her watch, eager to leave. From the moment she'd entered the restaurant, she had once again been reduced to the child that still craved approval from the formidable figure that was her mother. She wanted to shake off the infant that sat patiently waiting for any crumb of attention that fell her way. Why, after all these years, did this woman still hold such power over her?

After a perfunctory goodbye, where no pretentious effort was made at intimacy, Fran watched Alicia leave the restaurant and a question jumped into her mind: what would break first, the solid great wall or her? Fran left after seeking out the waiter to give him an extra generous tip and an apology.

The symptoms started in the car and she only prayed she would be home before her sight started to go. The sensation of her tongue thickening inside her shrinking mouth was the first indication of what was to come. Her breathing became hard and erratic and her hands were clamped around the steering wheel for dear life.

With effort she managed to enter the safety of her home before the shutters on her eyes came down. She felt her way to the kitchen, retrieved a carton of orange juice and started to pour it quickly into her mouth. Greedily she swallowed, forcing the liquid past her tongue. The shaking hands caused some of the contents to gush down over her jacket and shirt. Her fingers would not remove themselves from around the carton. Her breathing had become jerky and irregular as she made her way to the sofa, still clutching the juice. The pounding in her head banged in time with the thudding of her heart. She was afraid it might break through her breast and escape.

She sat in the darkness, the feeling of impending doom turning her stomach inside out while she waited for it to pass. She knew what it was: it was a panic attack. It was frightening and it was lonely.

And it only happened once a month.

CHAPTER 4

Fran

Fran's first memorable lesson from her parents was that a rational explanation should be offered for even the most childish wonderings. There were no moo-moos or tweet-tweets, only cows and birds. Signs, typed and laminated at her parents' office, were used to educate her around the house. The TV sat beneath a sign stating 'TELEVISION' followed by a red cross. Fran learned at an early age that the red cross meant she wasn't allowed to touch. She also learned that the only appropriate goals were what her parents termed 'achievable'.

As Fran was nearing her tenth birthday her favourite teacher called her mother in for a private word about her daughter's artistic ability.

'I have to say, Mrs Thornton, that your daughter shows an incredible amount of skill for her age. With the correct tuition this could be nurtured into a formidable talent. In all my years of teaching I have never seen this kind of expression in one so young. It really is quite remarkable.'

Fran sat on her fingers, trying to curb the excitement. Her mum would be so pleased that she could do something better than all the other children. Her mum would turn to her and smile, praise her for her pictures.

'Please tell me how you can see this in a clutch of childish drawings. They look nothing more than finger-painting exercises.'

Fran's legs became still. She was supposed to be happy.

Flustered, the teacher tried to make her point. 'Oh no, Mrs Thornton, they show far more than that. It is her use of colour and light and the imagination that she puts into—'

'So you're telling me that with the extra classes you're suggesting, my daughter will grow up to be a revered and prominent artist. That she will be the best.'

'Oh no, I couldn't possibly promise that at this stage but she could have a wonderful future.'

Alicia stood and smoothed her knee-length skirt. 'I assure you that she will have a wonderful future whichever route I choose for her, Miss Nightingale, and as you cannot promise that she won't starve in a garret in Paris I will not be taking you up on your offer.'

'But surely…' The teacher's words trailed off as the eyes stopped her dead.

'Second best is not acceptable. Do I make myself clear? Come along, Frances.'

The teacher swallowed and nodded as Fran trailed behind Alicia out of the classroom. She wanted to go back and say sorry that her mum had been so rude but Alicia was already storming towards the end of the corridor.

That night Fran's paints were removed without explanation. They simply disappeared. Three days later, in her search for the art equipment, Fran wandered into her father's study. It had always been out of bounds to a child that might disturb the controlled order of paperwork.

Her mouth gaped open at the rows of leather-bound books that stretched from the thick, plush carpet to the detailed coving at the high ceiling. She ran her hands lovingly over the cold, smooth leather bindings then quickly snatched them away. Her father might know that she'd touched them.

Her attention was caught by photograph albums on the fifth shelf. They were arranged methodically in date order, clearly labelled: who, where and when. By standing on her father's office chair on tiptoe she could stretch her slender body high enough to reach one that had her name on it. To remove any footprints she rubbed at the soft, cool leather with the hem of her nightdress.

She sat on the floor, her frilly white dressing gown splayed around her, gazing at images of herself in pretty dresses with gleaming red hair, sitting demurely at a photographer's studio. In every picture she was on her own.

Two short rings of the telephone disturbed her quiet concentration. Her heart leapt a beat – that meant her parents were on their way home. The call served as a signal to Mrs Thomas to be ready for their arrival, whatever the time.

Fran jumped to her feet, clambering back on to the chair to replace the album. In her haste the wheels of the chair rolled slightly, causing her to fall back against the bookcase. The movement disturbed other albums, which crashed down around her.

'Oh no, oh no, oh no!' she whispered while trying to gather them together.

As she struggled to lift two at the same time something swooped down from side to side through the air, like a feather. It landed beside her.

Mrs Thomas barged into the room, one curler dangling over her forehead, smelling of Fairy soap.

'What are you up to, child?' she asked, her voice fraught with panic. It lost some of its anxiety once she surveyed the limited damage. 'You know you're not allowed in here. You'll have me sacked.'

Fran covered the stray photo with her hand. 'I'm s… sorry.'

'Go on, upstairs with you, child! I'll sort this mess out and we'll say no more about it.'

She nodded gratefully, closing her hand over the photo, but she dared not tell Mrs Thomas about it. They'd never have time to find its home.

Once safely in bed she glanced again at the black and white print of a woman with long, unkempt hair. She examined the slightly familiar features that stared back at her with pure joy shining from the dark eyes. She hid it inside the back cover of *Bleak House*, where it remained, forgotten, until she was sixteen years old.

'But, Mother, I'd work just as hard if I went to a local school.'

'Frances, we have this argument every time you return for the holidays. It's a good school.'

'But I'd rather be here with you.'

'Nonsense,' Alicia sniffed, her jaw tightening at the open emotion. 'You're a young woman of fifteen. You should be making friends, the right friends,' she said pointedly.

'But, Mother—'

'No more, Frances. That school should be teaching you the discipline you obviously need. Your arguments are based on emotion, not reason.' Alicia held up her hand to signal the end of the discussion.

Fran stormed upstairs to pack. Reason, not emotion – had her mother forgotten she was at home and not in the courtroom?

For six weeks she'd done everything to be the model daughter. She'd worn her hair tied back tightly, worn designer slacks instead of jeans, walked slowly around the house just as her mother wished to prove that she was growing up and could be what Alicia wanted.

'All for nothing,' she stormed, throwing the navy blazers into her case. All she wanted was the opportunity to be a part of their lives. She slumped down into the cane chair beside her bed. What more could she do? She had tried to be everything her mother expected, yet it wasn't enough.

While her parents had spent the summer defending a very important client, whom Fran suspected was no less important than Jesus Christ himself, she had taken the time to catch up on reading, discovering a love of Tolstoy. More than once her hands had itched for a paintbrush or a pencil, often when images filled her head of the sumptuous ball gowns she had imagined while reading *Anna Karenina*, but the thought of Alicia's disapproving expression kept the pencils hidden in her school bag.

She kicked idly at the frilly covers overhanging the double bed. For some reason she longed to ruffle the bed, pull down the lemon canopy overhead, anything to disturb the quiet order of the bedroom.

For as long as she could remember the stuffed toys had sat on the ottoman at the bottom of her bed and the collection of china dolls were always placed just out of reach on top of her dressing table. If she'd wanted to hold one when she was younger she'd had to ask Mrs Thomas to reach one down. She glanced again at the stuffed toys that were not worn and ragged as they should have been. She'd never been allowed to get attached to one cuddly toy; they'd been replaced with a new, fresh model as soon as they showed any signs of love.

Frances picked up Pooh Bear from the ottoman and placed him on top of her pillow. She liked the homely look of him sitting there as though waiting for her next visit. For a few moments she sat back, listening for the sounds of home to take back to school with her. She tipped her head. Every house has its own noises, she thought, its own form of breathing. Strange sounds that are inexplicable but show that the house is alive. Only silence met her keen ears.

She carried her cases downstairs, aware that her mother would disapprove, and waited for Mr Thomas to carry out his perfunctory checks to the tyres and mirrors of the Mercedes. Her father was still at the office so there would be no goodbye from him and her mother had disappeared, as she always did when Fran was about to leave. When she was younger Fran had thought it was because she was tearful at watching her daughter leave; she now knew it was to avoid any open displays of emotion.

Fran took the opportunity to dart upstairs to grab *Bleak House*, a book she hadn't read for years. Her room felt suddenly different, alien already, yet she'd only left it ten minutes earlier. Something had changed. It wasn't until she was halfway to the train station that she realised: Pooh Bear had been placed promptly but definitively back on the ottoman.

'Hiya Fran, glad to be back?' asked Kerry, her best friend, roommate and the only person allowed to call her Fran.

'Remind me…' she said, eyeing the narrow single bed, desk and plywood wardrobe '…why exactly do our parents pay those big bucks?'

'In the name of education, my dear, but you forget, I'm on a scholarship. Nothing but my own excellent grey matter brought me into your sad, dreary existence,' she claimed dramatically.

Fran threw her pillow, hitting Kerry full in the face. 'Yes, imagine, if not I might have had someone decent to share a room with.'

'Quick, Fran, quick, quick, take it off!' Kerry shouted urgently.

'What?' Fran looked around her, startled.

'Your mother's voice.'

Fran scowled as Kerry wandered over to the mirror to check her lipstick.

'I do not sound like my mother,' she stated in a clipped voice that was exactly her mother's.

Kerry's reflection met her eyes. 'Not normally no, but every time you return from "Straitlace House" I have to mould you back into a real person and cut away the strings.' Kerry walked towards her, imitating a puppet.

'That's not true. I'm the same person wherever I am.'

'Yeah sure, anyway a few of us are going over the wall tonight. Are you up for it?'

'No, I need to catch up on some studying.'

'Please yourself. I'm off to give those lads hell.'

'Tart!' laughed Fran.

'And she's back, the Fran we all know and love. A round of applause, if you please.' Kerry spoke into the hairbrush.

Fran began to unpack as Kerry added mousse and then back-combed her hazel hair for more volume. She applied lip liner to a mouth far too sensual for a fifteen-year-old and clipped pink, spiral earrings on to her lobes. Fran worried about those earrings – one wrong turn and your throat was cut.

'Sure you won't change your mind?' she asked again.

'Nah, see you later, alligator.'

'In a while, crocodile,' Kerry replied in what had fast become a ritual.

Fran braced herself for the slamming of the door. Kerry didn't do anything quietly. She settled herself cross-legged on her bed with her biology material and remembered that Alicia had told her to ring the moment she arrived. Was it some latent concern for her safety? Fran doubted it. I'll let her wait a while, she decided, and continued to read the sections that she'd marked, chewing the end of her pencil.

What was Kerry doing? she wondered. Kissing boys, more perhaps? Was she being held, hugged? Fran recalled an incident when she was about seven. She'd run across the gravel drive, full of excitement about the ponies Mr Thomas had taken her to see. She fell, grazing her knee, causing a gravel rash. As what felt like hundreds of bricks entered the raw cut she cried out in pain. The tears were immediate as she ran inside to her mother, who was on the telephone in the White Room. She held up her hand to stop Fran entering while she finished the conversation.

Fran stood there with silent tears running down her cheeks as her knee and hand stung. Alicia replaced the receiver and moved towards her. Fran held out her arms ready to be pulled close.

Alicia stopped two feet away from her, remaining within the boundary of the White Room. 'Call Mrs Thomas to see to Frances,' she instructed Mr Thomas, who was breathless from running after her.

'She's in town—'

'Oh yes, of course,' Alicia stated, flustered.

She looked around for assistance. Knowing that Mr Thomas would not be able to help in such a situation, Alicia did the only thing she could.

'Mr Thomas, drive Frances to the hospital. It may need a stitch.'

Mr Thomas nodded and returned to the car. When her mother smiled, as though she'd solved a problem, and turned away, Fran followed Mr Thomas.

She sat on a stretcher while an elderly nurse tended her wounds, shaking her head every few seconds. Even Fran knew that her injuries didn't warrant a hospital visit. She returned home after tea and went straight to her room. All she'd wanted was a hug.

Fran realised how long she'd been studying only when she attempted to move from her cross-legged position to get a packet of crisps from her bedside cabinet. She shuffled like a hunched, stumbling wreck. As she tried to loosen the set muscles in her thighs she cursed. Finally upright, Fran made her way through the congregating crowds of schoolgirls who stood talking animatedly of foreign holidays and shopping trips. Having nothing to contribute she continued on her way to the communal phone points.

She was back in the dorm when Kerry returned.

'Oh my God! What happened here, World War Three?' she asked, surveying the strewn boxes and clothes that littered the room.

'I'll clean it up,' Fran sniffled from underneath a blanket of loose, unruly curls.

'Hey, hey, what's wrong?' Kerry asked, sitting beside her.

Fran struggled to find the words. The red-hot tongue of anger still coursed through her. 'They've gone.'

'Who? Where?'

'My parents, to the Caribbean,' cried Fran.

'Yeah, so?'

Fran turned her red swollen eyes on Kerry. 'I've just been home for six weeks. Every single day they've had to work, yet the day I return to school…'

'You didn't know?' Kerry asked incredulously. 'I'm sorry, Fran, I don't move in a world where people just up and go on exotic holidays. My parents know six months in advance about a week at Butlins.'

Fran shook her head. She'd had no idea.

'Ignore them. Parents were only invented as a character-building exercise for us teenagers. Imagine them thirty years from now when they'll be begging for the angina tablets and you'll take your time.'

Fran chuckled at the image.

'That's better. Now what you need, my dear, is to get out a bit more. The boys we met tonight were fun. Come tomorrow?' Kerry asked.

Fran opened her mouth to refuse the invitation, as she always did, but the words that came out were, 'Okay, I'll come.'

It was later, much later, after Kerry's deep breathing confirmed sleep, that Fran let the tears fall. She stared up at the high ceiling, visions of her parents jumping into a car ten minutes after she'd left, laughing at how gullible she was. She'd held the tears back while Kerry worked hard to keep her spirits high but she couldn't hold them any longer. The fact that their cases were packed, the tickets arranged and not one word to her. The tears slid silently from her eyes while she lay and made excuses for them. There had to be a reason; she just knew it.

By the time half term began to approach Fran knew she had a problem. She checked her diary. Her index finger shook as she physically counted off the days to be sure.

'Nine days. I was right the first time.' The diary dropped to the floor with a resounding thud.

'Don't panic, don't worry. Now let's think—'

'WHAT?' Fran screamed. 'I'm dead, twice!'

Kerry paced the room. 'First, we have to get it confirmed. We'll go to Boots and get a test.'

'Oh God, Oh God, Oh God!' Fran lamented, rocking to and fro, holding her stomach to keep the nausea down. 'What am I going to do?'

'Look, don't panic… you might just be late.'

Fran shook her head. 'I'm not, I can tell. I feel strange… sick. I just want to die and that choice won't be mine once my parents…'

'It may not have to get that far.'

'How am I going to hide it? What am I going to—'

'There are other options.'

The meaning of Kerry's words stilled her rocking. She shook her head vehemently.

Kerry let out a huge breath. 'You can't have it both ways. You don't want your parents to know yet I think they may become suspicious when you take it home for the holidays.'

'What have I done? I didn't even enjoy it,' Fran cried.

'I hardly think that's the point at this stage, do you?'

Fran remembered the night it happened. It could only have been one night. Justin had sneaked her into his dorm and she had known what was about to happen and she'd welcomed it. Sex had to include hugging. It just had to.

Justin had paid attention to her from that first night she'd gone with Kerry. He'd complimented her, made her laugh and held her hand. A few kisses and furtive gropes beneath layers of clothing to protect against the late October wind had failed to satisfy him or produce any response from her. In the silence of his dorm it had felt comfortable to have his arms around her. His skin had felt warm against hers. His kisses had been pleasant and undemanding. But when he had entered her it hurt more than she'd expected and only made her want to cry. She'd read about it in magazines but the few chaste kisses had not prepared her for the reality. A few seconds of pain followed by even less time humping and pumping had failed to bring her to even a moderate sweat. Fran had decided it was a cosmic joke that she was now part of. It hadn't made her feel any of the things she'd hoped for: no bond, no connection, no love.

Without warning, like a tropical storm the tears coursed down her cheeks. 'Kerry, I'm scared,' she whispered.

But Kerry had no soothing clichés to offer. For once she was stuck for words so she did all that she could: she held her friend while she cried.

Fran didn't need to face the agonising torture of telling her mother. That was done for her when she fainted during English Literature.

The revealing blood test and physical examination were nothing compared to the coldness she received from her mother. The situation was not discussed; no decision from Fran was necessary. It was taken totally out of her hands and decided by Alicia and the school headmistress.

'It's settled then. Frances will go to Inverness until it is over,' Alicia stated flatly.

Fran stroked the invisible mound that contained *it*. She didn't raise her head as her mother and Miss Milton discussed her. Instead she focused on a loose fibre protruding from the slate-grey carpet tiles that mirrored Miss Milton's complexion.

The cold emotionless voice continued. 'As I said before, I want no contact with any of the pupils at this school.'

'Have arrangements been made?' asked Miss Milton softly. Her concern was abruptly met.

'Don't concern yourself. It will be placed appropriately.'

'I meant for her schooling,' said Miss Milton abruptly.

'Yes, yes,' Alicia waved away the principal's concern. 'Her fees have been paid to the end of the year and I would hope that I can rely on your discretion even though I could not rely on your protection.'

'Of course,' replied Miss Milton sourly.

'Are you ready, Frances?'

'Y… yes… Mother.' Fran was startled. It was the first direct address she'd received from her mother since she'd arrived three days earlier.

'Then I suggest you go and collect your belongings.'

'Yes, Mother.'

'Oh, and Frances…'

She turned and faced the emotionless eyes that burned through her. '…Be sure not to leave ANYTHING behind.'

Fran closed the heavy, carved oak door behind her, understanding fully her mother's words.

'Is it time?' Kerry asked as Fran slowly opened the door.

She nodded. They sat together on Kerry's bed, staring at the suitcase by the door, both of them afraid to speak. 'Will you see it before it's taken?' Kerry whispered.

'No, Mother says it will be taken immediately.'

'God, Fran, I'm going to miss you so much!'

Fran sat beside her, letting herself be held by her best friend as they both cried, afraid to let go. It was then that Fran realised she was leaving home.

Kerry shoved a piece of paper into her hand. 'This is my address, write to me.'

Fran nodded blindly. 'How will I manage without you?'

'Don't, Fran, we'll see each other again when it's all over.' But the words sounded hollow. Fran knew they never would. Her mother would never allow her to carry forward any links to this shameful event. She disengaged herself from the embrace, unable to stand the pain any longer, and picked up the case.

Kerry stood. 'See you later, alligator.'

Fran forced a watery smile. 'In a while, crocodile,' she whispered, closing the door behind her.

Without once addressing Fran directly, Alicia instructed Mr Thomas to drive to the train station. Fran took her suitcase from the boot of the car and saved the tears until she was on the train, alone. Mrs Thomas could not be spared to go to Scotland with her – Alicia needed the housekeeper too much.

The woman ensconced in the small cottage could not have been a better choice as far as her mother was concerned, Fran quickly realised. As a devoutly Catholic spinster who had aged prematurely, she was perfect. Fran knew only that her name was Maria and that she'd been the resident nurse at a girls' school for over twenty years. She would have liked to form a friendship with the stern woman but she betrayed her moral superiority with the thin mouth and narrowed eyes set in a gaunt, worn face that mocked Fran every day. My, how the mighty have fallen, her expression said. Her obvious intolerance of the wealthy and their disregard for morals made the days very lonely.

It was hard to tell what day it was other than the weekly phone call from her mother. The ringing of the telephone jarred Fran from the seclusion she had found inside. She waited hopefully as Maria gave the weekly progress reports on her health, diet and appearance. Each week she wondered if her mother would ask to speak to her – she didn't.

It wasn't until the baby kicked that she finally thought of it as a life growing inside her. She was sitting by the river when it happened. Immediately she stood up. The movement filled her with an undeniable joy that she desperately wanted to share but her only companion was Maria so she sat back down and remained where she was with her hand placed protectively over her stomach.

Gradually she stopped seeing the bulge through her mother's eyes. No longer an embarrassment, an indiscretion from which she would return to a normal life, it was a baby, a child – *her* child. The feelings of warmth and protection that she'd felt at the very beginning of her pregnancy had been hidden behind the fear of her mother's disappointment and disapproval.

She talked to the child of everything, every day, almost like a diary. She decided it was a boy and named him Jamie, explaining to him that it was a temporary name, that his new parents would give him another.

She walked all day, climbing the tree-lined hills of the U-shaped valley in which the cottage stood. Each day she fell short of the previous day's resting-place as her stomach got bigger.

During the long walks she described the changing season to Jamie. The biting winds that were being replaced by chilly breezes. The softening of the frost and the rebirth of the trees. She described it daily in detail as though painting a picture for him. The thought of his new parents brought a gnawing ache to her heart, which she tried to banish in case he felt her sadness.

She was returning from a short night-time walk when she had the first pain. A warm stickiness crept down the inside of her thighs. Clutching her stomach, she stumbled to the cottage door.

'He's coming, Maria! My baby's coming,' she cried, breathlessly.

Maria made no attempt to help her and instead strode to the phone.

'She has started, her waters have broken,' she explained unemotionally. She nodded at whatever was being said on the other end of the phone then placed it back in the cradle without any salutation.

'They will leave in the morning. I am to make you comfortable.'

'What do you mean in the morning? Why not now?' Fran stormed hysterically. I need my mother, I need someone, she cried inside. I'm frightened. What if I die?

How could they just go back to bed knowing that molten spears of pain were searing through her body? Surely her mother could remember that. Who was going to help deliver him? What had she done to make them hate her so much?

A pain that felt like a lightning strike cut through her stomach and she screamed out. Maria busied herself in the kitchen while Fran placed a cushion between her teeth as a relief from the pain.

'Don't push,' were the only instructions given to her.

She lay for twelve hours drifting in and out of consciousness. The sweat that had poured from her matted the red curls together and welded them to her neck. Her jaws ached from the pressure of clamping them together.

Finally the sound of a car raised her hopes. They were here now, everything would be okay; the pain would stop.

At the last possible second Maria materialised beside her and began wiping her brow as though she'd been there all night.

Through the haze borne of pain and exhaustion Fran could see that they'd brought Doctor Treadwell, their family doctor.

Alicia stood over her. 'It's nearly over, Frances,' she said almost warmly. She made no effort to touch her daughter.

The doctor examined her and whispered a few words that Fran didn't hear.

'Mother,' she croaked as loudly as she could. She had to tell her mother her decision; she had to tell her now. It was important to get the words out.

Alicia moved closer.

'I want…' she swallowed in an attempt to moisten her throat '…I want to keep my baby. I want to keep Jamie, he's my…'

Alicia moved away quickly and whispered something to the doctor.

'This is for the pain,' he said without emotion as a long needle pierced the skin of her thigh. Within seconds the room spun and a black curtain descended over her eyes. She didn't know where it came from but she welcomed the peace it brought.

It was the soreness that woke her. Her whole body had been tortured. Cuts and bruises must be covering her skin, she thought, automatically reaching towards her stomach – a sterile dressing stretched across the width of it.

The motion brought Alicia to a sitting position.

It took a moment for Fran to remember what had happened. She lay back down when her head threatened to spin so hard it felt like it might disengage from her shoulders and whirl off into the distance.

'You're awake,' Alicia stated.

'Where is he?' Fran croaked, listening for his cries. In spite of the pain and soreness that consumed her body, her arms needed something to do. They knew they should be holding something.

'Where is he?' she asked again with a little more strength.

'Try to rest, Frances. Drink some water.'

The glass shook slightly as it came towards her. Something was wrong, she knew it.

The glass fell between them as Fran made no attempt to grasp it.

'Mother, where *is* he? Where's my son?' she screamed.

Alicia shook her head sadly. 'I'm sorry, Frances. He's dead.'

Fran stared at her mother's face, bored into her eyes, waiting for the punchline. Any minute now the doctor would appear, place a blanketed bundle in her arms and congratulate her on a bouncing, healthy baby boy.

Her mother's set expression told her that it was not going to happen.

She'd never grieved for anything in her life. Not a dog, hamster, nothing. She wasn't prepared for this: to grieve for her own child. No, this was sick, it was wrong. It couldn't be happening. Maybe she hadn't woken up yet. This could be a nightmare, but as she looked at Maria's slightly hunched back in the kitchen she knew it wasn't.

This was a pain she couldn't bear. It ripped at a part of her so deep she didn't even know it existed. The physical pain could have been no worse had they ripped out one of her kidneys but at least that she could have lived without.

Fran made no move as her mother left her to rest for a few days before Mr Thomas drove up to collect her.

'We'll talk about school when you get back,' Alicia said as she closed the door behind her.

Fran stared at the wooden door. Fuck school, who cared? She wouldn't go back to school. Who could even think about school? She'd lost everything. She'd lost her hope, love, future, everything and her mother was concerned about school.

Maria waited for the sound of the car to disappear completely. 'Here, drink this,' she offered, her voice a couple of degrees above freezing.

Fran took the glass and sipped, guessing it was brandy. She drank it greedily and welcomed the rush to her head. At nine o'clock Maria said goodnight for the first time since she'd arrived and mounted the timber steps.

Fran struggled to the kitchen and found what she was looking for: the brandy. She drank from the bottle, standing in the
kitchen, her bare feet oblivious to the cold stone tiles. The pain
had to stop. If it didn't, she would die from it. The liquid burned
her throat and made her choke but the bottle remained glued to
her mouth. She felt the moisture on her cheeks; she didn't know
if it was the brandy, saliva or tears and she didn't care.

Her son was gone. Jamie was dead, and now, so was she.

The day she returned from Scotland Fran cleared out her room. The
stuffed toys were placed in disposal bags and her early drawings,
sketches and paintings ripped into shreds. Her books were catego-
rised into childhood and adulthood. Only one book caused her to
pause: *Bleak House*. She turned it over and flicked through the pages.
A creased photograph fell on to her lap. For a moment she studied
it and recalled the day she'd found it. She still had no idea who the
woman was and if she was completely honest, she didn't care. She
placed the photograph and the book back on the second shelf beside
Madame Bovary. The childhood books were put into the bin.

She removed the flowery quilt cover from the bed together
with the scarf that had draped fashionably over her lamp, giving
the room a warm glow. Her walls were stripped of anything not
connected with academic achievements and her drawers emptied of items she no longer needed.

She instructed Mrs Thomas that she wanted everything
white: new sheets, pillow slips, everything. She also informed
her mother that she wished her room to be painted white. The
existing pastel shades prompted emotional responses, reflec-
tions, hopes and dreams. White demanded nothing.

Fran watched as the occupants of the house went calmly
about their business as though nothing had changed. But ev-

erything had changed. Everything was gone, but for them everything remained the same. The familiar crunching of BMWs, Mercedes and Bentleys on the gravel drive, the dinner parties, the featureless cotton napkins, the conversations about law, the subscriptions to the 'fashionable' charities, the choice of which always seemed to be set by her mother. And Fran's exclusion from the whole thing.

One night, in an effort to learn anything about her mother, Fran sat in the hallway just outside the partially closed double doors listening to her parents' laughter. They gave wonderful parties, everyone said so, and she enjoyed the gaiety that met her ears. It was like listening to another woman. It wasn't the mother that ate occasionally at that table with her discussing exams, achievements, targets and goals. It wasn't the wife that dined there with her husband speaking seriously but animatedly of loopholes in the law and case studies. It was a third Alicia that was light, amusing, even entertaining. That was until her tone became uncompromisingly harsh as she loudly berated Mr Thomas for not turning the wine bottle as he poured, spilling a drop of red wine on the antique tablecloth.

Realising that the mother she knew so well was there, but thinly veiled, Fran shook her head and sought Mrs Thomas in the kitchen.

'About time, child. I was thinking I might have to throw this casserole away.'

'I'm not hungry, thank you, Mrs Thomas. I'll just sit here a while.'

Mr Thomas entered the kitchen with cheeks the colour of the wine he was holding. 'That damned woman—'

Fran realised he hadn't seen her sitting there. The colour in his cheeks deepened as he noticed her.

'I know, Mrs Forbes-Grant is horrible, isn't she?' said Fran, easing his discomfort.

He smiled gratefully as he left the kitchen with another bottle of wine.

Fran no longer had anything left to talk about with Mrs Thomas. Meal times in the kitchen had been her opportunity to discuss school but she hadn't been for over six months so that topic was out, as well as what had happened in the last six months.

Her father's concerned question, 'Are you better now, dear?' had set the precedent to be followed. It had been an illness, an interlude from which she was now expected to return unchanged and unharmed. The subject would not be discussed.

Fran offered to clear the last few things away for Mrs Thomas, insisting she go to bed. Reluctantly the housekeeper left the kitchen. Ten minutes later Fran was in her room, clutching a bottle of white wine possessively.

It occurred to her as she drank the last mouthful that she'd finally got what she'd always wanted: she was to complete her A-levels at home. Be careful what you wish for, she thought in a drunken haze, because you might just get it.

'Hmm, not bad,' stated Alicia, reading Fran's exam results.

Not bad, not bad? she thought angrily. Top marks and she's mildly pleased. What more could I have done, achieved world peace in my free study periods?

'Your father will be pleased,' she said, pushing the paper across the coffee table to her.

And what about you, Mother, are *you* pleased? she thought, angrily.

'What career did you have in mind?'

'Maybe something creative,' Fran said, hopefully.

'No, dear, too unstable.'

'Maybe something to do with travel?'

'Too common.'

'Working with underprivileged children?'

'Too depressing.'

'Hospital work?'

'Too gruesome.'

'A lawyer,' she said, resigned.

'Very good idea, Frances.'

At her mother's insistence she applied to Oxford and Cambridge. She submitted a third application that she didn't mention and was accepted by all three.

'So, Cambridge it is,' stated her father.

'I think I'd prefer the University of Wales,' Fran offered meekly.

It was further away and although she knew that the geography wouldn't solve her problems, it might help.

A look of horror crossed her mother's face. '*Wales?*'

'Frances, your mother has always hoped that you would follow in her footsteps and receive your education at Cambridge.'

The words from her father were unnatural. His opinion was rarely given and even more rarely asked for. Fran looked from one to the other, praying for one of them to be on her side for once. She buckled under the weight of their unanimous disapproval.

'Okay, Cambridge it is,' she conceded.

She didn't enjoy college life. The process of learning she thrived on but she shied away from the camaraderie and team spirit of her three roommates. She thought about her parents often though months would pass without a telephone call either way but through the blue-blood network her mother was informed that Fran was no fun at all, choosing to remain in the dorm studying every available minute. To see her face without a law book in front of it was a rare occurrence. Fran was aware of these progress reports and guessed that Alicia would not be displeased with what she was hearing.

At the beginning of her second year Fran found a part-time job clerking for a small firm of solicitors employing no more than five staff. Her clerking included coffee-making, breakfast-fetching and just about anything that no one else wanted to do. Her colleagues thought her rather unsociable and withdrawn but she made good coffee. Fran did as she was instructed without question just as long as she received her pay packet each week.

The weekly pittance she received enabled her to move out of the dorm into a studio flat that would have given her mother palpitations. Everything was crammed into one room with no obvious border marking the end of the living room, bedroom or kitchen. A thin grey wall covering had been placed on top of a darker, bolder wallpaper so the bawdy flowers showed through. In total it was smaller than her bedroom back home, but even if the dust that lay forgotten in the corners and the old, cheap furniture offended her sense of style and taste, the solitude compensated for it.

Gone were the in-depth discussions on hair, cosmetics and electronic tweezing appliances and her half-hearted attempts to appear interested. She no longer had to pretend. She didn't believe in the solidarity of her peers; she believed only in reaching her target as quickly as possible. If she got lonely, she read a book.

The lecturers and tutors showed their pride in her. She excelled in every area and could cite at least three cases to prove an argument.

During her final year, she and her fellow students were taken to a courtroom to plead a theoretical case. The court was real, the female judge was real and on the first day, Fran was the prosecution.

She approached the jury and leaned on the wooden panel separating them. Her casual cream slacks and matching silk shirt, with the top button open at the collar ensured that she looked exactly as she'd intended: smart but relaxed. She looked around and sighed.

'Ladies and gentlemen, I'm sure you're all wishing you were somewhere else at the moment, either at work, home, on holiday. I certainly wish I was,' she smiled.

A few of the jurors smiled back.

'I had a whole speech prepared for you today but quite frankly I threw it in the bin…'

They watched her with interest.

'After looking at you, at your attentive expressions, I questioned myself, "Who am I to treat these people like idiots and spell out the details of this case?" You're not children. You are educated, intelligent people who can be trusted to follow the intricate details as they emerge. Also, I am not here to bore you.'

They chuckled appreciatively.

Fran smiled engagingly at them. 'Please try not to see this as an infringement on your time. Quite frankly I'd rather be somewhere else at the moment too, but I hope you will realise the importance of your job here today. It is an opportunity for you to see that justice is done. Your chance to witness that the law is your friend. That it is not *above* you, practised only by wealthy, over-educated people, but *by* you, the real people. Please take pride in your task here today. I thank you for your time, ladies and gentlemen.'

The jurors were rewarded with a friendly smile as she re-took her seat. She was one of them. The feathers had been visibly puffed and the solemn, bored demeanours replaced with proud, straight postures.

Fran was rewarded with a sour look from the defender, who had no choice but to outline the technical aspects of the case, which gave the jury the impression he thought them stupid. Had he tried the same approach as Fran the jury would have thought him unoriginal. She sat and stared forward, feeling the vibrations of the jury's impatience and boredom: the case was hers.

The second day she was defence. She watched as one of her classmates, who was confident to the point of arrogance, repeated her speech from the previous day word for word. He relaxed the jury to the point of lethargy. With a smug look on his face he re-took his seat.

Fran approached the jury, smoothing down her double-breasted jacket, bringing attention to her appearance, which contrasted with his. The top button of her shirt was fastened and her hair pulled back into a neat bun.

'How dare Mr Miller treat the law as though it were a joke? By his very decision not to present any facts to you he is contradicting himself and treating you like children or imbeciles.'

Members of the jury began to straighten in their seats. The judge sat forward with an interested smile.

'I will present the facts of the case in my capacity as defence counsel with the knowledge that these details will be heard and understood with the clarity of mind that I'm sure you all possess.'

She sent a withering glance in the general direction of the prosecutor that told the jury she thought him incapable of practising law.

Norman Miller then presented a perfect case. She searched the papers on her desk. There had to be a flaw; it was finding it. Her client had attacked and mugged an eighty-eight-year-old woman. The prosecution's witness was a priest so there would be no joy there. She couldn't find one possible way to defend him, yet she knew it had to exist. That was the rule: the defence may be obscure, but it was there.

It occurred to Fran that there was a similar case receiving high media attention at the moment: a youth, like her client, had mugged an old lady for about seven pounds.

An idea started to form. She checked the jury papers and found what she was looking for. Her eyes perused the members of the jury and one face held her: a man with shoulder-length curly hair in his mid-thirties whose expression held a quiet confidence whenever he looked at her. She studied him at length. His expression never changed. He had a secret and she now had her defence.

'The prosecution rests, Your Honour,' said Norman Miller.

The judge nodded, satisfied with his presentation of the case. No fireworks but competent, her expression said.

Fran stood and approached the jury. She held no papers, no files. They were all neatly packed on the table as though she was ready to go home.

She paced up and down before the jurors' box.

'Terrible business. Hard to believe that anyone could cause an old lady such pain and suffering for no more than seven pounds.'

The jurors were all nodding in agreement.

'In fact there's a case in the media at the moment about this same thing. Are you aware of it?'

They all nodded.

'May I approach one of the jurors, Your Honour?' asked Fran, with respect.

The judge's eyebrows lifted a little but she motioned to proceed.

She stopped and turned to juror number four. 'Mr Hunter, am I correct in thinking that you know a little more about that particular case?'

The judge leant forward as the juror blushed slightly. All attention turned towards him.

'I… er… umm…'

'Would I be correct in assuming that you in fact live on the same street as the old lady who was mugged?'

'I... d... don't...'

'And of course your involvement in this trial would be totally unbiased, wouldn't it, Mr Hunter?' she asked sarcastically.

She turned to the bench. 'Motion for a mistrial, Your Honour.'

The judge nodded towards her. 'Motion accepted.'

Her parents' house felt different when she returned after finishing university. Still as threatening but not quite as confining. She wondered if that was because she wasn't staying.

'Well done, Frances. No less than we expected,' were the congratulatory words from her parents followed by two swift handshakes. She felt more like a colleague than a daughter.

Before dinner she took the opportunity to inspect her bedroom, imagining it unchanged in her three-year absence. Meetings with her parents had been conducted in Cambridge. Normally a lunch or dinner appointment when one of them was in the area. These occasions had always been stilted and uncomfortable and Fran had been glad when they were over.

The door handle turned easily within her grip. There was no squeak of tired hinges as the door opened before her. In fact there were no door squeaks anywhere in the house. 'No squeaks allowed', thought Fran, imagining a sign on the front door.

The quiet smile froze on her face as she entered. White walls had been covered with wallpaper the colour of melted honey. Two brown leather chairs sat before a brand-new fireplace. A caramel-coloured Persian rug lay in the centre of the room beneath a glass coffee table. To the right of each chair stood side tables that housed identical reading lamps.

Fran backed out of the room shaking her head. Be reasonable, she told the hurt that was building inside, you're twenty years of age, they knew you'd never come back home to live.

She agreed with this reasonable voice inside her head. But why didn't they tell me? her emotional voice screamed.

Slowly she walked back downstairs wondering where her constant was. Everyone had a constant, she was sure. Something on which you could always rely. Just one thing that remained the same even when everything else in your life was changing.

'My room...' she managed as she sat at the dining table.

'Oh yes, dear, your father wanted a reading room and we just didn't know where else it could be. We knew you wouldn't need it any longer. Your things are in the chests in the attic. Mr Thomas will get you anything you want to take back with you.'

In chests in the attic, Fran thought angrily. Am I dead? It was a six-bedroom house. Was there really no other room that was suitable?

As if reading her mind her mother said, 'The light and view in that room is perfect.'

Fran merely nodded. What was the point? There were two sitting rooms on the ground floor and they each had a study. The reading room must have been imperative.

'So, Frances, have you decided what side you're batting for?' asked her father.

'I'd like to try prosecuting for a while. My tutor said—'

'Do you really think so?' asked Alicia, making no attempt to hide her disappointment as she idly pushed a sliver of carrot to the side of her plate.

'I enjoy the challenge of making a case instead of just defending. Making a case is creative and intriguing, like painting a picture...' Fran caught the tolerant smile that passed between them '...and I really think I can do some good,' she finished lamely.

Alicia placed her knife and fork soundlessly onto her plate. 'It's hard, thankless work, long hours, low pay and you don't get to pick and choose your clients. You'll be assigned any old riffraff cases. You'll spend all your time in a dingy office in some horrible council building.'

'But I enjoyed—'

'And it will not do your long-term career any good at all. Prosecutors are merely numbers called upon to send the dregs of society to prison. They become bitter and twisted and quite often fall away from the legal scene, especially young ones.'

Fran couldn't take it any longer. The disapproval and disappointment that came at her in waves was too much.

'But defending isn't bad—'

'Good decision, Frances.' Her mother talked over her cheerfully. 'I took the liberty of calling Geoffrey Windsor at Windsor and Travers in Birmingham. It's a wonderful firm of young solicitors and they owe me a favour or two. They want you to start on Monday.'

Fran was just too tired to argue and left the house as the dessert dishes were being cleared.

The drive back to her tiny bedsit was long and miserable. She tried turning on the radio to distract herself from reflecting on her own weakness and stupidity. It didn't do any good. All it did was help to scramble her untidy, crowded mind. Only one thing would bring order to the chaos and there were bottles of it in her pantry.

She'd opened the pantry door before she removed her coat. The bottle accompanied her everywhere – the kitchen, the bathroom and the bedroom.

As the empty vessel fell to the floor she realised that she had tried on for size the person her mother expected her to be, and found that it now fitted her perfectly.

'Good morning, Frances, we've heard many good things about you,' said Geoffrey Windsor warmly as he shook her hand.

He was just as she'd imagined him – tall, thin with a bald patch that he tried to disguise with hair that should have arced over his ears. The mouth smiled while the eyes appraised every detail of her jet-black, well-cut trouser suit. He observed the wild red hair that remained tightly shackled to the back of her head. Yes, definitely a friend of her mother's.

Her first few cases were bread-and-butter cases, testers to see how she coped. She impressed them all, but as her office grew bigger and the cases more sought after, her popularity waned in the eyes of her peers. Fran understood: you were allowed to do well, but not *too* well.

Three days after her twenty-second birthday she was asked by her mother to defend the son of a personal friend. As usual she tried to say no and failed. The knowledge that her mother would be in the courtroom ensured she had a bigger breakfast – must keep her strength up. She drank two bottles of vodka instead of one.

I can't fail, I can't fail, she chanted to herself. She's behind me, third row on the left. She's watching and she's judging. I can't fail. How will she look if I fail, how will she explain to his father that I messed up? She's never watched me in court before. I just can't fail.

Fran realised a second too late that everyone around her was standing. She stumbled to her feet. Bloody good start! No lost cases, I won't fail.

She almost slept through the formalities and knew she'd come alive once the case began.

'Objection!' she cried as it occurred to her that the prosecutor's last question was misleading.

'On what grounds?' the sour-faced judge asked.

She couldn't quite remember; she sat back down.

She studied the judge's face and found his solemn, unchanging expression amusing. Was that a mask? Was the real judge in his chambers drinking tea?

The vision forced a slight chuckle from her lips. Furtive glances her way told her she'd done something wrong. She coughed, thinking it was the best thing to do.

She looked sideways at the eighteen-year-old on trial for a hit and run. He hadn't even had a licence; he'd just taken off with Daddy's sports car. Pillock, she thought, watching his face as it grew pensive. You should go away for years, you toffee-nosed little git! The realisation that she was his defence lawyer almost caused her to laugh hysterically.

He looked sideways at her again. Oops, should she have raised an objection to something? Never mind, it was too late now.

She straightened up in her chair. I can't fail, she told herself, trying to force some clarity into her cluttered mind, but the yellow legal pad lying on the desk looked so comfortable, almost like a fluffy pillow. If she could just rest her head for one minute, she'd be fine.

'Would counsel approach the bench, please?'

By the time the delay mechanism in her sozzled brain heard the words the little git was pushing her towards the bench.

She focused on the middle judge and aimed straight for him, battling with a floor that was like a swirling tornado trying to pull her down.

The prosecutor was smiling at her. She smiled back.

'Miss Thornton, are you feeling yourself today?' the judge asked.

She almost said, 'Well, it's been so long I'm sorely tempted', but she stopped the words just in time.

'I'm fine,' she said as clearly as she could, focusing on a huge red spot on the end of his nose. She only hoped she could get away before it exploded.

He continued talking to her in a harsh tone. 'If this continues I'm afraid alternative counsel will have to be arranged.'

His frowning features brought a picture of the Seven Dwarfs into her head. 'Okay, Grump... I mean, Your Honour.'

She turned to walk back to her chair but the swift movement made her head spin. The observers mingled into one and they were all laughing. What were they laughing at? Why hadn't they told her the joke? She could do with a good laugh.

Only one person was not laughing: her mother. Uh, oh, thought Fran, she's got that look. What have I done this time?

Two steps forward and Frances fell unconscious to the ground.

CHAPTER 5

Kit

'Kit, Kit, wake up! It's me, Mark.' He shook her roughly.

'NO!' she screamed through the tears. Her flailing arms caught the side of his head.

Mark caught her shoulders and lifted her top half up from the bed. Her body was covered in beads of perspiration. 'Come on, Kit, it's over!' he shouted. He turned and motioned for the other occupants of the house to return to their rooms.

Her eyes slowly registered that it was Mark sitting on the bed beside her. Relief suffused her body as she fell against his broad, bare chest. He comforted her while leaning slightly forward to switch on the bedside lamp.

'Same one?' he asked as the tears began to subside, leaving occasional sobs that surprised her.

Kit nodded weakly. She knew where she was but she didn't yet feel completely safe.

'Tell me about it,' he urged.

She shook her head.

'It's okay... they're gone,' he whispered softly. He held her for a few more moments until her shallow breathing became more normal then he held her gently but firmly away from his half-naked body. 'Do you want to talk?' he asked, moving further down the bed.

'No, you've heard it all before.'

'So bore me,' he offered.

'Will it ever be behind me?' she groaned.

'You know it will. It's only been three months, Kit, and six weeks of that was in the hospital. Stop pushing so hard.'

'I can't. I want it gone. I want to be clean—'

'You *are* clean,' he snapped as his eyes bored into hers. 'You're not dirty, Kit. It's a part of your life, which happened, and you can't ignore that but don't let it shape you now. It's your turn to decide what you want to be.'

She fought back the tears and pointed to her chest. 'It doesn't matter how many times you tell me, I don't feel it.'

She wanted him to wave a magic wand and make the past disappear, erasing the bastards who had abused her body and ate away at her soul.

'You're in limbo at the moment. They still taint your life because you had to bring them with you here, but this is your time to cleanse. When you leave here you have to leave them with me.'

'But—'

'You don't have to leave until you're ready. No one is going to force you, but there will come a time when you want to. You'll itch to move on and explore places and experiences where *they* have no place or association. Then you'll be able to leave the past behind.'

Kit so wanted to believe him. She tried to attach meaning to his words but it didn't feel real. She only knew that in the confines of the small room, with Mark sitting on the bed speaking softly to her, she wanted to believe it would all be okay. She felt her eyelids begin to droop as though magnets drew them down while the sound of his voice comforted her. Her last thought was the realisation that Mark was getting to know her a little too well. That was the trouble. People got to know you, sucked you in, gained your trust and then spat you so far away, ripping your heart so far out of your body, that it took years to wash away the blood.

Kit walked down the stairs of the three-storey Victorian house. The bawdy pattern of oversized flowers on the aged carpet grew faded in the middle of each tread. A small puff of dust rose up from each harsh footstep that was almost a stamping of the feet.

She checked her appearance in the hallway mirror. Yep, her hair was suitably spiked and the habitual black make-up littered her features. Charcoal eyeliner emphasised the sleeplessness of the previous night. She wiped away a smudge of black lipstick and smiled. No one could see through her today.

'Message by the phone for ya,' said Mara, a recovering crack addict, as she passed by, munching on a piece of jam-drenched toast.

'*Me?*'

Mara nodded disinterestedly as she mounted two stairs at a time.

Great, Kit thought, glancing at the back of an old envelope. Just a number. It was pointless shouting after Mara to find out who had called. Most days the teenager had trouble remembering to take her dressing gown off before she left the house.

She punched in the numbers, a little bemused but curious at the same time. The phone was answered after two rings by a boyish childlike voice. Kit rolled her eyes: this just got better and better.

'Hello, my name is Kit and someone there wants to talk to me,' she said, gently, trying to use her voice to find a rapport so as not to scare the child.

'Bugger off!'

Charming, she thought and was tempted to replace the receiver but curiosity got the better of her.

'My name is Kit!' she shouted, hearing raised voices of more children in the background.

'Yer name is tit? Tit, tit, tit, tit!'

She decided to use words this child was likely to understand. 'Okay, you little shit, go get your mum or dad!'

The line went quiet for a few seconds and the shouting in the background faded into the distance.

'Kit, is that you?' said a breathless voice that was vaguely familiar. Kit stepped away from the phone cradle despite the fact that the handset was still against her ear. The voice didn't yet have a name but if she recognised it, that could only mean it came from her past. And there was no one back there that she wished to know.

'It's Carol.'

'Carol who?'

There was a slight pause. 'Your sister.'

Kit's spine stiffened. 'Don't call yourself that because it just isn't true.'

'Just give me a minute.'

'Whatever you're selling, I ain't buying,' she murmured, moving the handset away from her ear.

'Kit, wait, I need to talk to you!'

'Sorry, recipe swapping isn't my thing,' she snapped, as bitterness surged through her body. She made no attempt to stop it. Instead she welcomed it. It was comforting. Familiar.

'I know you're angry but this isn't about—'

'Now why on earth would I be angry with *you*? I could stand here and list the reasons but funnily enough I have to be somewhere in about eight hours so I just don't have the time.'

'It's Bill, he's dying.'

Kit's eyes glazed over. The messages on the noticeboard in front of her blended into one mass of murky grey paper. Her surroundings dissolved as visions from the past surged into her head. Memories of a damp, dark house in a road where the sun never shone roared up and blinded her mind's eye. Her brain closed down as she travelled back through the years to the night when Bill had robbed her of the only thing that had not been infected with her life. The memory of his bloated, sweating body humping on top of her returned with the clarity of the present. Suddenly the stench of stale whisky filled the small hallway. Low animal grunts like wheezing last breaths sounded all around her. The foulness of his urine soaking the bed beneath her seeped through her black canvas jeans.

'Kit, are you still there?'

She used the sound of Carol's voice to claw her way out of the memories. 'Y... yes.'

'He's dying, and he wants to see you.'

Kit woodenly replaced the receiver, mounted the stairs and closed her bedroom door behind her.

'You off to AA?' Mark asked, checking his watch as she walked into the kitchen.

'For fuck's sake, Mark, get off my back!'

'Well, are you going?' he asked, unperturbed.

'Leave me the hell alone!' she roared. 'Just get out of my face, Mother Hen! Piss

off and peck at someone else!'

Mark tidied away the dinner plates. 'Just doing my job.'

'Exactly, it's your fucking job! You get paid to piss us off. I just wish you wouldn't take your work so seriously.'

'What's your problem, Kit?' he asked, adding milk to his coffee.

'*You!*' she screamed. 'You pretend to care but it's nothing more than a job to you. You get paid and that's it.'

'Yeah, and look at the rewards.' He gestured around the cramped kitchen. 'I have all this. I live in two rooms, I have no social life and you get to bitch at me whenever you feel like it. Christ, I am one lucky bastard!'

'It's your job, so deal with it!' Kit sneered before leaving the room. She grabbed her jacket and slammed the front door hard.

Kit walked, and thought. She had consciously decided not to tell Mark about the phone call from Carol. She didn't want him interfering in yet another part of her life. This was a decision she needed to make without his help. She wished now that she'd given a false name and address to Mark as her next of kin and told him she was an orphan, but she hadn't. Stupid, stupid, she chastised herself. If she'd known that Carol would be informed of her whereabouts she would have told him nothing. And now this call, this intrusion into her new life. The fucking cheek, she thought, unable to suppress her anger. Why the hell should she care if the old bastard was dying?

And she cared less that he was asking for her.

His face jumped into her head. A face she had so desperately tried to forget. A face that had forced her into a world of sleaze and filth so deeply ingrained into her pores, skin grafts wouldn't get it out.

In London Bill had come to her in many different shapes and sizes. Some young, some old, fat and thin. It didn't matter, every punter had worn Bill's head. And that woman, her sister, had the nerve to ask her to go to Liverpool. She had two hopes, none and Bob.

The numerous pubs and wine bars that she passed beckoned to her. Each one a separate battle to fight. Laughter found its way outside to her. How long since she'd laughed, really laughed? It would be so easy. Just one drink. Only one. She could handle it. Just one drink to banish his face from her head. She had to, needed to. Okay, so the tremors, sweating and anxiety had passed but the need for a drink to guide her back to blissful oblivion remained. Things were so much easier then. It was all still there, she knew that, but she'd been able to hide it, veil it. Now her past slapped her around the face at every opportunity. She craved the numbness of being drunk. Her shaking hand met with the brass of the door handle.

'Kit?'

The low voice from behind startled her. She turned and breathed with a sigh of relief.

'Frances. What are—'

'My car is parked over there. I couldn't get a space any closer.'

Kit remained motionless. Her hand still dangerously close to the brass handle. Her toes pointed towards the door.

'Look, a packet of nuts just isn't worth going in there for,' Fran said, taking Kit's arm. 'Come on.'

She guided Kit to the cafe they'd gone to before. Kit hadn't realised how close she was to the AA meeting room. Fran went to the counter and ordered two coffees.

'Here, drink this instead,' she instructed.

'What the hell is with you? Are you my mother?' Kit snapped. The last person she wanted to display weakness to was this woman.

'I'm just trying to help.'

'Regular Mother Teresa you are.'

'And a regular pain-in-the-ass you are,' replied Fran, without batting an eyelid.

Kit smiled. 'Touché!'

'So was it a bag of dry roasted or a packet of crisps that you just couldn't live without?' asked Fran, referring back to the pub incident.

'Both. I'm going for an eating disorder next.'

'Christ, at least your teeth will survive the acid in your mouth and they'll be able to identify the body!'

'Ooh, is that the lawyer talking, Miss Thornton?' Kit asked appreciatively.

'Do you want to talk about it?'

Do I want to talk about it? thought Kit. Not a fucking chance! What would this tight-assed bitch think of her life story? She watched as the steam swirled upwards from the coffee.

Why had she not been able to quickly dismiss the phone call earlier? Did some hidden part of her want to confront him? Was there a part of the masochist left in her?

Kit looked into the eyes opposite. They held no pre-judgement and no malice. Do I want to talk about it? Do I want to see that heart-shaped mouth turn up with distaste? Maybe if I tell her something she'll be so disgusted she'll piss off.

'Let's just say my stepfather, who loved me a little too much when I was younger, is dying and wants to see me.'

'Are you going to see him?' Fran asked, stirring her coffee.

'Yeah, and I'll take him some grapes as well.'

Fran thought for a moment. 'Or you could go and stick a knife in the bastard?'

Kit almost spat coffee across the table. From what she'd seen of Frances Thornton so far that counted as an outburst.

An uncomfortable silence followed. Kit wasn't sure what to say next. She watched as the redhead bent pensively over a coffee stirred so many times it was beginning to thicken.

She'd admitted as much as she had to get rid of the woman and yet she still sat there. Staring and stirring. Christ, wasn't there a polo match or society dinner she had to be at?

Kit didn't really know what to do. This woman had saved her from going into a pub. Whether she would have had a drink she didn't know, but at least she'd been stopped. A shudder ran through her.

'So, what's hiding in your walk-in closet, Frances Thornton?' Kit asked.

Fran smiled sadly. 'How long have you got?'

Kit checked her watch. 'About ten minutes,' she joked.

Fran didn't see the humour. 'Try ten hours,' she murmured sadly as Kit watched a multitude of emotions flit across her face.

Kit sat back. She needed to be careful; her guard was coming down a little. To walk away would be rude, which wouldn't normally bother her with a toff like Frances, and especially a lawyer. But now she felt like she owed the woman something and she hated feeling indebted.

'Come on, if anyone could change their life it's you. You're so controlled,' said Kit.

'You think so?' Fran laughed harshly. 'Yes, I'm so controlled I passed out drunk while defending an MP's son on a hit-and-run charge.' She lowered her voice. 'Take her away, M'lord. Drunk in charge of a court case.'

Kit sat forward. This woman was growing in her estimation by the minute. 'What happened?'

Fran thought for a moment. 'My mother signed me into a private rehab centre. She declared me a danger to myself so I couldn't leave until I was dry.'

Kit watched the hurt build in her eyes. Obviously that woman was still a very strong influence in her life.

'When I was released I went on a bender that made George Best look like a choirboy.'

'Act of rebellion?' asked Kit.

'Most definitely yes.'

'But why would you do that after being sober for days?' Kit asked, amazed. What she wouldn't have given for an all expenses paid stay in a posh clinic.

'Because I wanted to return to the place that had once protected me,' she admitted. 'I felt bare, naked, as though everyone could see through me. I wanted to cover up.' She straightened in her chair. 'And I wanted to do it my own way,' she said harshly, pointing over the road.

'Did it not occur to your mother to try to help?' Kit asked, convinced everyone else's mother had been trained on *Little House on the Prairie*.

'Not a chance!' snapped Fran harshly. Her mouth turned upwards in a definite smile. 'To be honest, I'm not sure I'd have done her social connections any favours if she'd taken me home.'

Kit leaned forward. 'Why?'

'I was allowed to attend one of her dinner parties when I was about seventeen. As a lesson in social etiquette I was allowed a glass of wine. Of course Mother was unaware that I'd consumed two bottles beforehand. The only thing I can remember is that Mrs McGee, my mother's best friend, had such a huge nose and buck teeth I became confused. After listening to her talk about her love of horses I could certainly see the resemblance and offered her a nose bag.' Fran tipped her head and thought for a moment. 'I can't actually remember her visiting after that.'

Kit laughed at Fran's expression but wasn't sure what to say. The ice princess was melting and becoming a real person.

Fran broke the silence. 'I won't bore you any longer. I'll save it for the day that you stop me from going into a pub. But for goodness sake, call me Fran.'

Kit nodded although she couldn't quite picture Frances... Fran in a pub. A wine bar, restaurant or hotel but definitely not a pub, not Frances Thornton.

'Are you going to see him then?'

Kit shrugged. She had the feeling that time was running out on her. The last few grains of sand were falling in the hourglass. Bill's condition pressured her into a decision. Even now it was not completely her choice. He was running out of time and therefore so too was she.

'I think you should go,' Fran stated definitely.

'Easy for you to fucking say!' Kit snapped.

Fran nodded. 'But do you still think about it? Do you hate yourself for being weak and pathetic and not doing anything to help yourself? Do you still lie awake at night feeling like she… I mean *he* controls you?'

Kit knew Fran was no longer talking about her. She looked around to see if anyone was looking at the raised voice – they weren't.

'I'm sorry,' Fran apologised, regaining her composure.

Christ, thought Kit, even her straitjacket is from Harvey Nichols.

Fran finished her coffee and picked up her jacket. 'But if he's dying you're not going to have too many chances, are you? Go for yourself, not for him. My God, you shouldn't do anything for him! But see it as part of the healing process. He can't hurt you any more. What he did back then hurt you. What more can he do to you?'

'But it'll bring it all back,' said Kit, not quite as convinced as she had been.

'Bring what back? It never left you anyway.'

Maybe Fran was right. Maybe it would be better if Kit went. The thought terrified her. Just the idea of seeing him again scared her rigid. But Mark was right also: Bill was here and until she faced him, he would follow her everywhere.

What was her main fear? The terror of seeing him again or letting go of a deep, dark hatred that ran around her body carried within her blood which would then force her to move on? But would she regret it if she didn't go? She realised that the decision was not as cut and dried as she'd thought.

'So, you gonna charge me for this hour or what?' Kit asked with a wry smile.

'No, it's on the house,' Fran said, returning the smile as she walked away.

CHAPTER 6

Fran

Fran catapulted from the uncomfortable blue chair before the words 'lunch break' had left the speaker's mouth. Having been wedged between a portly barrister and a homely paralegal, she was relieved to feel her body adjust back to its natural shape.

Seminars arranged by the Law Society had never lit fireworks in her soul but today's offering, focused on a Criminal Defence Service update, had so far failed to turn up anything she hadn't already digested from the newsletter.

The feeling of disinterest that had accompanied her every waking breath had not lessened during the train journey into Euston, passing through one suburban backyard after another. The manila folders had remained unopened in her lap, her mind unmotivated by the same old stories inside the covers. Instead, she had settled back, content to watch the steam lift from the rooftops as the early morning sun had warmed the frosted tiles.

She headed towards the front entrance of the Trafalgar Hilton, eager for some air. The boardroom had been filled to capacity and stifling. Her gaze rested on the entrance to the National Gallery and instantly recalled a school trip when she was fourteen. The first day of the four-day stay had been spent inside that building and somehow the visits to the Planetarium, St Paul's Cathedral and Tower Bridge had failed to live up to the wonder she had felt on that first day. Instantly she visualised some of the exhibits within and a bubble of excitement formed in her stomach. How she would love to re-visit those works of art with a deeper appreciation for colour, depth and expression.

She imagined returning to the buffet lunch on the first floor of the hotel. The finger food would be flattened by droll conversation that never veered from the topic of the day. Prosecutors, defenders, barristers would soak up the moisture of the air with their arid conversation.

Her gaze returned to the gallery like a pirate spying a hoard of buried treasure. Dare she venture into the unknown for just an hour?

Like a gatekeeper, her mother's voice wafted into her mind like someone else's cigarette smoke, uncomfortable and unbidden. Get back upstairs and network, Frances. Use this time to further your career. Make contacts for the future.

She shook her head to rid herself of the unsolicited advice. Stronger was the urge to free her analytical mind, if only for a short while.

Blimey, I used to be indecisive but I'm not so sure now, she thought to herself as her legs moved of their own volition. Maybe, just a quick scoot round some of the rooms and then back for the second half of the seminar, she told herself as she entered.

By the time she'd visited the micro gallery Fran knew that she would not be returning for the second part of the seminar. With the decision made she waited for a drum roll and the appearance of the National Guard, on her mother's payroll, to escort her back to the hotel. When none appeared she collected floor plans and set off on her wondrous journey.

She passed a group of schoolchildren resplendent in navy uniforms and hats. They walked behind their teacher with forced solemnity and boredom. From twenty feet away they looked identical. Fran wondered idly if their parents would notice if they were switched for the school holidays.

She began at the Sainsbury Wing, pausing to admire Mantegna's *Agony in the Garden* and Bellini's *Madonna and Child*. She moved on to the West Wing and perused works by Poussin, Rembrandt and van Dyck, unaware of the time. Prolonging the anticipation of the impressionism of the East Wing, she paused for coffee. The schoolchildren had morosely followed their teacher in another direction and although other visitors milled about conversation was minimal. It was a place of observation and, to Fran, reverence, but she almost laughed out loud at the efforts of one woman who was tiptoeing along as though surrounded by eggshells. To her acute embarrassment, her four-inch stiletto heels clip-clopped along on hollow flooring.

One particular painting entranced Fran. *The First Outing* by Renoir featured a young girl observing the crowds at the theatre. She had always favoured the French artist after reading that for the last twenty years of his life he had been forced to paint with a brush tied to his arm after his hands were crippled by arthritis. She admired and respected his determination to share his gift with the world at great pain to himself. How wonderful, she sighed, to be able to produce such beauty from a memory, a vision. To paint something that came completely from within. To let your mind and hands wander experimentally over canvas. To practise with colours, textures, ideas.

'Beautiful, isn't it?' said a soft, husky voice from behind. Fran started. She'd been so entranced by the innocence of the young, unsophisticated girl that she hadn't heard anyone approach.

She turned to agree. Her eyes rested on a face not far from her own. The first thing Fran noticed were the piercing blue eyes set in a face devoid of all make-up but more beautiful than anything she'd ever seen. Perfectly shaped eyebrows gave her features a striking intensity. Fran did a double take.

The woman's soft pink lips formed a slow smile as she looked back at the painting. Fran appraised her briefly, a habit inherited from her mother. She guessed her to be around thirty, slim with a long graceful neck, accentuated by the short, blonde hair that was almost white, giving her an angelic quality. She wore light blue jeans and a white silk shirt. Inch for inch she matched Fran's height.

Fran wanted to move away – she felt gawkish next to this paragon of grace – but she couldn't. She was curious, the way an average child at school is in awe of the beautiful people.

'What is she thinking, I wonder?' the stranger asked.

Fran pulled her eyes back to the painting, the faint smell of jasmine surrounding her.

'I think she's innocently envious. She feels young and awkward and envies their age and sophistication.' Fran spoke quietly in the library atmosphere but her opinion was definite. She became lost in the brush strokes of the painting; she could have been talking to a tree. 'I don't think she looks comfortable in the surroundings. She's on the outside looking in, almost.'

'Hmm, possibly. Or does the flash of dark red hair, visible below the bonnet, tell us she has spirit and will be what she wants to be?'

'Maybe both,' agreed Fran, enjoying the conversation.

'Red hair, not dissimilar to yours,' observed the stranger.

Fran smiled at the comparison.

'Do you think we'd make the same observations about her if the artist had gone with his first impression, no pun intended?'

'I don't know what you mean,' admitted Fran.

The woman moved closer and pointed. 'Originally there was a male companion at her side. That gentleman there with his back to her, his jacket formed part of the figure.'

Fran enjoyed the sound of the husky voice with a slight accent that she couldn't place. She observed the painting thoughtfully. 'No, the effect would not have been the same.'

'I agree.'

'Do you paint?' asked Fran, wishing to prolong the conversation.

'Goodness, no! I'm merely an observer of fine works. You?'

'No, I'm a lawyer. I enjoyed art as a child.'

'Does that mean you don't paint any more?'

Fran shook her head.

'You should, it's a shame to waste artistic ability.'

Fran took a step backwards. 'Excuse—'

'I'm sorry,' the woman apologised. 'I didn't mean to be rude but an expression of longing passed over your face. That must mean that you miss it.'

Fran folded her arms in front of her. The perceptiveness of the figure disturbed her. 'I'm a lawyer,' she repeated.

'Yes, you said. That's what you do, not who you are.'

Colour suffused Fran's face.

'I'm sorry, I'm a little forthright sometimes. I shouldn't have said anything.'

Fran smiled to ease her discomfort. She liked the openness with which the woman spoke.

'Frances.' She held out her hand.

'Martine.'

They both looked around uncomfortably for a moment. Neither knew whether they were saying hello or goodbye.

'Umm, I don't mean to be presumptuous but I haven't eaten yet and my stomach tells me it's after six. Would you like to join me?'

Fran hesitated. She ought to be thinking about getting home but she was intrigued by this woman's easy manner, the quiet confidence that surrounded her. Fran wasn't sure she wanted their meeting to end just yet. She realised that she was hungry and her only other option was to endure the plastic, half-frozen offerings on the train.

'I'd like that,' she replied with a sense of rebellious freedom.

'Great, I know a lovely little Malaysian place not far from here.'

'I don't have a car. I'm only here for the day.'

'I don't bother when I'm in London, it's easier to walk or take the tube.'

Well, that explains the svelte figure, thought Fran.

The restaurant was small and dimly lit; the décor was dark and close. Low-wattage bulbs shone just a little light from diamond-shaped downlighters reflecting back off the wall. The tables were low and intimate, yet there was something revitalising about removing one's shoes to sit on the floor to eat as though it were an occasion not a necessity. Tantalising aromas of strong herbs and spices greeted them as they sat.

A mahogany counter shielded the open cooking area from the rest of the restaurant. Immediately Fran felt at ease.

'It's lovely,' she breathed.

'I make a point of eating here every time I'm in London.'

'You don't live here?'

'God, no! I love London. The vitality and life here refreshes me. It's busy and exciting but I couldn't live like that permanently. It's too exhausting.'

Fran felt the same way. It was a city that took your breath away. The sheer history was overwhelming.

'I think when people make the mistake of moving to places they fall in love with, the magic dies, don't you think?'

Fran watched the animated face before her. She could listen to this woman all day and not be bored. There was vitality about her that brought Fran out of herself. They had met only an hour earlier but she felt instantly at ease. She would have liked to see her mother's face at the vision of her sitting on the floor, barefoot, about to eat.

She'd never eaten Malaysian fare before and so deferred to Martine, who ordered Loh Bak (spiced pork roll) for starters,

Rendang Daging (beef curry) for main course and they jointly decided to wait for dessert.

The waiter took their order while Martine described an art exhibition she'd recently attended. Fran craned her neck to watch the activity behind the counter. She could hear the lull of the sweet voice and when she turned her head Martine's amusement was obvious.

'Or I could be boring you to tears.'

'I'm sorry, it's just—'

'Come on.' Martine tapped her hand and began walking towards the counter. Fran followed.

'Excuse me, my new friend is having trouble listening to a word I'm saying. She finds the activity here far more riveting. Would you mind if we watched for a moment? Then I might be able to hold her attention.'

The three chefs agreed with laughter, enjoying the opportunity to create for an appreciative audience.

Fran could have died with embarrassment. 'You're mad,' she whispered into Martine's ear, again overcome by the captivating aura surrounding her. She could see that people reacted positively to Martine.

Both watched in fascination as the intestinal tracts of the prawns were hooked out. They were then shelled and chopped to a fine paste. Spring onions, soy sauce, water chestnuts and other ingredients were added to the mixture, which was teaspooned into individual bean curd skins and then deep-fried.

'Are you happy now or would you prefer to watch everyone's meals being prepared?'

'No,' laughed Fran. 'It's just so different to microwave lasagne.'

'Ah, a lawyer's lifestyle!' Martine lamented as she sat crosslegged opposite Fran.

'It's just not worth the hassle for one.'

'No husband?'

Fran shook her head as their starter approached. The smell of the food made her realise how hungry she was. Martine ordered a dry white wine. Fran ordered orange juice, claiming alcohol didn't agree with her.

While they ate they talked about food, art and music. Fran found they shared a love of foreign, haunting melodies that gripped your heart and wrung it out. 'The type of music you listen to with someone you love,' whispered Martine with a far-away look in her eyes.

Fran watched as Martine travelled somewhere alone and dark. She observed the pain in her eyes and the sadness that pervaded her body.

'I'm sorry, I just lost myself there for a moment,' Martine apologised, reaching for the tiny cup of black coffee. 'Did you say you were here only for the day?'

'Hang on, I have a call to make.' Fran grabbed her handbag and walked outside, dialling the number of The Waldorf. After making a reservation for one night she pinched her nose tightly and, using her best flu voice, left a message on the company's answering machine.

She returned to the table. 'Definitely until tomorrow,' she answered Martine's previous question. 'Tomorrow is Covent Garden, I adore that place.' Fran took a deep breath. 'Care to come?'

Martine nodded and they arranged to meet in the square at midday.

Alone in her hotel room Fran wondered what had come over her. The old Frances was somewhere in Birmingham eating a meal for one out of a plastic tray, watching cable TV while looking over work notes. She could see her. What was she doing in this place, fascinated by a stranger who'd spoken to her in an art gallery?

She had no idea but she wanted to find out; she was on a roller-coaster ride and although it was new and scary she couldn't get off. She wanted to see where it was going. She only knew that, like a kid on Christmas Eve, she couldn't wait for tomorrow.

She slept fitfully and woke with the knowledge that she had dreamt about Martine. The haziness and distortion she couldn't accurately recall or even the subject matter but the characters were very real and if she didn't hurry she would be late.

She dressed quickly and paused only to apply coffee lipstick to a slightly trembling mouth. She conceded defeat when it became obvious that her lips looked almost double the size. After wiping the colouring off impatiently she walked briskly to their meeting point.

She hopped from one foot to the other as she checked her watch again. Fourteen and a half minutes past. A feeling of dread formed in the pit of her stomach: Martine wasn't coming. For some reason she'd changed her mind. Fran felt the disappointment rise in her throat.

'God, I'm sorry! Problems at the shop. I couldn't get away. You okay?'

Fran nodded, feeling her heart lift at the sight of the breathless woman with a package in her hand.

Martine held out the small parcel. 'For you.'

Fran smiled with delight. No one ever gave her presents. She unwrapped the package like a small child to reveal a framed A5 print of the painting she had been admiring yesterday. 'It's beautiful,' she smiled. For once she didn't know what to say.

'Come with me,' Martine instructed. 'I'd like to show you where I work.'

Fran merely followed, trying to fight down the relief that Martine had turned up. She finally came to a halt in front of a small-fronted beauty salon that was occupied but not heaving with activity. The name above the door seemed familiar. The word 'Images' was carved in gold lettering that reminded Fran of wedding invitations. She had the feeling she'd seen the same sign somewhere in Birmingham.

Martine pushed the door open to the surprise of the dark-haired girl on the reception desk.

'Martine… but… I didn't think you were coming back to-day.'

How lovely, thought Fran, to have a job where you could just do that.

'I won't get in your way, I promise, I just want to show Frances around.'

The girl smiled tolerantly.

'So you're a hairdresser,' observed Fran as she followed her through the salon. 'This is what you do.' She tried to keep the disappointment out of her voice. Somehow she had imagined something far more exotic.

Martine's amusement was obvious. 'Aha, perfect!' she breathed as the entrance door opened. Fran's gaze automatically followed. The woman had medium-length mousy hair that matched the colour of her tights and hung untidily on her grey rainmac. Wearing little make-up she appeared pale and drawn with her worries held in the visible sacks of flesh below tired eyes. She carried a green plastic shopping bag that had seen better days.

'Cut and blow dry?' Fran asked.

Martine's eyes held amused interest. 'Why do you assume that?'

'Well, it's, er…' She realised quickly how that had sounded.

Martine guided her to the rear of the salon. 'You're right about the fact that she's not very well off but it's not only wealthy people that come here. Our prices are high, yes, but we're the best at what we do.' She paused to look around the shop for an example. 'Mrs King-Thorne over there can afford to come every day if she wants to but Dorothy Tromans saves a little from the housekeeping each week and comes every three months. To her, this is a well-deserved treat.'

She gave Fran the chance to digest her words. 'Now for the guided tour. The whole of this floor is devoted to physical appearance. The salon is a small part of what we do.'

Martine guided her through a door that she'd assumed to be a storeroom. A short corridor, well lit and furnished with familiar prints, led to a sunny room where assistants were busy manicuring and pedicuring, chatting cheerfully with their clients.

The room leading off from that housed seven sunbeds and next to that a smaller room with two theatre-lit make-up mirrors for beauty advice and demonstrations. All of the rooms had speakers that played low instrumentals.

A second floor stretched above the store next door. The first room they entered was aromatherapy. Fran couldn't get enough of the smells of jasmine and lavender and many others that she couldn't name. She watched as an assistant mixed various oils and counted the drops. The assistant saw Martine behind her and explained what she was doing. 'I'm making up a blend for general relaxation.' She listed the various ingredients and the number of drops needed. Some Fran had never heard of. She watched in awe as the drops were painstakingly counted into the electronic mixer.

'Is this for a massage?' she asked.

'No, this is for a burner. With massage oils you have to blend to a base oil such as peach kernel or apricot kernel and add one drop to each millimetre of base vegetable oil.' She demonstrated. She then turned the bottle upside down a few times and rolled it between her palms to disperse the oil.

'Do you use all of that?' enquired Fran.

'No, a teaspoon is normally enough.'

'Do the clients choose their own ingredients?' Fran asked, entranced by the entirely relaxing effect that the room possessed.

'Once we've obtained a brief medical history, yes.'

Fran was intrigued. 'Why, surely the oils can't harm you?'

The assistant looked over Fran's shoulder and, seeing that Martine stood chatting to the woman lying face down on what looked like a hospital stretcher, continued to explain. 'Bergamot, for example, increases susceptibility to sunburn. Black pepper, cajeput and lemongrass can cause skin irritations. Camphor, fennel, hyssop and sage cannot be used on people with epilepsy and many of the oils such as cedarwood, clary sage and juniper, to name only a few, should not be used during pregnancy.'

Fran was amazed – she had no idea that oils affected people so strongly. She could have talked to the assistant all day but Martine pulled her to the far corner of the room so as not to infringe on the privacy of the client.

'That movement Anita is using is called effleurage. It relaxes the nervous system. The kneading motion that she'll change to shortly unlocks tense muscles, particularly the trapezium muscle.' Martine jabbed the area between Fran's neck and shoulders. 'There. You see she used both hands in a rhythmic sequence picking up and gently squeezing the tense muscle.'

'I'm going limp just watching,' said Fran, only half joking.

'Now she's using friction strokes to penetrate deep muscle tissue. Her thumbs are more effective for releasing knotted muscle.' Martine watched for another moment or two and content with what she saw said, 'Come on, reflexology next.'

Fran couldn't wait. She had no idea what that meant until she saw an assistant using small circular movements on the client's feet. The assistant appeared to be in trance-like concentration. Martine ushered her back out of the room. 'She's listening to the pain.'

Fran nearly laughed out loud.

Martine pointed to a huge picture of a pair of feet with shapes and arrows pointing to names of body parts. 'In the 1930s an American physiotherapist mapped the entire body on the tops and bottoms of the feet, but various forms of reflexology were used by the Egyptians 3,000 years ago.'

Fran was entranced. It was like another world.

'The theory is that the body is divided into ten zones that run lengthways from head to toe,' Martine went on. 'They're equally split either side of a vertical, central line. Organs on the left side of the body can only be influenced by the left side of the foot. If the constant flow of energy or "qi" is impeded by a blockage, a reflexologist can break down the blockage which enables the body's own healing mechanisms to kick in. It actually treats the whole body.'

Fran tried to digest all the information. Martine smiled. 'Just tell me if I'm going too quickly. I'm afraid I'm one of those sad people who lives to work.'

'What job do you do?'

There was an impish delight in Martine's eyes. 'Let's just say I oversee all aspects.'

Fran shook her head, realising the truth. 'You own Images. Oh my goodness, and I called you a hairdresser! I'm so sorry.'

'I'm not offended, I love what I do.'

Fran sensed with regret that the tour was coming to an end. Transfixed by this woman's pride in what she did, she admired Martine's passion for her work.

'Does all of this work?' Fran asked as they returned to the salon.

'Different techniques work for different people. Every woman has beauty, many only need to discover it within themselves.'

Easy for you to say, thought Fran, who now knew that nothing about this woman was artificial. Only foundation and a touch of lipstick were used to enhance the ethereal beauty.

Martine nudged her in the direction of the reception area. 'I think that lady is ready to leave.' Again, Fran followed her gaze. Her sharp intake of breath brought a triumphant smile to Martine's face. Fran didn't mean to stare at the sleek hairstyle that cupped the attractive oval face or the expertly applied make-up or the confident stride with which the woman now moved. 'Goodbye, Mrs Tromans,' Martine called out pleasantly.

'Wow, I can't believe that's her' whispered Fran.

Martine turned satisfied eyes towards her. 'Now you understand what we do.'

Fran tried to hide her discomfort as she followed Martine out of the front door.

She felt like a schoolgirl as they toured the market stalls. She fell in love with the specialist boutiques, like Nicole Farhi, where she purchased a silk scarf.

They sat on the edge of the square eating hot dogs layered with mustard. 'So where exactly are you from?' asked Fran as they each took bites. Martine chewed for a moment. God, she can even make eating a hot dog look graceful, thought Fran.

'Good question. Listen carefully, it gets complicated and there'll be questions later. My mother is half Italian and half English – killer combination,' she joked, looking at the hot dog. 'I get to love the food that I eat and then feel guilty for it.'

'What about your father?'

'French, hence the name. We moved from France when I was three so I don't remember much about it but they still live in Cornwall and are as sickeningly happy as they were twenty years ago,' she said fondly.

Fran felt a pang not unlike homesickness yet there wasn't anywhere to be homesick for. She thought of her own parents. To her they were like the perfect figures atop a multi-tiered wedding cake: isolated and alone. She remained on the bottom layer of the cake with all the icing she could eat but not a soul for miles.

'Did they listen to you?' she blurted out.

'Oh yes, I think that children who are ignored grow up with less social skills because they didn't have that total security in which to practise, so by the time they experiment with humour and opinions with their peers, one mistake, one ridicule and they withdraw.' She chuckled, low in her throat. 'My father and I debated what day of the week it was. Every time I formed an opinion I would go home and test it out on him. If I could maintain my argument against my father, the opinion was mine forever. We argued one day about drink driving. The debate became quite heated. I stormed off in anger unable to believe that he agreed with it. He waited for me to cool off in the garden before he explained that he did in fact agree with me, but it was arrogant to ignore the point of view of another person just because you don't agree with them. I never forgot that lesson,' she finished fondly.

Fran tried not to be envious. One memory like that. Just one to remember, to share.

'Anything else you want to know?' Martine asked.

For some reason everything, thought Fran. 'Anything you want to tell me?'

Martine moved away slightly as though uncomfortable with their proximity. 'Let's walk,' she murmured quietly.

They wandered through Leicester Square and pushed through the crowds along Piccadilly without realising how far they'd walked, talking of past experiences, education, family, school and food. Everything except partners and spouses.

They wandered up through Shepherd Market, which was quiet, after the stallholders had left. Small groups of people lazed under canopies, drinking cappuccinos in the late afternoon sunshine. Sunglasses and mobile phones littered wrought-iron tables.

They stopped at a small corner coffee shop boasting one outside table beneath an arched entrance way leading towards

Mayfair. Window boxes filled with marigolds, ivy and trailing fuchsias decorated the old, brickwork archway.

Fran sat back in her chair while Martine fetched coffees, letting the sunshine bathe her. The busy roads and heaving crowds could have been miles away; the only sounds present were quiet voices and muffled laughs of complete relaxation.

'Lovely, isn't it?' said Martine, reading her thoughts.

'Mmm… I could live here. Just in this corner.'

The surroundings were conducive to honesty, Fran thought, and realised she wanted to know more about this enigmatic woman she'd known for just twenty-four hours.

She decided to push. 'Last night in the restaurant you left me for a while. You looked pained. Lost love?'

'Or you could ask me something simple, like have I got a dog?'

'Don't hedge. You can tell me or not.' Her gaze didn't waver as she waited for an answer.

'Are you sure you want to know?' she asked seriously.

Fran nodded.

Martine took a deep breath. 'Quite honestly I lost a limb. At least that's how it felt. I could still do things but not as easily. Do you know what I mean?'

Fran shook her head. To be perfectly truthful, she didn't.

'You're very lucky. Quite simply I lost the only person I've ever loved.'

Fran heard the soft, husky voice begin to shake. She hated causing the pain that was like a freshly opened wound in her eyes but she had to know more. She placed a reassuring hand on Martine's arm and squeezed.

Martine didn't look up. 'Her name was Cristina. She was Portuguese. We met here in London and clicked immediately. We shared each other's thoughts. She was bubbly and outgoing, the life and soul of everywhere she went. In private things were different. Her mood swings were like nothing I'd ever seen before. We'd been together about four months when I realised that the extreme nature of her personality was due to a medical condition.' Martine turned haunted eyes full of pain towards the sky. 'She was a manic depressive, bipolar.'

Fran had heard the term but wasn't sure of the details. 'To quote Cristina, she was either on the ceiling or on the floor but never on the sofa. Sometimes she'd want to stay up all night and talk and other days she was unable to leave the bed and talked only of wanting to die. I learned to recognise the signs. I knew when dark days were coming and I was able to rearrange my schedule so I could be with her.'

Martine ran her graceful fingers through her short blonde hair, which fell back into place. 'I'm sorry, I shouldn't…'

'Please carry on,' urged Fran. For some reason she had instantly known that it would have been a woman and she didn't know why. What she hadn't expected was the stabbing jealousy that was forcing her jaws to clench.

'During a two-day visit to her mother's house in Greenwich she was persuaded that her problem was due to her "unsavoury lifestyle". Cristina called and told me she wouldn't be coming back. I accepted this as a period in her life that she needed to work through. You see, I'd come to accept what and who I was at a very young age…' Martine's voice became no more than a whisper. 'Two days later she killed herself.'

The lump that had formed in Fran's throat was not for Cristina – she was now at peace – but for the woman before her who was not.

They sat silently while Martine composed herself. Fran had no words of comfort. Martine broke the silence. 'Well, I sure am glad I didn't put a damper on the day. When do you have to leave?' she asked.

Never, if you don't want me to, thought Fran, surprised at how drawn to this woman she was. Her mind was in turmoil. Strange emotions and sensations warmed her body when she was close to Martine. It was strange, scary, new and exhilarating at the same time. All she knew was that Martine transfixed her; brought out in her feelings she didn't know she had. She felt she could share anything with this woman and not be judged.

'Do you feel it too?' Martine whispered.

Fran needed no explanation. 'Yes.'

Suddenly her life in Birmingham flashed like an explosion before her eyes. Her mother, her job, her flat. The safety. She had to get back. This was not her sitting in the middle of London like a bohemian with no responsibilities and alien sensations. She became choked, suffocated. Something was under threat and she didn't know what. She needed to get back to the neat, tidy existence at home that held no surprises.

Blindly she stumbled to her feet. 'I have to go,' she blurted out and ran away from the woman who, too shocked to move, sat rooted to the spot.

Fran ran as fast as she could to the road and jumped into a taxi. That was when she heard, above the bustle, the solitary sound of her name being called from the distance.

CHAPTER 7

Kit

The smell invaded Kit's nostrils as soon as Carol opened the door. A childhood smell of overcooked cabbage mixed with damp, it sickened her. The two women did not touch and Carol guided her inside, speaking quietly even though Bill was ensconced permanently upstairs and wouldn't have heard them.

'I'll go and tell him you're here,' said Carol. 'Then we'll have a cup of tea and a chat.' She was gone before Kit could remind her that they were not friends, they were not neighbours and she had no desire to make small talk with a woman she barely knew.

Nothing had changed in the dark, poky kitchen that sat between the living room and the bathroom. The only window looked out on to a six-foot fence separating them from next door, ensuring little light managed to creep into the kitchen. The yellow vinyl-topped table was no different except for a few extra scratches. Nothing had changed. Kit half expected her mother to come through the door at any moment with carrier bags from the supermarket. The sights she saw held no fond memories for her.

'We should talk,' said Carol as she entered the kitchen.

'About what, Carol, the weather?'

'About what happened.'

'I have nothing to say to you. You left home, not the planet.'

Kit looked into her eyes. The weakness reflected there was obvious. 'You had to know, you were much older than me. You had to have some idea what you were leaving me to. I can forgive everything else but you were my sister and you did nothing. There you go, we just talked.'

Carol moved towards her. 'Kit—'

'Don't touch me.' Her eyes flashed.

Carol sighed and leant against the sink. 'You scared us, Kit. Even Mother and especially Dad, they didn't know how to act around you. We were all the same. You see, she could see our lives before we could, and she was right. But not you. You were different. Self-sufficient and demanding at the same time.'

Kit fought hard not to be interested in Carol's words. She'd never talked about her childhood with anyone – she had no idea what she'd been like.

Carol smiled sadly. 'We wanted sweets, money, new clothes… all the things that Mother couldn't give us but understood. You weren't interested. You had a lively mind and an imagination. You had a brain and a voice and you used them. Don't you see, Kit? Your individuality terrified and threatened everyone around you.'

But Kit didn't want to hear any more. 'Well, you must be so pleased to see how my life has turned out. Boy, did I exceed everyone's expectations!'

Carol shook her head and sighed deeply.

'You'll be shocked when you see him,' she warned as she filled the kettle, now burnt black. She moved around the kitchen with the natural authority of the elder sister.

Kit didn't answer. She had not slept for two nights and now that she was here she just wanted to get it over with and be on her way as quickly as possible. She looked closely at her sister. Eternal martyrdom formed her features as it had their mother's. She smiled, but never really smiled, Kit noticed.

She took the chipped cup offered to her and found it laughable that she sat so civilised drinking tea with the sister who hadn't given a toss about her, while the centre of her hatred lay upstairs.

There were no sounds from upstairs yet she sensed him and it frightened her.

'How long?' she asked.

Carol knew what she meant. 'Not long, Kit. He's been ill for years but his own laziness stopped him from going to the doctor and when he did it was too late to operate. It's in his stomach.' She glanced up at the ceiling. 'It won't be long now. Sometimes he doesn't even know what he's saying.'

'How can you stand to be near him?'

Carol weighed her answer. 'I suppose I convince myself that it's what Mother would have wanted. I do it for her, not him.'

Talking about him only made Kit feel worse. She slammed down the teacup. 'I'm ready.'

She walked up the darkened stairway and each step brought the bile higher in her throat. The creaking of the ninth stair caused her to stumble. It had been the warning of his proximity on that night long ago. The sound transported her back into the bed and the body of a fifteen-year-old frightened schoolgirl.

Kit sank on to the stair and pushed her back against the wall. She was so close but she couldn't do it. She could enter that room with the intention of wreaking vengeance but not offering forgiveness. How might my life have been different? she wondered, staring at the carpet that lay full of dust. Would I have let anyone use my body if he hadn't used it first? Could I have fought harder to stop him? The questions ran around her head urgently, seeking answers.

You bastard, she seethed inwardly. Even now you have some control over my life because you're forcing me to confront this now, before I'm ready to accept the full repercussions of that night. She couldn't do it. Then she thought of her life back in Birmingham and knew she couldn't return to it unless she did. She swallowed hard and entered the room wondering if the sour, stale odour of decay was real or in her mind only.

The curtains were drawn and her first thought was thank God, there's been a mistake, it's not him! In the darkness it looked as though the bed was empty and the blankets were ruffled. The lump atop it didn't look big enough to be a person. Then she saw his eyes. Her mind reeled and her legs went weak beneath her; those eyes bore into her soul.

Carol felt her weakness and supported her around the middle. 'It's okay, he can't hurt you any more. This is for you.'

Kit swallowed deeply suddenly inexplicably thankful for the presence of the sister she had never known. She swallowed her fear but it went no lower than her throat. Then she looked at him again. The obese stomach was gone; the rolls of fat that had hung below his chin were no longer there, leaving loose sallow skin in their place. Thick black hair had been reduced to two tufts behind the ears, which were now completely white. Skin hung on his bones like a badly fitting suit. His colour was ashen except for large black circles under his eyes. His chest rose and fell with the effort of laboured breathing. And still he stared at her.

The fear in her body began to drain away. She stood erect and inched away from Carol's grip. Slowly she moved towards the bed and stood level with his knees. His gaze never left her face.

'Kit,' he rasped. It wasn't a voice she knew. She was no longer terrified of the shrunken, sorrowful figure in the bed. She hated him and always would but the fear was slowly seeping away. It was a young girl's fear that she'd held since she was fifteen. Now she could let it go. She didn't feel pity for him either; she could not bring herself to be sorry that he was dying. He had killed many parts of her in the room across the hall.

The fragile, age-spotted hand moved slowly down the bed towards her. She ignored it. There was nothing else to do; she had nothing for him.

'Forgive… me?'

Unable to grant his request she shook her head. She stared straight into the eyes that were unchanged and had never left her mind. 'I wish I could for my own sake, not yours.'

Carol moved forward to stand by her side. Kit motioned for her to leave them for a few moments. She was safe – this thing in the bed could no longer harm her. And so she waited until the door closed and she heard Carol's soft footsteps going down the stairs.

She took a deep breath, her hands gripped tightly together. 'I can't forgive you, Bill, because that would indicate some form of understanding on my part that I simply don't feel. What you did to me I'll never forgive but seeing you suffer will give me the strength to move on. I can't give you absolution because you'll never know how much it affected my life. You stopped me from being the person I should have been.'

'I've… been… lon—'

'I don't care, Bill. Don't you understand? This is not about you. Maybe if I were a better person it could be, but it's not.' Anger bit at her stomach. She had done what she had come to do. She had come to judge the power he still held over her life and to put him firmly in her past. 'I'm not Mother Teresa, for God's sake! I don't care about the way you feel. I'm here to make sure that the guilt of what you did follows you wherever your excuse for a spirit wanders. I hope you rot in hell for what you did to me!'

Now she couldn't bear being in the room with him any longer. She wanted to get away from him and everything that reminded her of her childhood; she wanted to move on.

She walked briskly out of the room, eager to be away from him. The more he spoke the more he became Bill. She couldn't stand that. It was easier to deal with a silent stranger that lay unmoving in the bed.

She walked into the kitchen to find Carol sitting with her jacket on. 'I thought you might like to get out of the house for a while.'

Kit nodded. They walked to the park around the corner, which was no more than two swings set on a patch of tarmac. Like the rows of remaining terraced houses it too had been abandoned by the major regeneration project. They each took a swing.

'I couldn't do it, you know, forgive him.'

'It's your peace to make and you only have yourself to live with.'

'I couldn't lie, not even for the sake of a dying man. It's not even so much about the act any more,' Kit said, trying to rationalise the thoughts weaving around her mind. 'It's more about the effect of the act. Do you know what I mean?'

Carol looked away but not before Kit saw the pained expression in her eyes. 'We were all to blame for that. I could have helped, I should have been a better sister. If I'd stayed in touch you would have been able to come to me. If—'

'Leave it, Carol. If we both added up the shoulds, coulds and ifs, there wouldn't be a lot left for either of us.'

'We both know I failed you so let's leave it at that.'

Kit felt her anger towards Carol dissolving. Her sister was no more than their mother had moulded her to be. She had been just as desperate to escape the loveless house and once she found the chance she'd seized it with both hands and simply never looked back.

'What are you smiling at?' Carol asked, puzzled.

'I'm just realising how easy it is to blame everyone for the things that go wrong. At some stage I'm going to have to face that.'

'What now, Kit?'

Kit pushed against the tarmac and began to swing to and fro, enjoying the rocking sensation. She didn't know; she only knew that something inside was happening. She wanted something but she wasn't sure what. A question occurred to her. 'Did you ever hear from Dad?'

'No, but Mum did.'

Kit was surprised. 'I never knew.'

'None of us did. I found three letters from him after you'd left and I sorted through her things.'

'What did they say?'

'Only that he was sorry for deserting her and that he was never coming back.'

'And it took him three letters to say that?'

'No, in the last letter…' Carol paused and looked into Kit's eyes '…he said he'd been to the school… to see you.'

Kit's feet met with the ground. 'To see me… but why?'

'You still don't get it, do you? You were different. If we wanted to go left to the cinema, you wanted to go right because you hadn't been that way before. You intimidated us all because nothing ever fazed you. The rest of us needed each other, Kit, but not you. You didn't need anything.'

Kit nodded, recalling the hours alone.

'It could have been better. We could have tried to know you but it was easier to leave you to yourself. That's what you do with something you don't understand, you leave it alone.' Nervously she stared hard at her hands.

'It's in the past, Carol, we can't change it, no matter how much we'd like to.'

Her sister nodded. 'I don't know about you but I could do with a drink of something. Shall we…'

'I can't,' Kit said quietly. She took a deep breath. 'I'm an alcoholic, Carol. Recovering, I think, but I can't ever drink again.'

She realised it was the first time she'd ever said the words aloud. In fact it was the first time she'd allowed it to surface in her mind so clearly. Even now it would be so easy to take Carol up on her offer. She knew it was something that would be with her forever.

'Oh my God, what did we do to you, Kit? Why didn't I have the courage to get to know you?'

The words caught in her throat and Kit saw that it took an effort not to cry. Without realising what she was doing she leaned across and touched her sister's arm.

'Get to know me now.'

They returned to the house and sat up all night talking about the past. Carol gave her a picture of herself as a child. She tried to merge the two mothers, hers and Carol's, but it just wouldn't happen. For some reason it didn't matter any more.

At seven o'clock Kit was woken in the armchair where she'd fallen asleep to be told by Carol that Bill had passed away. Neither of them cried. Kit felt more sorrow for what had been lost between herself and Carol than Bill's death. They could have been sisters. It would have been nice to have a sister, Kit thought. She didn't try to force any sadness for Bill – that was too hypocritical.

By nine o'clock Kit was on the train back to Birmingham, to Mark.

The familiarity of the train station surprised her. She'd just left a place that she'd lived in for fifteen years. Each step nearer to the hostel confirmed to her that she was returning home. Home, a mending place where she'd lived for a couple of months.

She went through the ritual with the locks and entered to hear the radio playing softly in the kitchen. An instant peace stole over her as she observed Mark before he turned. She was unprepared for the lurch in her stomach that felt like her whole insides had just rearranged themselves.

'I've been waiting for you. How did it go?'

Kit shook her head, confused at her own feelings. He didn't look the same to her any more. He didn't look like safe Mark, caring Mark. He looked like a man she had missed more than she wanted to admit.

'I don't want to talk about it right now,' she said abruptly as she tried to control her feelings. She could feel the colour that had suffused her cheeks and the instant warmth that it brought.

'I think it's time I moved out,' she stated, unsure where the words had come from but the instant they were out of her mouth, she knew it was the right thing to do. She needed some distance from Mark. Her feelings were painted red with hazard lines, screaming danger. As the train had lurched towards Birmingham she had felt Mark getting closer, waiting for her. But worse, she had enjoyed the sensation that had rolled around her stomach, welcomed it. And that was the dangerous part. She had lived her life so far without coming to rely on anyone and that wasn't about to change now. She would not give anyone else the power over her life again.

'A bit sudden, isn't it?' she heard above the clatter as the kettle fell into the sink.

'I'm ready.'

She watched him nod slowly, without turning. 'I think you're right.'

Kit wasn't sure what she'd been expecting. Every nerve ending in her body told her that being near to Mark was dangerous. She knew that she had to put some distance between them.

Kit pushed open the doors to the employment agency. She'd lost count of the times she'd looked at the boards and found nothing but today she was determined. She took a number from the deli-like queuing system and sat in an easy chair. Two men next to her discussed their families and failed interviews like old friends. Looking around the room, Kit realised it was much like a gentleman's club for the unemployed.

'Ninety-two!' a monotone computerised voice boomed. It was her turn. She walked towards a woman sitting at a square desk with a selection of forms and a computer in front of her.

'Two sausage rolls and a quarter of boiled ham,' Kit joked as she sat down. The woman looked at her blankly as she folded her hands together in a 'how can I help you?' stance. Kit realised this was no place for humour. 'I'm looking for a job.'

A bored expression modelled her features. The new Kit tried not to be irritated.

'And what can you do?' the woman asked in a voice that said, *Astound me.*

Kit would quite happily have reeled off her previous job description but feared that this caricature of a public servant might actually begin to grind the two protruding front teeth that shaped her top lip.

'Not much. I'm coming on to the job scene a little later than most people.'

'Hmm, any qualifications?'

'No,' replied Kit, feeling guilty for breathing. The woman shook her head and disinterestedly pushed away the keyboard.

'What exactly did you have in mind?'

'Anything that pays more than Income Support,' she said pleasantly, trying to get the woman on her side.

'Well, your lack of experience and qualifications doesn't really—'

'There has to be something slightly more than sixty quid a week. I'll pack pies, I'll do anything.' Kit was trying not to let her anger show. The woman hadn't even looked. 'Look, I thought it was your job to try to help me find one.'

'Yes, but in view of your—'

'Listen, lady,' fumed Kit, losing patience with the attitude of the woman. 'I'm well aware of my shortfalls but you're not hearing me. I want to work. I don't care if it's washing dishes, waiting tables or working for some spotty teenaged manager at a burger bar, just have a bloody look, will you?'

The face six inches from her own turned a shade of colour that Kit felt sure a paint manufacturer would have found an attractive name for, like Perspiration Pink, Rebuked Red or even Chastised Cherry.

The woman scrolled through her computer screen quickly. She paused and then moved on.

'What was it? Tell me, I'll do it,' cried Kit, looking into the dusty back end of the computer.

The woman scrolled back to it. 'It's data input. Very boring and not much money.'

'It sounds perfect,' replied Kit. 'But don't you need qualifications for that?'

The woman looked across the desk at her. 'No, only fingers and you have those. There's just one thing and I think this may be why we haven't filled the vacancy yet. It's near Sutton Road.'

No further explanation was necessary. Kit knew the area and avoided it like a slug in a salt mine. Just outside Edgbaston it was known as the most prolific place for prostitution in the area. She took a deep breath and raised her head. 'Yes,' she breathed. 'I'm interested.'

A brief phone call later and Kit was walking down the Sutton Road to the interview. Practice, she repeated to herself over and over, it's just practice. They'll never hire me but at least I can see how a real interview works. If I can just keep my mouth one step behind my brain I might be able to get through this okay. What do I do when I go in? Shake hands, curtsey, beg and roll over? I'll play it by ear, she decided, as she reached the front door of the company named on the piece of paper clutched inside her hand.

A portly middle-aged woman opened what looked like a serving hatch as Kit's nervous fingers rang the bell a few too many times.

Kit formed her lips into what she hoped was a pleasant, friendly smile but could have appeared a constipated grimace for all she knew. She waited to be asked to come though the door next to the serving hatch. Instead the woman came out to her.

Ten minutes later, after a conversation that involved Kit very little, she was ushered out of the door with instructions to return the following morning.

It wasn't until she let herself into the hostel that she realised that she actually had a job.

'I got it, I got it!' Kit exclaimed excitedly to Mark as she bounded into the kitchen.

He stood and hugged her. 'Well done! Your natural good humour and charm won them over.'

She pulled away quickly. 'Please, Mark, you know I hate sarcasm. And yes, either that or the fact that I don't mind being mistaken for a prostitute on my way to and from work.'

'So, we'll celebrate with a cup of coffee.'

'Whoopee!' she replied, unable to tear her eyes away from the muscles in his shoulder blades as he stood with his back to her. Yes, the sooner she moved out of the hostel, the better.

'What about the college courses we talked about?'

Kit tried to focus. 'No problem, I can do evening classes.'

'I wasn't sure you'd want to carry on with it.'

'Oh yeah, this job fulfils every one of my career ambitions,' she retorted.

'And what are they?'

'I don't know yet. Just somewhere I fit at the moment.'

'How about in a three-bed semi with a husband and two-point-four kids?'

She raised her eyebrows. 'Yeah sure, men like that fall for girls like me all the time and I'll surely catch one while I'm walking up and down Sutton Road.'

'Don't you ever hope?'

'No. At the moment all I want is to be independent and able to give myself choices of what to do next. My life is never going to be glamorous, I know that.' She paused, choosing her next words. 'But I want the things that other people take for granted. This brain seems to enjoy the input of knowledge and that's my goal for now.'

Mark reached across the table and held her hand. She enjoyed the touch of his cool, rough hand much larger than hers but removed it swiftly.

'Why do you do this job, Mark?' she asked.

'I just do,' he answered shortly.

'Good answer, cryptic though,' joked Kit as she left the kitchen.

'So, you buying the coffee tonight or what?' Kit asked sharply as she moved her chair back to the edge of the room.

Fran nodded distractedly.

'Christ, I don't want to force you! It doesn't mean you'll have to bear my children or anything.' She looked around to make sure no one else was listening. 'And I wanted to, you know, umm, thank you for encouraging me to go to Liverpool. It helped,' she admitted.

'So shouldn't you be buying the coffee?'

'Yeah, but you've got more money than me so…'

Fran nodded and followed her into the cafe.

'So, how did it go?' Fran asked once they were seated at what was now their table.

'He's dead and I'm not nice enough to say that I'm sorry, but I'm glad I went.'

Kit hadn't said much to Mark about the visit. She hated his pity and wanted to move away from it. She'd tried hard to dis-like this woman but she couldn't. The fact that Fran had a drink problem told Kit she wasn't perfect and her attendance at AA told her that she had the balls to try to do something about it. She ignored the fact that Fran was a lawyer.

'So what you been up to?' asked Kit, curious about life in paradise.

Fran shrugged, biting her bottom lip. 'Nothing much.'

There was a story there. Kit could feel it. 'Fine, I tell you something I've told barely anyone and you blank me. Yeah, that's fair!' Kit grabbed her coat, angrily. 'I was right about you all along, Frances Thornton. You think you're too good for—'

'What on earth are you talking about?' Fran asked softly.

'Last week I told you about what Bill did to me. You listened and you gave me advice but now when there's something wrong with you I'm treated like the hired help.'

Fran shook her head, denying Kit's words. 'Sit down, people are looking,' she grated.

'So fucking what?' Kit shouted. Frances Thornton was ex-actly how she'd first imagined.

'Okay, okay, sit down,' Fran instructed. 'Let's just say I met someone I'm attracted to and I'm not too happy about it. Talk over.'

Kit sat back down. 'Is he married? Is he older than you, younger than you? What?'

'None of the above,' said Fran miserably.

Kit studied her face. Something was wrong. 'Oh I get it! He's not in the correct tax bracket for you? What is he? A lowly en-gineer, waiter…'

'Wrong again and the tax bracket means nothing.'

Yeah sure, thought Kit, I can just imagine you in the local greasy spoon with Mr Builder. 'What's wrong then?'

'It's, umm, difficult. I'm not ready yet. It's...' Her words faded away.

'Yes...'

'It was a woman,' she said, forcing her chin forward defiantly.

'Yes...'

'Well, what am I going to do?'

'You're gonna have to be a bit more specific, Fran. Is she married? Does she have kids? Is it the two heads putting you off?'

'Aren't you shocked?'

'Come on, Fran, you know my life! Should I be?'

Fran pulled at her hair in frustration. 'But I'm not a...'

'A what? A woman capable of being attracted to another woman? Don't give yourself a label.' She pointed to Fran's Gucci jacket. 'You wear enough of them. Just give yourself a chance to find out how you feel.'

'But what would people think?'

Kit translated this into 'What would my mother think?'

'Who gives a flying shit what your... anyone thinks. From what I've seen you've spent your whole life worrying about what other people think. You still try to please them now. I'm not telling you what to do. It's your decision and it's a hard one to make. But Christ, Fran, it's not weird or anything, it's just life. Get to know the person, not the gender.'

'It feels good to tell someone. I can't eat, sleep, everything I look at reminds me of her.'

'That settles it. Either have a go or die from hunger and exhaustion!'

Fran smiled weakly. 'Easy for you to say.'

Kit could see the emotions crossing Fran's face: loneliness, hope, fear… She felt for her. 'Come on, Fran, you can tell me. How did she make you feel?'

She thought for a moment. 'Scared, safe, excited, confused. Pick an emotion and I felt it, but more than that. I wanted something and I don't know what. I've tried to put a name to it but I can't.' She looked pained. 'Have you ever felt that, Kit, that you want something so bad it hurts?'

Kit tipped her head. 'Actually yes. When I was about six a girl who lived two doors away came back from a day trip to Black-pool with one of those snow scene things that you shake. God, I thought it was magic the way the snow swirled around the top of the tiny Blackpool Tower! It was so beautiful I couldn't take my eyes off it. I begged her to let me shake it but she wouldn't let any of us touch it. I went to sleep that night thinking of the snowflakes and glitter being swirled around by the water inside and ached because I wanted something as pretty as that.' She smiled and shook her head. 'It was so rare to find anything magical in the poverty of our street, I never forgot it.'

'Here I am telling you that I think my whole life is about to change and you tell me about a snow scene.'

Kit shrugged. 'Well, you did ask.' She observed Fran's discomfort. 'I bet it's bloody killing you,' she observed accurately.

'What?'

'You've actually come across something over which you have no control. That must hurt.'

Fran smiled sadly. 'You have no idea,' she answered honestly. 'Anyway enough about me, what's new with you?'

Kit grudgingly told her about her plans to move out of the hostel and her new job.

Fran leaned forward, her eyes wide. 'Pretty boring week then?'

'Can we talk about something else please, like the merits of alcoholism and drug addiction.'

'Ouch, the spikes are out!'

'I'm not spiky, it's just boring!' she snapped.

'Fine, so bore me. Where is the job?'

'Sutton Road,' stated Kit, enjoying the shocked expression in Fran's eyes.

'Isn't that…?'

'If you must know, it's data input.'

'Yes…'

'What?' asked Kit

'Well, judging by the tone of your voice I guessed there had to be a punchline.'

'Let's talk about something else.'

'Why are you so defensive? I'm not judging you. Believe me, the way my life is going at the moment I don't have the right so for goodness sake, loosen up!'

Kit laughed loudly, scarcely able to believe that uptight Frances was telling her to loosen up. 'Okay, you asked for it,' said Kit, sobering. 'You make me feel stupid. No, actually it's just me when I'm around you. There you sit in your designer labels with your fancy job. How can you really be interested in what I do?'

'Firstly, what makes you think I have a great life? Secondly, I think you're my friend and thirdly, that woman over there is wearing Armani. Should I go and ask her if, because she wears good clothes like me, she understands the hell I go through every time I pass a wine bar or my uncontrollable envy of people in restaurants who can drink in moderation?' Fran paused. 'Why do you find it so difficult to believe that I like you?'

Kit didn't look up from her coffee. 'I'm sorry,' she said genuinely.

'So you should be, Miss Mersey Tunnel Mouth. Anyway, what sort of prospects are there in this job?'

'Christ, Fran! Am I dating your daughter?' An uncomfortable expression passed over Fran's face. 'Anyway, did you always want to be a lawyer?'

'No, I loved art first but realised quite early on that it wasn't realistic and that I needed a career like my parents.'

'You see, Fran, that's the difference between us. You talk of prospects and careers. I talk of jobs and rent.'

'Yes, but we both have to want to get up in the morning,' replied Fran, unable to keep a harsh note out of her voice.

'Have you noticed what stage of friendship we're in?' asked Kit to break the atmosphere that had become heavy.

Fran shook her head.

'Well, there are five stages. The first stage is where we're polite to each other. Well you are because I'm naturally rude. This is where we tread warily, eyeing each other up to see if we like what we see. Then there's stage two. Here we decide we like each other and decide to meet again. The third stage is more interesting. This is when we begin to open up a little more, confide small things but keep the big stuff to ourselves. Stage four is the juiciest bit. We get to know each other's deepest and darkest secrets. This is when I'll tell you about the time I was abducted by aliens. Stage five is when we know everything about each other and I tell you to sod off because you don't interest me any more.' Kit sat back with a satisfied smile on her face.

Fran cocked her head to one side. 'I'd guess we're at stage three, am I right?'

'Buggered if I know, I just made it up!'

They both laughed.

'Well, fellow party animal,' said Kit, reaching to the back of the chair for her coat. 'My curfew awaits me and although I'd love to stop here and chat all night, I'm also rather fond of having a roof over my head. At least until the weekend.'

'Kit, I want you to take this,' said Fran, handing her a business card.

'Hmm… Thanks, but I couldn't afford you,' Kit said dryly.

Fran chuckled. 'My home number's on the back. Ring me if you want to talk.'

'Yeah, whatever. See you next week,' said Kit as she put the card into her pocket.

CHAPTER 8

Fran

Fran watched as the jury took their places and knew their decision immediately. She succeeded in keeping her face expressionless. Jurors two and seven had glanced in their direction with a hint of a smile. She'd won.

She looked sideways at Philip Tranter, whose hawkish eyes darted around the room, anxious for the verdict. By a slight squeeze of the arm or half smile she could let him know that he was free and clear. But she chose not to. She felt no emotion for this man who was guilty as hell of two counts of GBH but she had been assigned to defend him. And she had. She stared at the legal pad in front of her while the formalities took place. When the words 'not guilty' eventually came Fran was already filling her briefcase.

'You were excellent,' he beamed, encasing her in a rough hug.

'Just doing my job,' she stated with distaste as she disengaged herself. She didn't like him. She didn't have to, and she meant what she'd just said.

'I picked a fucking winner in you! I'm just glad you didn't interrupt your record of victories with me.'

Fran snapped the briefcase closed. The gratitude of this bastard who had quite openly admitted to her that he'd beaten his wife and child, purely because he had disturbed them when he was trying to watch football, made her feel sick. He strutted out of the courtroom arrogantly and she thanked God she didn't have to see him again.

The usual tricks had worked for her once more. He'd been cleaned up, his beard shaven off – Fran knew that facial hair made the jury think that the defendant was hiding something – and he'd attended two elocution lessons. She'd brought in three colleagues from the bank where he worked to testify to his generosity, shyness and efficiency. The jury's perception became that of a stereotypical 'nice guy', just as she'd intended. They had been unable to connect a wife and child beater with the well-spoken, well-dressed gentleman before them. The proof had been there, but public perception, as Fran knew, was much stronger.

The stuffy courtroom was nearly empty. Her watch told her it was four thirty. Lesser mortals would have been tempted to go home but Fran could see a few hours of work instead.

'Good one, hope you're pleased.'

Fran looked up startled. She'd thought she was alone. 'Just doing my job, Keith,' she defended.

The prosecutor eyed her from his chair. 'How the hell do you sleep at night after defending scumbags like that?'

Fran understood his anger. The emotional part of her would have liked to see her client being dragged away kicking and screaming. She'd seen the police photographs but the professional side of her had been tasked to take on this case by the two senior partners of the firm for whom she worked. It was actually her first case back in court and she could only marvel at their faith in her ability. She had pointed out that there were better-qualified people in the company to try this case but they'd pressed her to take it.

'Do you get any satisfaction at all from your work? This is our eighth meeting, and incidentally my eighth loss, but you sure don't seem to be enjoying yourself.'

'I won, didn't I?'

'Yeah, but you wouldn't guess from the set expression of your face.'

'Is that sour grapes I can smell from a sore loser?' she asked.

'Oh no, I'm not the loser! I get to go home tonight, eat dinner, listen to some music and watch TV without fear of the doorbell or the phone. You're not the loser either. You can go home. You can do whatever you do, which I'm sure involves some sort of surgical procedure to remove the bad taste from your mouth.'

'What the hell is your problem?' she exploded, angered by his attitude.

'Oh nothing much. It's silly really. It's just that poor woman who now has to live in fear of him finding them. Of course you realise he's done it many times but she never pressed charges because she knew if he got off he'd find her and it would be worse. The police convinced her that there was enough evidence to put him away this time. It took months for me to gain her trust.' He turned away in disgust.

'Someone has to be defender, Keith. I have a job to do and if you're pissed off because I do it well, then I'm sorry but I'm not prepared to fail just to please you.'

She grabbed her briefcase roughly and turned to storm out of the courtroom. Keith's huge bulk stopped her. She looked up into the knowing face of her sometime adversary and stubbornly refused to back away. Without realising it, he'd tapped into that secret stock of guilt that she kept hidden but fed regularly.

'You have all the answers, don't you? It's cut and dried, black and white. Be careful, Fran, or you'll make the same mistake as the African tortoise.'

'The what?'

'It's a myth about an arrogant tortoise who decided to gather up all the wisdom in the world to hang from a tree so that everyone would respect him. He tied his bag of wisdom around his stomach and climbed the tree but the bag kept getting in the way, causing him to fall. The arrogance in him forced him to keep trying until a little, foolish snail suggested that he attach the bag to his back.'

'And did the big tortoise climb the tree after the little snail helped him?' asked Fran scathingly.

'No, he abandoned the whole project when he realised that all the wisdom in the world was not in his bag.'

'Interesting story.'

'All I'm saying, Fran, is don't assume you have all the answers. You don't.'

She strode from the courtroom without a backward glance.

Less than two minutes after reaching her office, her secretary Dawn entered with a cup of black coffee, a notebook and pen.

'Congratulations.'

Fran merely nodded without pride as the door opened without the usual knock first. Geoffrey Windsor, one of the senior partners, moved towards her with his hand outstretched. 'Well done, my girl,' he said, smiling. 'I think you're on your way back.'

'Thank you, Geoffrey,' she said, trying to muster some feeling.

'A rather interesting case came in this morning. Thought you might like to take a look. Another GBH. Police officer used a little too much force with a hoodlum. The internal inquiry produced nothing so the boy's mother is bringing a civil case. I've arranged a meeting with the police officer for tomorrow morning. Dawn will brief you on the details.' Once again he congratulated her and left.

'Is it something about me? Why all the GBH cases?'

Dawn looked uncomfortable. Fran tried to raise a smile. 'I was only joking.'

She'd never quite sussed Dawn out. She'd inherited her when she joined the firm. In her early fifties Dawn had been with the company since it began. She knew more about the place than anyone.

There was a quiet dignity about Dawn that gave the impression she knew more than she was letting on. Fran never had cause for complaint about her work but they'd never really talked to one another. She'd worked with this woman for almost two years and didn't even know if she had children. It wasn't necessary information as far as Fran was concerned but her typing speed was.

She sat back in her chair. 'So, what have we got?'

'Another tough one. They're not being too co-operative about the photographs of the boy's injuries.'

'I'm the defence, for Christ's sake!'

'It's a civil case now. The force couldn't care less. That officer is on his own.'

'How old is the boy?'

'Eighteen. He was being brought in on a shoplifting charge, tried to get away. The officer used what he termed "acceptable force", which resulted in a dislocated shoulder, cuts and bruises and two missing teeth. And the kid is black.'

'Shit! How the hell am I supposed to do anything with this? It's a bloody minefield.'

'Yes, just like the last one,' Dawn said quietly.

'Right, get on to the hospital and get the photographs, it'll be quicker. Find out if anyone was with him. Find out the last person to see the lad before the incident. I want names, places and exact times. Also, speak to whichever school he went to. I want to know about any fights he had or any trouble he got into,' stormed Fran, her mind working with the speed and efficiency of a Grand Prix pit stop.

'What was he trying to pinch?' she asked, hoping it was a sawn-off shotgun.

'A box of condoms.'

'Bloody hell, this gets better! Not exactly one of the Kray brothers, is he? I'm not sure I'm going to be able to put him on trial for trying to practise safe sex.'

'Winner or not?' asked Dawn.

'I'm not sure. I'll see what they've got, so the photographs are urgent. Then I'll see about plea-bargaining. If not, then I'll try to provide reasonable doubt as to how he got the injuries.'

'But how can you do that?' queried Dawn. She often acted as a thinking board for Fran, not least because she was interested.

'Depends on who was with him before the incident. I'll try to prove that he could have got into a fight before the police officer apprehended him.'

'Tricky though.'

'Any better ideas? With this political nightmare I'd love to hear them.'

'Yes, don't take the case. Have some time off. Call in sick so they have to pass it to someone else.'

Fran stopped scribbling. For Dawn that was an outburst. 'Is something wrong?'

Again Dawn looked uncomfortable. 'I just think you could do with a rest.'

Fran's suspicions were aroused. 'Is there something going on that I don't know about?'

The pencil rested alongside the notepad in her lap. Dawn wrung her hands nervously. 'Well, don't you find it strange that you've been on desk duty for weeks and then instead of breaking you in gently you get lumbered with these two difficult cases one after another?'

Fran leaned forward. She could see what was coming. 'And...'

'I've seen them do this before.'

'Go on,' urged Fran, feeling an anger build inside her. She remained outwardly calm.

'Well, they're hoping you'll slip up. Make an awful mistake that will then give them reason for letting you go.'

Fran shook her head, bewildered. 'So they're setting me up. I've never lost a case, yet the first one I do, they're going to sack me.' She couldn't believe it. 'But why?'

Dawn's embarrassment grew. 'Well, I think…'

Fran saved her any further unease. 'It's because of the alcohol, isn't it? My record has a black mark on it. Not quite the image they would like to promote. I see. But if that's the case why didn't they fire me earlier?'

'I overheard snippets of conversations while you were, umm… away. I think your mother…'

'What?' she cried. 'What has my mother… Oh my God… she called in a few favours, didn't she? Jesus!' Fran buried her head in her hands. The humiliation was too much to bear. She could just imagine what was being said about her behind closed doors.

She needed a moment alone. 'Thanks, Dawn. I really appreciate what you've told me. I know it must have been hard.'

Dawn jumped to her feet and ran out of the door as though being chased by a tornado.

Fran wasn't sure which betrayal she was having more trouble with. She had always seen this as a place of safety; where she was taken on her own merits, that she kept her job based on her performance. She had the highest rate of wins in the company, yet that counted for nothing if your face didn't fit.

This company, whose reputation was based on trust and loyalty, had betrayed her. This makeshift family that had protected and nurtured her had now, like a pack of dogs, turned on her and waited only until they found her weakness before they'd pounced. She was no more than a tiny cog in a well-oiled machine. An efficient, unforgiving machine that would rip your hands off if you didn't follow the safety instructions.

It would take some time to digest the information and once she had she would need to decide where to go from there.

She checked her watch; she was late. Kit would be wondering where she was and she had yet to find the flat. She left the office earlier than usual creating a few raised eyebrows as she went.

She found the flat easily enough from Kit's directions. They'd decided to skip AA tonight and conduct their own counselling session: admitting her own shortcomings and weaknesses to Kit was easier than to a room full of strangers.

More different they could not be; Fran knew that. But one thing bound them together. They shared an addiction that had nothing to do with which side of the tracks you were born on. And she had to admit she'd never met anyone quite like Kit before. Such people didn't exist in her world. With Kit what you saw was what you got; there were no hidden motives. You knew where you stood and you didn't need to read between the lines. And she was the first genuine friend Fran had had since Kerry.

'Welcome to my humble abode,' said Kit as she opened the door.

'Forget you, what's that delicious smell?'

'That's my dinner. Chicken roasted with garlic and mushrooms and a couple of jacket potatoes.'

'You shouldn't have gone to so much trouble,' insisted Fran, removing her jacket.

'I didn't. There's a tuna sandwich in the fridge for you.'

'Ha, ha! It smells wonderful.'

'Well, you're my first guest so I thought I'd better make an effort. Next time you can bring your own.'

Fran surveyed her surroundings. It was small but cosy. Nothing matched, which she felt suited Kit perfectly. Two sofas faced each other across a rectangular wooden coffee table that had seen better days. The kitchen led off the lounge separated only by a round dining table that couldn't decide where it wanted to be. There was little else in the way of furniture present. But more than anything Fran noticed that it was already like a home: it was lived in. She'd been in her flat for almost two years, yet it didn't feel like this.

'I like it,' Fran stated honestly.

'It's a hole, but it's *my* hole.'

'Come on, Kit, for someone who's never had her own place before it must feel pretty good.'

'Christ, Fran, it's only four small rooms but I just keep walking from one to the other to make sure I'm not dreaming! I've only ever lived in one room, and sometimes even then not alone and I keep wondering if I'm being greedy, having all this space. I find that I want to be in all four rooms at the same time. Stupid, huh?'

'Not at all,' she laughed. 'Here's another secret for you. My flat was undecorated when I moved in. With a huge black marker pen I defaced every wall with obscenities and then painted over them. That peach magnolia hides a few secrets.'

'Fran, I'm shocked.'

'I just wanted to make it mine.'

'I think I'll just buy a plant,' laughed Kit. 'Mind you, I bet it's quieter here than your place.'

'How so?'

'Well, the Changing of the Guard all the time must get on your nerves.'

'Shut up and feed me, will you?'

'Yes, master, straight away, master,' Kit chuckled, curtseying.

The meal was consumed over chatter about books and music. 'Jeez, what did you do to that chicken? It was gorgeous!' complimented Fran before placing the last piece in her mouth. 'God, I hate girlie nights like this!' she commented as they left the dirty plates on the table and claimed a sofa each. 'Food, non-alcoholic wine, music…Incidentally, Kit, what sort of crap is this?'

Kit chuckled. 'It's a Gregorian chant, and if you don't like it, piss off!'

Fran sat back from the coffee table and pulled her legs up in front of her. 'You know what I mean. It's comfortable.'

She rested her chin on her knees and wrapped her arms around her legs. It was a new experience for her. This was something she'd never had before and she couldn't understand why. It was like a pyjama party for adults. She'd chosen not to have friends at college. Even your best friend was permanently in competition. Who had the best jewellery, the best wardrobe and the latest smartphone? Within the circles that she moved friendships were not formed, only alliances made. Merely connections that could be used at a later date.

She'd be more comfortable if she could rid herself of the alien sensations that refused to leave her alone. She could imagine Martine right now – her voice, her laugh. If Fran closed her eyes she was back in London, in the art gallery, the restaurant. It was so close she could almost smell the jasmine that surrounded Martine. She could even picture the tiny scar on Martine's chin from a bike-riding accident when she was a child, which had shown Fran that the perfection had a slight flaw, making her more human somehow, even fallible.

They had known each other a matter of hours but for that short time she'd experienced feelings she'd never known before. Like a quenched geyser lying dormant in the pit of her stomach it ached to be released and to surge upwards through her body.

Fran thought about the nights when she couldn't sleep, forced awake by shadows that danced across the ceiling that eventually came together to form Martine's face on the ceiling. But why was it, when she tried to tell her active mind that it was over, finished, it refused to believe her?

* * *

'Keith Milton is here to see you,' Dawn said into the intercom sharply, obviously to impart to Keith that unscheduled appointments were not appropriate. Fran wondered if Dawn might have been a bull terrier in a previous life.

The impromptu visit surprised her. He'd never been to her office before. Her expert eye quickly scanned the neat, separate piles of folders on the desk before her, methodically labelled and arranged for ease of use. No photographs or other frivolous trinkets littered her desk. No, there was nothing there that he could not see.

'Send him in,' said Fran, assuming he was there to apologise for his conduct the previous day.

She stood up to greet him and pointed to a chair, watching as he sat and pretended not to notice that the two chairs on his side of the desk were much lower than hers, giving her the position of power. He glanced at the certificates adorning the wall behind her. Another imposing gesture. He sat easily and Fran noted that outside of the courtroom his huge bulk looked better suited to a javelin thrower.

'If we keep meeting like this, there'll be gossip,' he warned with a smile.

Fran had never seen him smile before. It suited him. She decided to make it easy for him. 'I see you've left your mean face in the courtroom, and you come to offer peace.'

A slow smile spread across his pleasant features. 'So you think I'm here to apologise? No chance! I meant every word. I'm prosecuting for Edwin Smith.' He let the information register. 'I just found out you were defending and thought it might be useful if we had a chat.'

Fran moved slightly backwards, away from him. 'I was given the case yesterday. I've only just read the file.'

'Charming man, your police officer,' he said with derision.

'Give me a chance, Keith. I haven't even met him yet.'

He threw a package from his briefcase on to her desk. 'Take a look.'

She guessed it would be the photographs. Slowly she looked at the glossies one by one. Close up and full face, taken from different angles. Even behind the swelling Edwin Smith looked like a child. That did her case no good. The jury would take one look at him and it would be over. And if that didn't do it these photos would. Fran kept any emotion hidden while she surveyed the mess his face had been made into. He looked like the Elephant Man. His top lip was swollen like an over-inflated beach ball and one particular cut, precariously close to his right eye, stretched two inches towards his ear. She looked closely at the bruising to his forehead and cringed. She could just make out, on his coffee-coloured skin, a footprint that ran almost the entire length of his brow. That one injury sickened her above the rest. It was the deliberation with which that blow must have been dealt that gave her the chills. She put her personal feelings aside and made a mental note to begin work on any motions to delay. There was no way they could go to court if any of these marks were still visible. Photographs were one thing, 'in your face' injuries quite another. She returned the photos to the envelope and pushed them back towards Keith.

'*Quis custodiet ipsos custodes?*' Keith quoted.

'I know, who guards the guards?' she replied with a smile.

The telecom light lit up. Fran answered and assured Dawn she didn't need to stay. A quick look at the clock told her it was nearly six.

'Acceptable force, huh?'

'You can't prove he didn't have any of these injuries before his incident with the police officer.'

'My God, you'll try anything, won't you?'

'Let's not get into that again, Keith, we won't agree.'

'Okay, say you took that defence, you know the balance of probabilities. I'll get it hands down.'

Fran was well aware that the balance of probabilities would not go her way. In civil cases the burden of proof was less about 'beyond a reasonable doubt' and more about 'less or more likely' to have occurred. 'Yes, but if not, the burden is on you to prove your case, not me.'

'I don't think I'll have much trouble doing that, do you? And I have a witness.'

'It doesn't say anything about that in here,' said Fran, beginning to get frustrated as she watched the odds stack against her. This case was turning into a bloody nightmare. 'Come on, Keith. What are they after? How many channels did they try before this?'

'Oh, you'd love it to be about money, wouldn't you? Sorry, Fran, you miss again. The boy's mother is a single parent. She tried to make a complaint at the police station, nothing. She wrote a letter to the Chief Constable and the Police Complaints Authority, again nothing. Not even an apology.'

Fran smiled. 'You realise that goes in my favour.'

'And mine. David and Goliath works every time. Only this time it's true. You know it's real people on the jury, Fran. They'll see this one right away.'

'So what are they asking for?'

'That he quits his job.'

'Is that it?'

'If we can settle out of court, that's all they want. They don't want money from him. Cynical people would be suspicious, wouldn't you, Fran?' he smiled.

'I do find it hard to believe, yes.'

'Why? Are you so jaded that you think everyone is after something? These people only want to make sure he doesn't get the chance to do this again.'

Fran sat up straight. 'I have a meeting with him in the morning.' She stood to inform him that the discussion was over. 'I'll give you a call tomorrow.'

Keith stood up to leave. Fran's mind was already elsewhere, the fury churning around her stomach. They had given her this case because they knew her first instinct would be to fight. To get up in court and play a few tricks and do what she always did: try to win. And it was her first instinct. She did want to take a man she'd never met into court just to prove she could win the case.

'Fancy a coffee somewhere?' Keith asked easily. 'I'm not done arguing with you yet.'

Fran opened her mouth to say no but she needed to get out of this office. It didn't look the same to her any more. And she liked Keith, even though they didn't agree on legal fundamentals.

'I'd like that,' she said.

CHAPTER 9

Kit

Kit's office resembled a box. The only things that decorated the wall were a health and safety poster for the use of a visual display unit that was held to the plyboard by yellow insulation tape and a wall-planner three years out of date. The dust that rendered them a filthy grey told her that the office didn't get cleaned too often. That and the fact that she had to wipe her hands every time she touched something.

Her box held a desk with an ancient computer from the Jurassic period that would have given Bill Gates a coronary. It took up most of the desk space and rumbled with every new piece of information that she entered. On her first day she'd jumped up from her chair thinking she'd broken it but when no flames or smoke materialised she knew she was safe. She only wondered if the dinosaurs had had as much trouble using it.

She'd picked it up quite easily. Exceptional keyboard skills were not necessary – the computer could only digest three words per minute anyway. Most of the input work was numerical and when narrative was required, she found two fingers served her fine.

Her boss was a middle-aged woman named Dorothy who was seated and working before anyone else and remained seated after everyone else had left. She'd heard it said that Dorothy was a long-serving employee who had given up all rights to a personality for the good of the company. At first she'd bustled down to Kit's office in the bowels of the building to check on her twice daily, but after being assured by her that it wasn't rocket science the visits had stopped, leaving Kit with no disturbances other than the sound of footsteps of maintenance engineers as they passed her door to fetch stock from the stores.

She'd met a couple of them briefly during her first day when a leery, balding plumber had suggested that he could sort out her pipes any day of the week. She had quite seriously replied, 'My name used to be Karl, but if you're game then so am I.'

After watching him squirm in front of his mates for a couple of minutes, she'd put him out of his misery. They'd all had a laugh about it but they got the message.

Later on she'd gone looking around at lunchtime for a bit of company. She'd found Dorothy alone in her office. She'd watched as the woman speared a slippery piece of pasta from her lunchbox and turned the pages of a knitting magazine. She paused at a white-cabled Aran cardigan.

'The canteen is on the second floor, you can't miss it,' Dorothy said, wiping the inside of the lunchbox with a sterilised wipe.

'You not going?' Kit had enquired.

Dorothy had smiled. 'No, dear, I find that I get much more out of my girls if I let them have a good old moan about me over their crackerbread and limp lettuce. It releases the tension.'

Kit had laughed and gone in search. It hadn't been hard to find. The cackle had guided her. She glanced in and half expected them to be leaning over a cauldron citing 'legs of toads, hair of spiders'. The reality had not been much different. No one was unpleasant, but she didn't stay. There was something about groups of women that she didn't like. She could imagine that behind your back they were quietly stabbing you in it. She couldn't be bothered.

She had wandered back down to what she now called her play-pen and found a group of engineers eating their lunch. She took her cheese sandwich and joined them. At first they seemed a little uncomfortable but after three of her best dirty jokes they were at ease and treated her like one of the lads. This had become her routine now and it was her favourite part of the day. In spite of her past she enjoyed the company of men. It suited her; she could be her normal sarcastic self. Most women would take offence at her humour but the men enjoyed it so she spent more time with them.

On the first day of her second week Kit was startled from her work by shouting in the stores. As there were no windows she sat back and tried to listen. By the sound of it they were right out-side her office. She recognised the gruff tone of Trevor, the stores manager. His low, smoke-aggravated voice suited his bearded ap-pearance. She craned her head but she couldn't place the second, well-spoken voice, which remained controlled, even in anger.

The door to her office opened and a man, as surprised to see her as she was to see him, stopped in his tracks. 'Oh, I'm sorry. I didn't realise this office…' He looked around and she could see that he questioned the term 'office'. Trevor was right behind him and she realised they were coming in to finish their discussion. Kit stood. 'Should I leave?'

'No, no! Never mind.' She could see that the pause in the argument was giving them both some time to cool off. The man in the suit turned to Trevor. 'I want a stock list on my desk Monday morning.'

'But that means Saturday…'

The suit raised his eyebrows. 'The stock is going somewhere so they can all help with the stock check. And it won't be at overtime rate.'

Trevor paused as though he wished to continue the debate but saw from the unyielding expression that faced him there was little point. He shook his head and left the office.

'Tyler Morrison, assistant manager,' the suit stated, thrusting his hand forward.

'Kit Mason, resident inmate,' she said, indicating the cell-like enclosure.

He smiled. 'Sorry about that out there. I don't normally use that type of language, especially when ladies are present.'

It took Kit a moment to realise that he meant her and that he was being serious. She didn't know what to say. 'Is there a problem?' she asked.

'The stock doesn't add up, again. We have a constant problem with missing items. I don't suppose you've noticed anything suspicious?'

Kit looked at the plywood surroundings and looked back at him.

'Yes, I see what you mean,' he agreed with a smile.

He wiped a small section of the desk with a white cotton handkerchief and perched his backside on the edge. Seeing the colour of the fabric, he rolled it into a ball and threw it in the bin. 'How do you like it?'

'That's a little personal. We've only just met.' The words were out before Kit could stop them. 'I'm sorry, I…' she stuttered. She'd observed other demeanours at work and realised that she would have to hold her tongue, although in her case it was like trying to hold an over-zealous eel.

He laughed and Kit noticed what great teeth he had, emphasised by a fading but visible tan. His navy blue suit looked pricey, she thought, but if he was one of the bigwigs it would be.

She guessed him to be in his early thirties, with lines around his eyes that looked as though he had laughed too much. His dark, almost black hair, worn a little long, emphasised the darkness of his eyes.

'Are they keeping you busy?'

'Yes, thank you,' she said primly.

'Please, don't close up on me. I have enough trouble sitting down upstairs.'

'Uhh?'

'Well, I have to remove at least three people from my backside first,' he declared with amusement and a little arrogance.

Kit laughed.

'That's better. Sometimes it's good to be around real people. Upstairs they have to share a personality. No one has the courage to have one of their own.'

'Charitable sort of bloke, aren't you?'

'Bored of idiots would be more accurate,' he said.

A sudden thought occurred to Kit. 'May I make a suggestion?'

There was barely concealed condescension in his eyes. 'Go ahead.'

'It's about the stock. I mean, I know I don't know anything, and I have no idea how the place runs, but Trevor works a day shift, doesn't he?'

'Yes, that's right. That's to cover as many engineers collecting parts as we can. I'm not accusing anyone of theft, it's purely that if Trevor isn't available they go into the stores, take what they need and don't bother to log it on the form. Ultimately it's stock we can't account for.'

'But wouldn't it make more sense to have Trevor on early shift when the stock is going out?'

Tyler said nothing and continued to stare over her head.

Kit felt herself blush self-consciously. 'I'm sorry,' she apologised, realising that, as usual, her mouth was ten minutes in front of her brain. 'And this is how you suck eggs.'

Tyler laughed out loud. 'Please, go on,' he invited.

'That's it really. I don't hear too many footsteps past my door after two thirty yet Trevor's still here.'

Tyler stared up at the stained ceiling. Kit couldn't believe he was giving it thought. She'd expected him to laugh in her face.

'Firstly I'm not sure Trevor would welcome permanent earlies...'

'I've heard him say he's an early riser...'

'And secondly, we'd still have a problem after he's gone.'

'I'm still here, couldn't I do it?'

His forefinger stoked his chin. 'And how do I know I can trust you with the keys to the stores?'

'Because I don't know the difference between an air-conditioning unit and a toilet plunger,' she replied honestly.

He looked straight ahead and said nothing.

She turned away from him. 'I'm sorry, it was a stupid idea. I'll just get back to my inputting.'

'The next time you have a stupid idea, Kit Mason...' she cringed as he stood to leave '...you give me a call,' he said pleasantly before closing the door behind him.

Maybe I'll just do that, Kit smiled to herself as the clock struggled towards five.

The short walk back to the end of the street was punctuated by a few nods to a couple of the regular girls touting for business outside a rundown cinema. She wasn't sure how that had started. Maybe there was an antenna that gave out a signal that could never be turned off, even when you thought you'd left it behind.

Without warning a shiver of fear pricked at the back of her neck. A sense of something dangerous stole around her shoulders. She turned her head quickly, her eyes alert, ready to spot anything different. Her gaze caught sight of a large figure dressed in black, ducking into a pastry shop some fifty feet away. Her heart rose into her mouth and choked her. In that split second she had recognised the tailored black jacket and the bald black head that dominated her nightmares. She could swear that the arms of the jacket strained against muscles that she knew so well. Feeling trapped and alone she walked on a couple of paces. He had found her. After all this time Banda had tracked her down. She stopped walking and turned around. She had to go back; she had to know.

She instructed her trembling legs to move forward towards the frontage of the pastry shop. She stood to the side and glanced in as though undertaking a covert police surveillance. Her heart raced and beat loudly against her chest. She could hear the blood pumping around her body. Stealing a look over the counter she inched forward, her view slightly obscured by rows of cakes and buns. She appraised each person in the queue and found nothing more than two pensioners and a teenage boy. She exhaled deeply and allowed the tension to leave her body. She'd been seeing things that weren't there. There was nothing frightening in the shop. Her mind had played tricks on her. She stood for a moment taking deep breaths, eager to get oxygen into her body before retracing her steps.

At the end of the road her mind thought 'left' but her feet had other ideas, taking her in the opposite direction to her new flat.

Each time she placed the key in the Yale lock a surge of pride shot through her. It was her flat, her home. She had her own door, her own postcode, even her own neighbours. Noisy sometimes but she found that more of a reassurance than a nuisance.

She loved her new home but missed Mark more than she'd thought possible. At one time she'd wondered idly if there could be something between them once she moved out. She now had to accept that it didn't matter: she was no longer his charge and yet he had not approached her. Contrary to her own feelings she had been part of his job. And yet try as she might to console herself with the thought she had to move on, she longed to see him again, not as a carer but as a man – a man who might be interested in getting to know the real person inside, without the cracks. Ha, who'd be that brave? she thought wryly.

Kit didn't even try and feign surprise when she realised where her feet had guided her, towards the safety of Mark. She was disappointed to see that the exterior of the old house had remained unchanged after her week-long absence. Why did the building bear no further scars to mark her departure? Why was it only clear to her that she no longer lived there?

Instinctively she reached for the key to the inner door before realising that she no longer had one. She knocked on the middle panel, feeling uncomfortably like a visiting stranger, and found herself hoping that Mark would answer the door and upon seeing her, his face would soften. Would he understand that of all the journeys she had made, this had been one of the most difficult? Would he fathom that this simple act could cost her so much?

The door flew open and Kit found herself looking into the expression of a stranger. The face was drawn and tight. Sallow skin hung from prominent cheekbones. Black, greasy hair straggled towards collarbones that almost protruded from the skin. Only the eyes were familiar; they were suspicious, wary and guarded and had once been her own.

'Is Mark here?'

The girl looked her up and down derisively before half closing the door and calling Mark's name. Kit felt the heat flood her cheeks. She was tempted to follow the girl and knock her to the ground. But she didn't. She had no right to simply walk into this house uninvited any more. It was no longer her home.

'Kit, hi, how are you?'

Again, it was not the face she had been expecting. Karen, who resided in the room next to the one Kit had previously occupied, beamed at her from the doorway. She opened the door wide. 'Come on in. Mark's busy in the kitchen.'

Kit stepped over the threshold and found herself wishing she'd gone straight home. The whole aura of the house screamed *Stranger* at her. She felt out of sync with time, as though she was walking back into the distant past and not the place she had been living a week earlier.

'How's the job? How's the flat?' Karen asked, excitedly. She had arrived at the shelter two weeks after Kit.

'Oh, fine, you know,' she answered vaguely. Her earlier excitement about the ideas at work had dissipated somewhere between the knock to the front door and the reality of Karen guiding her to the kitchen, as though she'd forgotten where it was.

'Hello, stranger,' Mark said, in a voice that she recognised, with a smile that she'd seen a hundred times before. It was the Mark that he used for everyone.

She struggled to find a Kit to match, a façade that would fit this occasion, but it was alien. She had not been backed into this corner; she had crawled there of her own accord, and now she felt trapped and vulnerable, like a rat scouring the rubbish bins.

'Just thought I'd pop by to tell you that I'm not missing you and I've forgotten you all already.'

'I'm sorry, and you are…?'

'Ha, bloody ha!' she said, standing awkwardly in the doorway.

'Are you staying for dinner, Kit?' Karen asked. 'Mark's making Spagretchy Bollocknoise.'

Kit smiled at the old joke the two of them had shared about Mark's speciality dish.

'Of course she's not,' Mark responded, as he stirred the mince. 'She's far too busy to hang out with a bunch of old memories.'

Kit closed her mouth, stung. The acceptance had been on the tip of her tongue.

An uncomfortable silence crowded the room. Karen hopped from one foot to the other. 'Erm… I'll just go and wash my hands before dinner.'

'Actually, Kaz, I could do with an extra pair of hands to help me serve this up,' Mark said, without turning.

Kit heard the message and understood it fully. He had no wish to be alone with her. The words were emblazoned on a neon sign hanging around his neck. 'YOU'RE NO LONGER WELCOME'.

She stood in the doorway observing the activity of Mark and Karen as they dished up dinner with the trained co-ordination of a dancing couple. Karen held out a spoon for Mark to taste. He took the offering and smiled appreciatively. Kit realised that Karen had taken her place. There was no distinction between the way Mark looked at Karen and the way he had previously looked at her. She had moved out and someone else had taken her place. Any misconceived notions she'd had about occupying a special place in Mark's thoughts crashed to the ground.

Kit was sure that the delicious aromas that had tormented the already empty space in her stomach would combine to produce another of Mark's culinary masterpieces but by the time the food landed on the table she had silently left the house.

Kit walked into her office to find a clutch of yellow miniature roses, arranged in a small wicker basket, perched on the edge of her desk. The sheer brightness of the petals gave the surroundings a little sunshine. She read the card with anticipation. A little something to brighten your office, Tyler.

Kit placed the card in her drawer and enjoyed the feeling of warm honey that filtered through her body. She'd never received flowers before.

Trevor entered the office with a smile on his face that she could just make out beneath the heavy beard.

'Good news and bad news, which one first?'

Kit sat back in her typist's chair that had a screw missing so the back support rested against her bottom. 'Good news, please.'

'Well, it seems for once they've had a decent idea upstairs and they're putting me on permanent early shift.'

Kit began to open her mouth and then closed it.

'My missus will love that. She's always being offered overtime at the supermarket and she can never take it because of the kids coming back from school. The bad news is that you're being lumbered with the stock control once I've left for the day.'

He was waiting for a response. She was being silly. Why should it be known that it was her idea? Probably best it wasn't, she decided. The engineers might not take too kindly to a woman who'd been here five minutes sticking her oar in. That must be why Tyler had kept her involvement quiet.

'Yeah, great,' she said with a smile.

'You don't mind?'

'Trevor, who am I to stand in the way of your kids getting their jam sandwich on time?'

He smiled back. 'But the good news is I've been instructed to make a hole in your wall.'

'A what?'

'More instructions from above. I'm to knock a hole into the plasterboard and fit a piece of UPVC so that you have a window.'

His look said that obviously someone upstairs liked her. 'Oh, whoopee!' she cried in mock excitement. 'Now I'll be able to see the roller-shutter door all day. How ever will I cope?'

Hmm, she wondered, was this so that she could serve as a lookout for any missing stock items or was it really just a thoughtful idea? She pushed the suspicion aside and chastised herself for being so jaded.

Trevor glanced at her roses. 'Nice.'

'From Tyler, to brighten the office,' she said, raising her eyebrows.

Kit caught the concern that flitted across his features.

'Listen, Kit, he's all right as far as that lot go.' Trevor looked around as though Tyler might walk in any moment. 'But… just be careful,' he warned before closing the door.

Kit stroked one of the smooth sun-coloured petals and consciously discarded Trevor's warning. She no longer had anything left to lose.

CHAPTER 10

Fran

Fran usually loved Saturday mornings; the beginning of the weekend. Until recently she'd used it as an opportunity for some uninterrupted work. Time when she could get her head into legal problems without meetings, telephone calls and court appearances. But not today.

The briefcase lay where she'd thrown it on the smoked-glass kitchen table. Normally she would sit at that table wading through papers. Today she couldn't. Each glance towards the offending object curdled her stomach. It also made her think of Keith. She took the briefcase and hid it under her bed – she didn't need reminding of that episode.

In fact, she didn't need reminding of anything to do with work. The barely concealed smug expression that had collectively formed on the faces of most of her colleagues told her they knew what was going on. They were revelling in the fact that she'd fallen from her pedestal, thrilled that she was not immune to the steely discipline with which the company was run, and that she was not perfect. But one question remained refused to be muted. If she was no longer Frances Thornton, Lawyer Extraordinaire, ferocious lion in the justice arena, then who was she?

A stray pencil peeking out from under the sofa reminded Fran of her impulsive act the previous evening on her way home from work. She'd seen a gentleman closing up his arts and crafts store for the night. Impetuously, she'd stopped the car and rushed in. The tart smell of linseed and oil paints greeted her. She drank in the aroma that was the one childhood smell that had stayed with her forever. The expanse of white that stretched over the canvasses thrilled her.

The owner fuming, with not-so-secret looks at his watch, was ignored as Fran, with a building excitement, fingered lovingly the sketchpads, rows of watercolour pencils, oil paints and charcoal. She had grabbed as much as she could carry – she'd wanted it all.

That had been yesterday. The anticipation of creativity had been overwhelming. The promise of discovery by her own hands had urged her to lay out all her purchases in methodical order in her spare bedroom where the light was at its best. She'd already been in the room twice, circling the equipment with the quiet reverence normally reserved for libraries. In the cold light of practical day she didn't know what to do with the materials that demanded her respect.

The threatening glare of the empty canvas intimidated her, as it stood proud but empty on the easel. How could she release herself to explore? How could a mind so used to being analytical free itself to catch a moment? Her brain was conditioned to process data methodically and accurately. Irrelevancies were not allowed, so how could she remove the constraints that would enable her to receive creativity, ideas and stimulus?

She forced herself to reach for a sketchpad and retrieve the pencil. She enjoyed the feel of the hard lead between her fingers. Her right hand itched to move across the page. There was something inside her that wanted to escape, to become. Something needed to be liberated from her mind and immortalised on to the paper: a look, a smile, an expression. A face that she could not forget and ached to see again. A face that haunted her dreams and had last registered bewilderment as she had run away. But this was not the subject she wanted to draw. To do so was too intimate. The action would admit too much. Maybe more than she wanted to face.

She began to sketch the view from the window, focusing on the shapes and angles of the varying buildings. She could see it with her eyes, even her mind's eye, but her fingers refused to get the message. She looked at the lines on the paper. They were too soft, too curved. She scribbled it out harshly, causing the lead of the pencil to rip through the page. It had to come out. Before she could move on it had to come out.

Involuntarily her hand moved across the paper. At first it could have been the face of anyone but as the hair appeared, then the patrician nose, the knowing eyes, the strong chin and high cheekbones, it all fell into place. Fran stared at the haunting image of Martine.

The ringing of the telephone saved her. She dropped the materials to the ground, disturbed that her memory could recall every feature of that face perfectly and so easily.

'Fran, it's Kit. How are you, fine, good, enough about you, I need your help. I've got a date.'

'Calm down, calm down! Who with?' asked Fran, pleased with the distraction.

'A bloke from the office. He's been really nice to me and he's asked me out tonight. Fran, I've, umm… never been on a date before.'

Fran thought for a second. 'I have a wonderful idea. It's a surprise. Just be outside your flat in twenty minutes.'

It took less than five minutes for Fran to grab her coat and handbag but the Saturday morning traffic made the journey ten minutes longer. She smiled as Kit hopped from one foot to the other as she waited.

'Am I being kidnapped?' she asked, getting in.

'If that's what sails your boat.'

'Come on, where are we going? I have to get back to make myself beautiful for tonight.'

'No effort will be required.'

'So sweet of you to notice, darling, but you're not my type!'

Fran laughed heartily. With Kit she could be herself. No layers, no pretence. 'Don't flatter yourself. You're not my type either.' Fran negotiated a sharp bend. 'I meant that no effort will be required because of where we're going.'

'Where, to see a plastic surgeon?'

'No.'

Kit crossed her arms. 'Okay, you carry on playing your little games...'

'Oh, don't be so miserable, it's a surprise.'

A few minutes later they pulled up outside the Birmingham branch of Images.

She won't be here, Fran thought, with a churning stomach. She'll be in London, or somewhere else, but she won't be here.

'Umm... I don't mean to rain on your parade, but I can't even afford the free coffee they give in there.'

'My treat.'

'Now hold on—' Kit protested.

'Oh for God's sake, Kit, take a chill pill! We're friends, so stop being so damned stubborn.'

Kit's eyes opened in amazement. 'Well, slap my mouth and rip my tongue out, why don't you?'

Fran pulled into a parking space near to the entrance. 'Nothing would give me greater pleasure.'

They entered the salon and Fran breathed in the mingling smells of shampoo, hairspray and undertones of camomile, cajeput and the spicy, warming fragrance of cardamom. It had the aura of Martine.

As Kit quietly began to shake at the prices, Fran's eyes performed a surreptitious sweep of the salon. The rich wood panelling was the same, the shiny brass finish was also the same, but there was no Martine. She buried her disappointment. This was for Kit anyway, not herself.

'I'm sorry but if you're looking for appointments today, we're fully booked, but Monday…'

Fran leaned forward on the imposing reception desk. 'We plan on spending a huge amount of money. Are you sure there are no cancellations?'

Fran watched as the brunette struggled between company policy and the promise of good revenue. The profit margin won and they were asked to remove their coats.

They decided on massage, manicure and hair.

'Ooh, I felt like Julia Roberts in *Pretty Woman* then!' remarked Kit.

They were led to dressing rooms to change into pure white luxurious terry-towelling robes.

'Hey, Fran,' whispered Kit. 'Do you think this is like those posh hotels?'

'What?'

'You know, they actually expect you to nick the robes and stuff.'

Fran giggled. 'Don't you dare!'

Their clothes were neatly folded and placed in a cubicle. The attendant slipped a nameplate on to the door before guiding them into a room with three waist-high trolleys. Fran once again inhaled the pleasing aromas that leapt from the numerous small bottles that stood next to tiny individual mixing vials.

A second attendant entered the room. 'Could you remove the robes and lie face down, please.' The attendants then covered Kit and Fran's middles with warm towels.

Kit turned her head sideways as her masseuse stood at the bench mixing a massage oil. 'What's your name?' she asked.

The girl seemed surprised. 'Trudy…' she said with a hint of a question in her voice.

'It's okay, no one runs their hands all over my body unless I at least know their name.'

Fran reached across and slapped her arm.

'Do either of you suffer from epilepsy, high blood pressure, or are you pregnant?'

'No, no and damned no,' replied Kit. Fran shook her head.

Fran closed her eyes as the warm oiled hands met with the taut muscles in her neck. The mixture of the oils gave her a heady sensation. The camomile soothed in conjunction with the expert hands that worked together in rhythmic sequence, alternately picking up and squeezing her tense muscles.

She smelt a woody, smoky aroma work around from her shoulder blades as the hands switched between stroking and kneading. The thumb pressure released knotted muscle and she thought, 'Please don't stop', then she became aware of the heel of the hand or the fingertips working their magic and she thought, 'Don't stop that one.' Each movement was as deliciously relaxing as the last. Her eyes remained closed. Her mind focused and concentrated on the soothing, revitalising experience.

Every muscle responded to the manipulation of the hands that worked their way down her body, leaving flaccid, yet awakened muscles behind them. Fran thought of nothing but the experience of total relaxation as she felt palm pressure on either side of her spine. The hands bore down and then rotated outward towards her ribs as though the tension was being banished from her body. By the time the massage ended she was aware of her body like never before.

'Whatever you're paid, it's not enough,' Kit complimented, echoing Fran's sentiments.

It was during the manicure that Fran became inquisitive. 'So, where are you going tonight?'

'I have no idea,' replied Kit, totally relaxed as the manicurist massaged lemon into her nails and cuticles. 'He's just a bloke at work who's been nice to me. He's just a friend. I mean it's not like every man and woman who spend time together have to end up knocking boots.'

'Knocking what?'

'Hazard a wild one. No, he really is a nice guy. We just get on well.'

'Okay, Kit, enough! Quality of words gets your point across. Quantity makes you sound like a liar.'

They were guided gently into the salon, where they were offered every concoction of the word 'tea' possible. Both settled for coffee.

They were placed with heads leaning backwards into marble washbasins. Their hair was cleaned and conditioned and their scalps massaged. Fran breathed in the comforting aroma of freshly washed towels.

Her natural curls bounced halfway down her spine. Tight perfect circles gathered together. She settled on a trim.

The stylist asked Kit if she'd like to see pictures. 'No, I'll leave it to you. I am follicles in your hands.'

The stylist contemplated the length of her hair, the shape of her head and face and her bone structure. Even though Kit's hair was quite short, Fran could see that when the woman separated a portion on the top and held it upwards to check for length and texture, her eyes signalled that she had ideas.

Fran's stylist was busy running her fingers through the mass of deep red curls. 'The way to control this wonderful hair is not to tie it back and suffocate it. Let it be free and nurture it.'

'It's the frizz,' defended Fran.

'There is no frizz. The hair is silky, not dry. I think a trim and then a soft style to form the curls into loose waves. What do you think?'

Fran agreed. She knew that no matter how it was styled today, the curls would return to haunt her tomorrow.

The stylist caught her expression. 'It's not a curse. You have beautiful hair.'

Fran caught Kit's amused expression in the mirror, and then froze. The face that she had worked hard to forget was set in deep concentration at the reception desk. The face that haunted her dreams and now filled her desires. Desires that she buried in the cold light of day and pretended didn't exist. The beating within her chest confirmed that they were real. She watched with bated breath as Martine surveyed the register. A puzzled expression formed on her face as the blue eyes started to search the salon. They were just about to glance in her direction when the stylist blocked the view while reaching for the scissors. She moved away but it was too late, Martine had gone.

'Fran, are you okay?' Kit asked. 'You're as white as a nun's knickers!'

'I'm f… fine,' she stuttered, still searching the one-dimensional glass that remained empty. Suddenly Fran realised that for a split second the sun had come out. And now it was dark again.

She stared unblinking into the glass wishing for Martine to reappear, yet terrified she would. She wanted the stylist to hurry up, take her time. She didn't know which.

'What do you think?' asked the stylist, holding a mirror behind her head.

'That's lovely, thank you very much,' mumbled Fran as she darted out of the chair and headed towards the reception, eager to pay and get out.

Her hands shook as she signed the receipt and wondered if they'd accept the payment. It looked nothing like her signature. She almost ran out of the salon.

'Was that her?' asked Kit incredulously, as she tried to match Fran's stride.

Fran nodded dumbly.

'Christ, she's gorgeous! But she doesn't look…'

'Oh thanks, I suppose I do then.'

'I didn't mean that. It's just… Bloody hell, Fran, will you just slow down?'

Fran ran as though the devil himself were chasing her. Only when she was seated in the driver's seat of her BMW did she allow herself to breathe. Her hands gripped the steering wheel and her head fell on to it as she tried to stop her mind from spinning.

Kit waited patiently in the passenger seat.

'Kit, there's something I haven't told you. I tried to seduce a man,' Fran admitted.

'You did what?' asked Kit, her turn to be shocked.

'It had been another rough day at work. I was trying to come to terms with myself and I suppose I wanted to prove that I was… well, normal, I think.'

'What happened?'

'Well, Keith is very good-looking in a virile, athletic sort of way. He asked me out for a drink and I went. Two espressos later it seemed like a good idea. We tried but neither of our hearts were in it. He's happily married and I'm gay. So that was that.'

Fran did not want to go into detail. It wasn't distant enough yet to laugh about and still caused her to cringe inwardly. Had she still been drinking it would have been one more memory to be drowned amongst the others. But she wasn't so she had to face it.

She had instigated it, no doubt about that. From the outset it was a mission to prove that she enjoyed sex with men and Keith was very attractive too.

She had invited him back to her flat for a drink and had acted like a complete idiot when they got there. Her hopes for her sexuality had been increased when the feel of his lips against hers had been pleasant enough in an undemanding way. His tongue on her neck had made her want to collapse in giggles and when his hand ventured inside her shirt it had produced an automatic physical reaction but no enjoyment of it. Further attempts to infuse the moment with eroticism crumbled when they had both realised that his lack of an erection together with her lack of inclination was unconducive to good sex.

'Bloody hell, Fran! How much proof do you need? Even you have to admit that the jury is unanimous on this one.'

Fran nodded her agreement and started the car.

'You know you have to go back, don't you?'

Fran shook her head. 'I can't. I'm scared, it's not real,' she cried.

'Fine, go back and prove that to yourself. Be in the same room as her, talk to her and prove there's no attraction.'

'I don't know,' Fran whispered.

Kit got out of the car and leaned down on the open window. 'You're only hiding from yourself, Fran,' she said softly as she began to walk away.

'Hey!' shouted Fran as Kit reached the door. She turned. 'Knock him dead, I'll be waiting for your call.'

'Same here,' Kit replied with a smile as she hurried into the building.

Fran found herself driving back towards the salon, just one more look. She just wanted to see that face one more time.

The lights of the empty salon shone brightly from between darkened windows either side that were closed with the finality of the weekend. As she watched, Martine materialised before her eyes: tidying the workstations, putting the last few things away. Fran blinked hard. Was the woman a figment of her imagination? Had she wished her image to appear? She looked again. No, Martine was definitely real. The churning sensation in her stomach confirmed it.

Fran watched for a moment. The brightness of the salon against the darkness of its neighbours made Martine a solitary, lonely figure, pottering around the illuminated area. She watched the lithe movements and tried to commit them to memory for later and felt something she'd never felt before. It was a need that had lain dormant within her all her life and had been awakened by this woman. It was the vital ingredient that had been missing from all her previous relationships: it was a connection.

As though sensing she was being watched, Martine's eyes turned towards where Fran sat. Fran saw the intense eyes glance her way, although she knew that Martine could see nothing, looking into the darkness from a lit room.

Fran was tempted to drive away, but she couldn't. Twice her fingers rested on the ignition key. The third time she turned it and pulled it out. An invisible force that had nothing to do with the early evening breeze pushed her out of the car towards the salon. She had to know for sure.

She opened the door and stared straight into the eyes of a face that was more beautiful than she remembered.

Martine stepped backwards. 'Frances, but…?'

'I had to see you,' Fran offered, as if that explained everything.

Martine struggled to gain her composure. 'I wondered if you would come back.'

It was not a question and Fran was unsure how to respond. She knew she should say something about London.

'I'm sorry for the way I acted.'

'Okay.'

Fran recalled that there was very little small talk with Martine. Attempts at idle comments with no meaning were met with questions. All words have a reason, or they wouldn't be, Fran recalled Martine saying.

'It was obviously what felt comfortable for you.'

Again no question posed. No reply required. This form of conversation forced Fran to examine her feelings and admit them. Her legs felt shaky. She slid into the chair that Kit had occupied earlier that day.

'I was scared,' she offered.

'Of what?'

'Myself,' Fran admitted.

'Have you never been attracted to anyone before?'

It was hard to think with Martine so close. She thought she had but she'd never felt like this about anyone.

'Not like this.'

'Do you mean because I'm a woman?'

Fran realised she would get no easy ride with Martine. She raised her eyes bravely. 'Yes,' she said honestly.

Martine turned away from her and placed a hop cone into boiling water for her favourite drink.

'Why are you here?'

The shift in conversation startled Fran. She'd been on the verge of admitting her true feelings and Martine had turned away. She tried to hide her confusion.

'If there's nothing else, I have to carry on,' said Martine with an edge to her voice. Fran felt as though she was being dismissed even though there was unfinished business between them.

She cast a lingering look at Martine. 'I'll go if that's what you want.'

Her trembling legs carried her unsteadily to the door. She wanted to leave; she wanted to stay. Her right hand met with the cold perfection of the brass handle.

'I'm sorry.'

Fran heard the small voice and sighed with relief that she hadn't been allowed to leave.

'You just bother me.'

Fran turned. The sentence was unlike Martine, who was normally so precise with each word. Martine looked right back at her with an expression of honesty and determination rolled into one.

'Your fear of your feelings makes me want to apologise for who I am, for what I am.' The piercing blue eyes suffused with emotion. 'And I've never done that, for anyone,' she added forcefully.

Fran moved towards her. 'This is new to me, Martine. In London I was drawn to you and I didn't know why. As soon as we met in the gallery I felt something. After spending time with you I didn't ever want to be without you again. I've never had these feelings for anyone in my life.' She was begging Martine to understand. 'All these years, all the failed relationships, which were pleasant enough and filled a gap, it never occurred to me to question why I wasn't happy. The way you make me feel terrifies me. Not only because it causes me to question so many things about myself, but the sheer force of it.'

Fran couldn't stop. All the thoughts that had tormented her now spilled out of her mouth. 'Those days in London were the first time I ever connected with anyone. I felt that the world could swallow me there and then and that was okay, because you were with me.'

Fran leaned back against a work surface, unsure what it all meant.

'I do understand, Fran. I'm scared too. I seemed to know everything about you even before you spoke. When I saw you today I was thrilled that you were here. I thought, no hoped, that you'd come purposely to see me. Then I saw the shock on your face and knew it was purely accidental. It hurt. I understand how hard it is, but I know who I am, Fran, and I know how I feel, but this is new to you and I won't push you.'

Martine reached across the space separating them and took Fran's hand. The touch sent a shock through Fran's whole system. It felt right and with an honesty that surprised her, she realised that she wanted more.

Martine made no move towards her but caressed her thumb lightly. 'I have to go away again for a little while. How about spending a little time together when I get back? Go out, stay in, whatever. No pressure, no expectations and…' she shrugged her shoulders with an understanding smile '…just see what happens.'

Fran happily nodded her agreement. She left the salon with the imprint of Martine's hand wrapped around hers. As sure as she was of the sun rising in the morning, she knew that something was destined to happen between them.

CHAPTER 11

Kit

Her disappointment was not as acute as it should have been, Kit realised, replacing the receiver. From the gregarious background noises, barely muffled by his hand over the mouthpiece, it was obvious Tyler was somewhere that he did not want to leave. Her disappointment was due more to the fact that she felt good and thought that maybe she looked good. She smiled wryly at her reflection in the mirror. Well, maybe not fabulous but definitely different. She would have got away with it tonight, she knew she would.

Cashmere cardigans and satin wraps would have viewed her differently, decent men instead of prospective punters might have let their gazes linger on her a moment as they idly surveyed the restaurant. They might have done if she'd been able to go out.

She tried to analyse her feelings, still reluctant to remove her new image. She didn't blame Tyler, it sounded like a good party and she wasn't sure she'd want to leave it either, though she couldn't help being a little irritated at the lame excuse of his father's birthday. He would have known about that when he asked her out. No, the problem was that she wanted to be seen. She felt like she was a kid dressing up in her mum's clothes, eager to show someone how grown-up she looked. It was almost like a test. Could she dress like this without being laughed at and ridiculed for the fraud that she was? Well, she wasn't going to find that out tonight, she thought, heading towards the bedroom to change into jeans and a jumper. The entertainment was definitely going to be of the paperback variety.

The knocking at the door made her jump. She ignored it, knowing it would probably be her next-door neighbour's father, an elderly man who was constantly tapping the wrong door. The heavy knocker sounded again, louder and more forceful. Strange, she thought. He usually realised his mistake after the first knock and the frail little man who brought his son two cans of beer every Saturday night did not have the strength to knock that hard. She slipped her shoes back on and opened the door.

Mark caught his breath at the vision that greeted him. Perfectly applied make-up created the impression that she wore none except for the deep red that coated slightly trembling lips. A soft, sleek black helmet that ended untidily on her eyebrows had replaced the tufty backcombed style. The sides, which were deceptively long, tucked neatly behind her ears with an inch of length showing below.

He swallowed hard as his eyes registered the black stockings that encased the shapely legs fitted into high-heeled stiletto shoes. Just above the knee began the flowing material of a black dress that gathered in at the tiny waist. The top half of the dress rose up tantalisingly over perfect breasts and met in a halter-neck.

Mark's throat was dry. 'Umm… excuse me. I'm here to see your flatmate. Er… jeans, jumper, leather jacket, you can't miss her. Can you tell her I'm here? Actually, on second thoughts, don't bother!'

He saw the surprise in Kit's eyes harden. 'Come in, if you want to,' she said, walking away from the opened door.

He followed her inside as she sauntered with a walk that caused the flimsy material to caress her calves. A walk that could make grown men cry.

Her reason for looking this way occurred to him. 'Going out?' he asked, shortly.

'Supposed to be but I got stood up at the last minute.'

Mark didn't trust himself to ask by whom. He wasn't sure he could remain impartial. In fact, judging by the angry monster eating away at his stomach lining, he knew he couldn't.

'You look fantastic,' he said, unable to tear his eyes away from the length of her slim, firm legs.

She turned and the expression in her eyes rendered him immobile. Hurt and accusation filled every inch between them.

'Why are you here?'

He had known that his actions a few days ago had hurt her. He had wondered if he could gloss over the episode and pretend it had never happened. He could lie and claim that he'd just been having a bad day. He could name any one of forty problems jostling around his head but Kit was too intelligent to be placated with a banal explanation.

Should he tell her about the sleepless nights he had spent tossing and turning, chased by the memory of her standing in the doorway of the kitchen, looking lost and confused? Should he confess the weakness that had coursed through him upon seeing the assured woman who had walked through the door? Would she believe the hurt he had felt when she finally admitted that she didn't need him any more? Could she understand the despair he felt each morning he woke up knowing that she wasn't close by?

'You looked too good, too confident, too…' His words trailed off as he realised that the thought that had been so full and meaningful in his mind sounded pathetic in the open air.

'You blanked me because I looked good?'

'It was everything, the whole package. You looked different.'

Mark saw the changing emotions flitting through her eyes and he knew that he couldn't do this to her. She was on her way to getting everything that she'd ever wanted. She was finding independence and finally getting to live her own life. He couldn't burden her with his own selfish feelings. She had moved on. Clearly she didn't need him any longer and he had no right to cling to what he wished could have been: she deserved better.

'I'm sorry, Kit. It had been a shitty day, meetings with the accountants and crap that would bore you to death. I shouldn't have been so rude and that's why I'm here, to apologise.'

Mark had the feeling that there was something more that she wanted to hear but she nodded her acceptance of the apology, which sounded ridiculous even to his own ears.

'I'll just go get changed.'

'Why waste it? Let's go out.'

He waited for her refusal. He wasn't fussy. He'd spend time with her on the rebound if that was the only way; he could sit and listen while she cried on his shoulder and he'd just be happy to be there.

'You sure?' asked Kit, reappearing. Mark's breathing altered again. She walked with such confidence, such allure, that she was like a dark angel. A perfect vision but with hidden depths. And he wanted them all.

She put on long drop earrings that accentuated the slimness of her face and exaggerated an already graceful neck.

'You look... amazing.' It was all he could think of to say to her. During previous conversations he'd never felt like a drowning fool. He forced his gaze away from the contours of the legs that he wanted to stroke and kiss and feel linked around his back. He tried to force himself back into the old Mark. More so now than ever it was obvious that she'd moved on.

He barely spoke as he drove to a little restaurant on The Water's Edge, a new canalside development. Lights lined the canal walkway. The reflection that bounced off the water magnified when the slight breeze brushed above the gentle ripples. Houseboats were moored at various points along the edge.

The restaurant was dimly lit and reeked of expense. Mark was aware of the silence between them but barely trusted himself to speak. She didn't look like Kit, he wasn't sure she even sounded the same, and he didn't know how to talk to her. The subjects of their conversations to date did not fit the woman before him. She was not the woman he'd spent hours sitting at the kitchen table reliving her nightmares with. She was not the broken-spirited sparrow that he'd held when the sleep demons had caught her. It was all wrong, yet it was so right. He wanted to turn the clock back for his sake, take her back to the hostel, where she would be his Kit again.

'Nice informal place you picked, Mark,' commented Kit as they were shown to a table.

'Oh yeah, you'd really fit in at McDonald's,' he said, meaning her attire.

'I don't fit here.'

'Yes, you do,' he said meaningfully.

She blushed and averted her gaze to the menu. He laid his own menu down on the table.

'Do you have any idea how many men in this place are distracted by your presence? And how many women are exasperated by their husbands' lack of attention?'

'You're just trying to make me feel good.'

Her gaze swept the room and met with the sea-blue eyes of a good-looking man sitting alone at the bar. Yves St Laurent shirt with Gucci trousers signalled he was seriously 'on the pull'. Mark watched as the man's eyes found Kit's, held and flirted for a moment. Kit demurely returned her gaze to the menu. Mark saw the interaction and hated it. He had no idea how much longer he would be content to be her friend.

'My, they do some clever things here with potatoes!' Kit observed.

Mark glanced disinterestedly at the assortment. He couldn't think about food, only Kit and her nearness. Although they weren't touching he could feel the heat from her legs so near to his own beneath the table.

Kit settled on a salad of new potatoes, lobster and truffles. Mark agreed. As far as he was concerned anything would taste like roasted cardboard.

'Mark, what's wrong?' Kit asked.

He knew he was making her uncomfortable; he could even feel the frown that was forcing his mouth down but he was powerless to stop it. This wasn't the Kit that had needed him, relied on him. This was a strong, grown woman with a mind of her own. She could have any man in the room.

'Nothing,' he mumbled.

Kit threw her napkin on to the table. 'Christ, if it's so boring being here with me, piss off! I know it's only a mercy mission but if you didn't want to take me out, you bloody well shouldn't have offered,' she stormed. 'I feel like a can of beer at an AA convention, for God's sake!'

Suddenly his phone sounded. 'Excuse me a minute,' he apologised, as he left to answer it.

Mark called the hostel to find out that it was not an emergency and could be sorted out easily enough over the phone. As he re-entered the main restaurant he saw the Greek god who had been perched at the bar sitting in his seat leaning towards Kit.

Mark watched as he said something that made her smile. Her fingers played suggestively around the rim of her fruit juice glass. She tipped her head to one side as she listened to his words.

The wave started in his stomach and rose swiftly upwards, building into a tsunami until the feeling slapped his face. His mind screamed 'Get away from her, you bastard!' He wanted to charge across the room and kick the man's perfect teeth down his throat. 'You're not good enough for her,' a voice inside him cried at the pillock who only wanted what had been taken from her too many times already. Couldn't she see what was going on, that the man was trying to pick her up; that he just wanted a quick fuck? That he wouldn't hold her, caress her and treasure her.

Mark wanted to punish her. Insane jealousy raged around his body. He couldn't think straight. A surging avalanche had now flattened all logical thought balanced precariously at the top of the mountain in his mind. Blood thundered through his ears as he stormed towards the table, making him oblivious to the complaints as he pushed past the other diners. He grabbed her arm roughly. She turned in surprise. He didn't dare look at her companion.

'We're leaving,' he ordered, his grip on her upper arm tightening.

'But—'

'I said we're leaving.' He leaned over and retrieved her handbag from the table and thrust it towards her.

'The lady doesn't want to leave,' said her companion.

Mark looked once into the eyes already unfocused through alcohol. He moved as if to walk away, then turned back quickly, smashing his right fist into the man's jaw. The drunken face hesitated for just a second before the eyes closed and he folded to the floor.

He'd have been all right if he just hadn't opened his mouth, Mark thought, rubbing his knuckles.

'For God's sake, Mark—'

'Shut up for once!' he barked.

He dragged her into a narrow alley that separated the restaurant from a nightclub and pushed her harshly against the rough surface of the brick wall, anger and jealousy the only things that occupied his mind.

'What now, caveman, are you going to club me?' she taunted as her chest rose and fell.

'If I thought it would do any fucking good, yes.'

Their eyes met in the darkness. Fire leapt between them, both oblivious to the anonymous crowds that surged past, unseen, some thirty feet away.

He grabbed her shoulders roughly. 'No more, Kit, I'm not apologising for being a man any longer. I've treated you gently but I'm not one of the men that used you.'

Her eyes sparkled in the darkness. She attempted to move but his arms were fixed either side of her head. She tried to duck down but he only lowered his arm.

He looked into her eyes and knew she wanted exactly the same as him. He was shocked at the hunger he saw there. 'I've watched you change and I've held it in. I've stifled it and ignored it.' Her unblinking gaze dared him to act. 'But not any more. You should have looked like this for me, Kit, not some bastard who will never know you properly.'

Mark felt the shiver of anticipation that ran through her body. The breeze from the water whipped past them.

Her body gave an involuntary shudder. 'Let me go,' she murmured weakly.

'Not on your life!' His gaze didn't waver. 'I want you, Kit, every inch of you. I want to own you...' He looked down the length of her body. '...And I will.'

She licked her dry, shaking lips.

With his body pushed against hers they were locked in a world where nothing else existed. The Saturday night crowds that passed the dark alleyway were oblivious to the heat burning inside. Outside the world continued but in that dark, tight alley his world had stopped.

The movement of her tongue flicking lightly over the sensuous lips tore away Mark's last taut strand of control. Nothing else mattered, all he saw was her. All he felt was her; all he dreamt was her. His mind had been taken over by images of her. He couldn't take the madness any longer.

He looked hard into the eyes that dared him to take her, then and now. The eyes of a caged animal – excited, frightened, wary, but alive and waiting.

He grabbed her shoulders roughly and pulled her forward so that her face was closer. Without tenderness he ground his lips against hers, punishing her for the effect she had on him. He prised them open with the force of his own and felt her resistance melt. He used his lips, his teeth and his tongue to take possession of her responding mouth. He licked, she licked; he bit, she bit harder. He was losing control, his mind now in a place where fireworks exploded in his head and his body responded and acted without direction from him. He wanted to brand her, forever his own.

His hands held tight the taut skin that covered her shoulders. The only thing that mattered was his quest to the very soul of the creature before him, who had the power to make him lose his mind. He tasted blood on his tongue. He wasn't sure whose it was, but as he felt her arms snake around his neck and her body arch provocatively towards him, he didn't really care.

They scratched and bit like two wild animals feeding off each other. Skin bruised and fabric tore but as he lifted her legs and wrapped them around his back and entered her with neither concern nor care, both cried out like drowning souls.

Kit woke with a warmth pervading her body that did not come from the blankets. She stretched lazily; aware of her body as though it were a new toy she was excited to own. In one night

Mark had erased the men that had used her. She felt new, un-spoilt. And he had made love to her as if she were more precious than life. She felt like a freshly deflowered virgin but she realised, in effect, last night had been her first time.

She turned on to her back, allowing herself the luxury of recollection of the heated, frenzied passion they'd shared in the dark alley, where his touch on her bare arms had burned through her skin to the bone. Where she'd stood, helpless, like a ragdoll, aware of her body's betrayal against the fabric of her dress. The passion she'd seen in his eyes mirrored her own. And then later, here in this bed, his hands had stroked every inch of her body. He'd used his lips tenderly to refresh the bruised flesh before turning her on to her stomach to place delicate, cleansing whisper-kisses along the scarred flesh of her buttocks. Then he'd entered her slowly, kissing away her tears while building her arousal to a peak of torture and desperation before her body spiralled rapturously down from the highest peak of Kilimanjaro, where he'd caught her, kissed her, and tenderly held her until she slept.

The hardening of her nipples convinced Kit it was time to get out of bed. Her body was sensitive to the fabric of her satin dressing gown.

Her mind wandered off to the Planet Stupid. She searched for a little common sense. A ridiculous picture had formed last night as she'd hovered in that surreal, magical place that preceded sleep. A place of impossible dreams that in the cold light of day diminish in logic. It was the vision of a house and Mark and someone's kid playing in the garden. She forced the scene out of her mind. They'd only had sex, for God's sake. It wasn't as though he was now committed to marrying her. He was probably regretting his actions already.

She expected to find him in the living room. It was empty except for a used mug on the coffee table. She was disappointed.

Where had he gone? Her mind started to race: she was right, it had been a mistake. It shouldn't have happened and now he was out trying to think how to break it to her. Within seconds that was the absolute, unbreakable truth. After all, Mark knew everything there was to know about her; he'd seen everything, heard anything. There was nothing she'd hidden from him. There was no way he'd get involved with an ex-prostitute with her track record and quite honestly she didn't blame him. No, she didn't blame him at all. When she saw him again, *if* she saw him again, she'd do him a favour and pretend nothing had ever happened.

The door opened, startling her. Mark walked in with a smile and two carrier bags full of supplies. 'Checked your cupboards this morning…'

He saw the expression on her face. 'Hey, what's wrong?'

She shrugged him off roughly. 'Nothing.'

He smiled as he moved behind her and circled her waist. She tried to break free but he held her close. 'I had a meeting with my boss. Remember the text message last night? I didn't exactly have a chance to tell you, did I?'

She turned to face him. 'But what is this, Mark? Yesterday we were only friends and then last night we…'

'Remind me,' he said, pulling her closer.

She placed her hands on his chest to keep a little distance between them. 'Is this a fling, Mark, are we just having fun with each other? I have to know.'

The laughter left his eyes. His hand stroked her face softly. She felt tears forming at the corners of her eyes; she brushed them away. His tenderness had done this to her the previous night.

'I can only speak for myself, Kit. With your permission I will not let you go for the rest of our lives… actually, forget the permission bit, it's not optional.'

He guided her to the sofa and then sat down beside her, stroking her hair. 'From the first moment we met I've felt something for you that wasn't in my job description. I've buried it, hidden it and ignored it because it wasn't appropriate. When you came to me you were like a broken spitfire. You were an alcoholic with enough anger and hatred inside to eat you alive.' He kissed her gently on the lips. 'You were like a tortoise. Anything you didn't like, you just curled right back into your hardened shell, knowing it would protect you, but inside was a young woman who wanted to be normal. Not spectacular, just ordinary. You fought with your claws to keep me out of your hurt, but underneath you wanted help.'

'So, all that time…' Her words trailed off. So he'd felt like that all this time and hidden it for her own good.

He nodded. 'I don't expect anything from you, Kit. We'll take this at your pace, but you have to know that I love you and I will never hurt you.'

'Mark,' she whispered his name with a voice full of emotion. 'Take me back to bed.'

Two hours later, with a hunger that forced them out of the bedroom, Kit set about making a snack. Mark inspected the compact bookcase, to the right of the small TV, which was packed with tired-looking books of all descriptions. Others littered the room. He took a closer look and smiled at some of the titles.

'What are these?' he asked as Kit entered with fresh coffee.

'Umm, they're called books, new concept.'

He pulled one out. 'Falconry?'

'The second-hand bookshop on Bond Street closed down. On the last day they were more or less giving them away, so I brought back as many as I could carry.'

He pulled out another. '*Anna Karenina*, a woman spiralling into the depths of madness, this just for laughs, then?' he joked. 'What's this one?'

Kit knelt on the floor beside him. 'Chinese astrology.'

'Umm… interesting. Yin, yang, male and female…' he murmured, leafing through it.

'Actually no,' she stated knowledgeably. 'Most people think yin and yang are male and female but they're not. They're opposing forces like night and day, good and bad, positive and negative.' She smiled wryly at him. 'That's us for starters, you're positive and I'm decidedly negative.'

'What got you interested in this?'

'Dunno really. I look at that one small book and the knowledge it contains and I just want to eat it. The first page hooked me. It's based on an old myth that Buddha invited all the animals to visit him but only twelve turned up so he gave each animal a year that would be dedicated to them throughout history. The years were allocated in the order that the animals arrived.' Kit closed her eyes and counted on her fingers. 'That's Rat, Ox, Tiger, Rabbit, Dragon, Snake, Horse, Goat, Monkey, Rooster, Dog, Pig…' She opened her eyes, pleased she could remember. 'Sometimes you can tell what animal a person is by just looking at them.'

He closed the book. 'What am I?'

She pretended to study him for a moment. 'A Monkey.'

'Cheers!' he laughed, raising an eyebrow.

'Yes, definitely a Monkey! Characteristics are generous, tolerant, sensitive but also very opinionated. Typical Monkey occupations are theologian, bus driver, counsellor and therapist.'

'You've checked.' He grabbed the book from her hands. 'Bet I can guess what you are.' He read through characteristics applicable to each of the twelve animals. 'Tiger! You have to be a Tiger.'

'Give me that.' She tried to snatch the book away from him. He avoided her grabbing hands.

'Now, let me see… loyal, wise, daring, disobedient—'

'That makes me sound like a German Shepherd,' she interrupted.

'…Arrogant, impatient, domineering, aggressive, demanding, stubborn, quarrelsome.' He looked over the top of the book. 'I think I'll just get my coat.'

She slapped him playfully. He read it again. 'Did they interview you for this book?'

'I'm not that bad!' she cried. Her second attempt to grab the book was judged perfectly. 'It tells you how different animals get along.'

'What about us?'

She pretended to read; she didn't need to. She'd checked the day she'd bought the book. 'Umm, it's not good…' She shook her head with warning.

'What does it say?'

'Basically, we shouldn't be on the same planet.'

He considered her words. 'Yep, sounds about right.'

She kissed him lovingly before she went to get dressed.

CHAPTER 12

Fran

Fran felt that the situation was going from bad to worse. She'd just had her second meeting with George Harris, the police officer who had done a complete turnaround and decided to fight the case.

During their first meeting she had outlined the dangers of fighting as opposed to plea-bargaining.

'So you're saying it's unwinnable?' he'd asked.

'Mr Harris, no case is unwinnable but as your solicitor I am obliged to present the facts and they are that you could walk away from this without a job, or you could walk away from this with a debt hanging over you for the rest of your life, a "For Sale" sign on your lawn, and possibly still lose your job.'

'But this is a civil action. They can't sack me.'

'Come on, Mr Harris,' she had smiled realistically. 'Whether it's a civil action or not, your employers are not going to want you on their payroll if you're found guilty, are they?'

That was when he'd broken down and admitted to her that he had caused the injuries to the youth. He explained that during the internal inquiry he had, at every possible opportunity, tried to explain that the pressures of the job caused him to finally crack, but no one had wanted to listen.

After weighing up the options that Fran outlined, Mr Harris had agreed to resign. His marriage was under enough strain without having to tell his wife they could lose the house in which they'd lived for twenty-seven years.

As soon as he'd left the office Fran had spoken to Keith Milton, who had assured her that his clients would not take the matter any further. The following day she had received a call from the Chief Inspector informing her that Mr Harris would be allowed to take early retirement on the understanding that he at no time spoke to the press. Case closed, or so she'd thought until twenty minutes ago when Mr Harris had barged into her office claiming aggressively that he was not going to take this like a twat.

He had visited his doctor, been placed on sick leave and was using words like 'counter-sue'. Fran wondered who the hell he'd been talking to.

'Come on, Mr Harris, you're aware of the Police and Criminal Evidence Act and you've already admitted that you broke just about every code of practice listed,' she'd reasoned.

'And you must be aware that PACE is a standing joke in the force. Be serious, Miss Thornton, police officers have more to do than ensure that a police cell is heated to the proper temperature, that two light meals and one main meal is served each day. We have to give them refreshment breaks every two hours and we can't question at meal times. How the hell are we supposed to get a result? Half of these kids don't ever want to go home.'

'Whether or not you agree with the rules is irrelevant. What matters is that they can prove you totally disregarded the procedure to the extent of physical injury and it doesn't matter if every other officer ignores that code of practice, you do not have the weight of the force behind you in a civil action.'

Fran knew she was showing her impatience but she couldn't help it. She didn't like this man who sat before her with one foot resting on his right knee. The sole of his shoe faced her, forcing her to wonder just how much force he'd used to leave such a mark on the boy's forehead.

The handkerchief he'd used constantly to dry his sweaty palms during their first meeting was nowhere to be seen. His mouth seemed thinner than before or maybe that was because it was set in a superior grimace that was half smile and half sneer.

'Miss Thornton, as my solicitor I believe it is your brief to act upon my instructions.'

'That is correct,' she'd said coldly. There weren't too many clients that she did like, it was just getting harder to conceal.

'Then I would like to fight this case,' he'd said pleasantly as he licked his middle finger and traced it across his right eyebrow.

Fran had merely nodded while clutching the desk in an effort to busy hands that wanted to slap reason into him. She could only wonder at the complete change in his attitude.

'So, what happened next?' asked Fran on the edge of her seat. She was listening attentively while Kit reiterated what had happened with Mark.

Kit lazily stretched her legs and placed her feet on Fran's Regency coffee table. A coaster with nine-carat gold trim fell to the ground. 'Umm… I don't really think I should tell you any more. It might offend you. You know, with you being anti-men and all that.'

Fran threw a cushion at her. Celine Dion crooned in the background and Chinese take-away cartons littered the coffee table. It was Wednesday night and the AA meeting was being held in Fran's flat, between the two of them. Neither of them were responding to the AA meetings as well as they would have liked. Fran still felt as though she was being judged by everyone in the room even though their experiences were similar. In some ways the meetings made her want to drink more. During the time she spent in that room she could think of little else. Here, now with Kit, they talked of other things and gave each other the support they both needed and would need for a long time yet, but she at least managed to feel a little less of a freak.

'Carry on,' she said impatiently, watching as the stupid smile formed on Kit's lips. I want one of those, she thought. I want to glow too.

'We went back to bed. That's it.'

'My dear Kit, I think you are in lust,' said Fran, pouring more juice.

'I don't care what it is. I just feel like I've been deflowered.' She cocked her head. 'Isn't that a pretty way of saying it?'

'What about Tyler?'

'He apologised for standing me up. I just nodded politely and told him it was no big deal.'

'Didn't you say it sounded like he was in a bar or something when he called? Come on, Kit, that's a bit off, isn't it?'

'Yeah, but what am I going to say? Thanks for not turning up, it was the best night's sex I've ever had. I'm sure he'd love to hear that.'

Fran laughed. The change in Kit was amazing. There was an aura around her that reminded Fran of the old Ready Brek adverts. She looked like she had a secret that the world was yet to learn. She's like an out-of-focus photograph, thought Fran. Still the same but blurred around the edges. The sarcasm was still there but without the edge. It appeared that Mark had softened everything about her. She smiled with genuine warmth now. Her hairstyle had remained soft since their visit to the salon and the habitual black was often toned down with a softer colour. Fran noticed she wore little make-up these days.

'What about you, anyway? When are you seeing Martin?'

'Martine, you ignorant woman,' chuckled Fran. 'And I don't know. I'm waiting for her to call.'

Fran tried to keep the impatience out of her voice. It had been over a week and each day she hoped Martine would call. Fear mingled with excitement made her feel like she was in a never-ending queue for a roller-coaster ride. She'd checked the answering machine twice to make sure it was working properly. She'd asked Dawn to ensure that her phone was answered at all times. But still no call. A frightening thought had hovered for days. What if Martine had changed her mind and didn't want to spend time with her? What if she'd met someone else on her travels, someone like Cristina?

She pushed the thought away angrily. How could she be jealous of a dead woman? That was sick and she felt guilty for thinking it. But still…

'So are we going to see you on the gay protests for lowering the age of consent and all that?'

'Kit, you need to stop watching the television. Not every gay person feels the need to run around half-naked to prove who they are, just as not every heterosexual needs to. Some people, whatever their sexuality, just want to live a peaceful, happy life with someone they care about.'

'Ooh, this is getting deep!' chuckled Kit. 'But isn't that kind of selling-out? I mean, don't you have an obligation to fight for the rights of people like you? The sisterhood and all that?'

'If that argument holds weight then don't you have a responsibility to fight for heterosexuals?'

'I'm not the minority.'

Fran thought for a moment. 'But who do I help by throwing my sexuality in your face? If you don't mind gay people it won't affect you but if you are homophobic then my aggression in stating my case will only offend more. This isn't Vietnam, Kit. I'm not going to fight for a cause that I don't understand. I'm not saying our society is perfect but until it understands that we are real people trying to live normal lives we'll get nowhere.'

Kit prodded harder. 'But don't you want the same rights as heterosexuals?'

'In what sense?'

'I dunno, public displays of affection, that sort of thing.'

'Why does every couple you see feel the need to be kissing and groping every minute of the day? While they're having a meal, walking in the park? My God, I thought you had a better idea than this!'

'Oh, come on Fran! This is a hypothetical debate. I'm interested.'

'Maybe I'll feel different in ten years' time. At the moment I'm new to this. I've never stood out in a butcher's shop never mind a gay protest but all I want is what other people want: to be happy and content. I don't expect everyone to approve of marriage between two women, that will never happen.'

'But being gay is not your choice, so why shouldn't you?' Kit goaded.

'No, being gay is not my choice but deciding to embark on a relationship with a woman is. Now I have to decide whether I'm doing that for me or for the gay community.' Fran gave a little chuckle to lighten the atmosphere. 'I suppose I'm what you'd call a laid-back lesbian.'

'Well, I think…'

Kit was interrupted by the doorbell. Fran sat up startled. 'Who on earth could that be?'

'Hang on, I'll just get my crystal ball,' said Kit, removing her legs from the coffee table.

'But I'm not expecting anyone at this hour.' Fran checked the clock on the fireplace. It was after ten o'clock.

The doorbell sounded again. 'Well, we could sit here and guess for hours but you know what, why not just open the door instead?' Kit suggested, cocking her head.

Fran looked through the security hole carefully as though it might bite. She stood back and opened the door quickly. 'Father?'

He looked at her as though waking from a deep sleep. Fran saw instantly that his suit did not fit as it should; it hung like the skin of an obese person after a crash diet. His face was pale and drawn, with no sight of the ruddy, healthy complexion.

'Hello, Frances, may I come inside?'

Fran was shocked at his voice. It was the low, deep voice that she remembered but much quieter. Foreboding rolled around her stomach.

'Oh, I'm sorry I've disturbed—'

'No, no, it was time for me to leave anyway,' said Kit, rising from the sofa. She shot a questioning glance at Fran, who stood behind her father. Her slight shrug told Kit she had no idea what was going on.

'Father, this is Kit. She's a friend of mine.' Fran realised it would have been more accurate to admit she was the *only* friend of hers.

Patrick Thornton extended his hand. 'Do you work together?' he asked politely, taking in Kit's less than impeccable appearance. Her T-shirt wasn't sure whether it wanted to be constricted beneath the waistband or hanging loose. The dark blue jeans were slashed at the knees. The sight of the leather jacket brought a panicky look to his face.

'You're okay, you can keep your wallet,' Kit said sharply, seeing the result in his eyes of the instant appraisal. 'No, I'm not a lawyer. I actually work for a living,' she joked.

Fran cringed, knowing her father's opinion of Kit immediately. She was concerned only that Kit would not be offended by her father's demeanour.

Before Patrick could respond Kit was walking towards the door. 'Nice chap, your father,' she said sarcastically as Fran opened the door.

'That's him, not me,' said Fran, a little shakily.

'Hey, are you okay?'

Fran nodded. 'There's something wrong, he's never done this.'

Kit looked into the lounge and back at Fran. 'Want me to stay?'

The thought appealed to Fran. Let Kit stay. Let Kit tell her father what she thought of him. Sit back and watch while Kit said everything she should have the courage to say. The thought was tempting.

'No, go home. I'll be okay.'

Kit hesitated. 'All right, but call me when he's gone, whatever time it is. I'll bill you for it later,' she said with a reassuring smile.

Fran nodded gratefully and returned to face her father.

He was sitting as though he needed to, on the sofa nearest to the fireplace.

'Interesting girl,' he commented with obvious disapproval. Fran ignored the tone. He was right, 'interesting' was one word for Kit. There were many others but none he would understand.

She remained silent. Meetings like this were unheard of. Fran occasionally saw Alicia without Patrick but never the other way around. She'd often wondered if Alicia carried his lungs in her Chanel handbag – she was sure that was where she kept his backbone.

'Ah, Ming vase!' He nodded towards the centrepiece of porcelain. 'Alicia's favourite.'

'It's only a copy,' she said uncomfortably. Her father didn't fit in her home, especially alone with her. She couldn't remember when they'd last been alone together.

'You're not well, are you?' she asked without preamble.

'No, I've known for a while now. But that's not why I'm here.'

'Are you…?' Her words trailed off. She couldn't say the word.

He nodded. 'Yes, Frances, I'm dying.' He shook himself and rearranged his features into the mask that she knew so well. It was his courtroom face, the one taught him by Alicia, she was sure. The grey eyes held no warmth and no feeling. His chin was set and he stared straight ahead.

'H... how long?' she stuttered. Surely there would be words now, explanations; details of his illness.

'Not long. A month, maybe two.'

Fran wanted to scream at him. She wanted to know why no one had seen fit to tell her. After all she was their daughter. As she watched him amble to the window she knew it would do no good. Her parents had always played by their own rules; this time had been no different.

'The rest is irrelevant, Frances. I say again, that's not why I came.'

Fran wondered what sort of relationship it was that such few words were the total conversation that would take place about her father's terminal illness. Was she not allowed to show any emotion, even now?

'I failed you, Frances, I'm sorry.' The words were clipped and he didn't look at her. 'You've done well for yourself and I'm proud of you.'

How many years had she waited for those words, from both of them? And they came now, more or less in the same breath that he used to tell her that he was dying. 'The saddest day of my life was the day you were told your child had died.' He didn't turn; he spoke to the glass.

Fran seated herself on the sofa and waited. Why now? Why after all these years was he talking to her about something buried in the graveyard that was their family history?

'I waited, you know. I prayed for a sign that you would show some resistance to Alicia. That you would be worthy...'

'I was sixteen,' she defended. 'I told her I wanted to keep him. If he'd lived I would have fought. How can you blame me? My child had just died, what was I supposed to do?'

Fran could not believe what she was hearing. All her life she had fought a losing battle against the closed-off, exclusive unit that was her parents. Never could she remember either one of them spending any time with her as a child, other than to instil the sense of righteousness and rigidity that now controlled her life. Her heart cried at the injustice of his words.

'Father, I've lived with that loss inside me. I've coped with it and in true family tradition I haven't bothered anyone with it. Don't you think I wonder how different my life might have been if I'd been given the opportunity to love? I think about it, my God, I think about it, I've cried about it, but I can't bloody well change it.'

'But you can do something about it now.'

'I don't understand.'

Patrick opened his briefcase and extracted a thin white manila envelope. He laid it down on the sofa beside her. She didn't touch it; she just looked at him for an explanation.

'He didn't die, Frances.'

Fran had an uncontrollable need to laugh. Initially at the absurdity of the notion and then at the ridiculousness of her father making such cruel jokes. Her child alive, no, it wasn't true. This was just another sick joke instigated by her mother to torture her.

'Father, I don't know why you're here but—'

'It's true, Frances. Your son is alive but he was born—'

'I really hope this is a cruel joke because accepting the alternative is impossible,' she warned.

Patrick continued to speak as though she weren't there.

'He was born with an illness. Down's syndrome, they call it. We decided it was better that you didn't know.'

Fran slumped backwards. This was not real, only the sickness and the rising bile were real. She ran to the bathroom and vomited violently, still denying that he spoke the truth. They could not have kept her son's existence secret from her for eight years, no way. She would have known he was alive. Surely she would have felt that he was alive. She had mourned his death for eight years, blamed herself for it for eight years and all that time he'd been alive, without her. It wasn't possible.

Her head fell on to the toilet seat as sickness threatened her again. What parallel universe was she in and when had she changed over? Was it when Kit was here? After she left? When?

Her mind flashed back to the morning after his birth. Where was his body? Why had the doctor left so soon without making sure she was okay? Why had Maria suddenly been kind to her as though she'd been unfairly treated? Why the hell did she never ask these questions? Her mind roared.

Oh my God, it has to be true, she realised. My son is alive. Eight years old, and alive. She began to laugh, before the tears choked her and she was laughing and crying. Until she remembered her father in the lounge. And the deceit. Fran tried to regain her composure. She had to think straight; she had to get past the rock that was sinking lower in her stomach as a portion of her heart curled up and died. They were not important now, only her child.

'Where is he?' she asked sharply as she re-entered the lounge.

'It's in there,' he stated, indicating the envelope.

'What happened? Give me the facts and don't try to dress them up with caring platitudes, just tell me.'

'Frances, it was the best—'

'Tell me!' she screamed.

He took a deep breath. 'You were unconscious when the baby was finally delivered by caesarean section. You were exhausted and there was nothing we could do to help—'

'Father…' she warned.

'It was obvious immediately that there was something wrong with him. We all stared in silence at the bloated face with scrunched features, not knowing what to do for what seemed like hours. We looked at each other, waiting for someone else to decide what to do. Finally, it was decided by Alicia that you would be told the child had died.'

'You *do* surprise me,' grated Fran, feeling any trace of emotional attachment to these people disappear.

'Frances, you were young, sixteen, for heaven's sake! How could you have coped with a handicapped child? You were no more than a ch—'

'Then what?'

He took a deep breath that rattled in his chest. 'The arrangements for the baby were made by me. Alicia wanted no part of it; she just wanted it gone. I was the cleaner.' He paused. 'I have received regular progress reports since. Your mother has no knowledge of this.'

Fran cringed at the businesslike manner in which he spoke. There was no emotion behind his words. Progress reports, he could have been talking about a stock market investment. Easier to stomach but harder to believe was his secrecy from her mother.

The details of her son's whereabouts were just a few feet away. She had only to reach out and her questions would be answered. The black scar that had remained in her heart, closed and shrivelled up for years, now reached out to the envelope.

'Why?' she asked simply.

'He's my grandson.'

Her hand itched to move towards the envelope but she couldn't. Not yet. 'Why now?'

'Because I'm dying.'

Eight years of loneliness and lies were about to end and she would from this day on always know what her son was doing.

It was hard to accept so quickly. Fifteen minutes ago he'd been dead.

'Is he happy?' The question that had beaten all others jumped out of her mouth. This was one thing that she had to know. The details she would dissect later.

'Yes, as happy as he can be.'

Her heart clapped and cheered.

'What about Mother?'

'That is your choice. I am giving this information to you, it's all I have.'

He checked his watch. She saw his growing discomfort. Old habits die hard; he'd completed what he'd come to do, his purpose for seeing her over. But she wasn't finished that easily.

'Why, Father? One question you have to answer is why you wanted me? Was it a fashionable time to have a child? Did the housekeeper need something to fill her time? For God's sake, answer me! You owe me that much.'

He appraised her as her mother did. 'You should have been so different.'

His hand was on the door handle. He lowered his briefcase to the floor. 'One day you will understand why it was so hard to show you the love you deserved. Don't try to be like her, Frances. You are yourself. You are beautiful and intelligent. You have no reason to emulate Alicia.'

She ignored him. He hadn't answered her questions so his words were no longer important to her. Nothing else mattered now except her son and the fact that his life had been withheld from her.

'Father.' She looked into his eyes with complete control. 'Get out of my home and do not come here again.'

Before his surprised expression could form any response, the door was closed.

She stood rooted to the spot, bewildered by the events of their one conversation and the realisation that he had told her he was dying, he had told her that her son was alive and not once had they touched. Deep inside her she felt sadness for his illness, the way she might for a work colleague. She felt regret for the relationship they could have had but the door that had remained open and inviting for more than twenty years was now forever closed to her parents.

With trepidation and shaking fingers she opened the envelope as though it were a long-lost fragile treasure from Tutankhamun's tomb.

The envelope held one piece of paper containing nothing more than an address.

CHAPTER 13

Kit

The small table that rested halfway between the kitchen and living room looked good. She looked good. Now all she needed was Mark to appreciate the candles, napkins, tablecloth and flowers that sat waiting for him.

Huge steaks sizzled with mushrooms on her two-hob cooker. Black scorched grid marks were visible on the meat, just as he liked it. A crisp green salad waited in the fridge and a sexy black camisole beneath her jeans and sweater signalled she was ready. The luxurious material felt good against skin already sensitive from a red-hot shower. Its teasing delicacy promised idly what the night would bring.

She enjoyed making an effort for him. Because of his job she didn't get to see him as much as she'd like: there was always someone, somewhere in need of his services. She didn't mind, she'd been there – she just wished that sometimes he would be a little more selfish with his time. So nights like tonight were rare. Nights where they planned to stay in together with food, music, conversation and hopefully more.

Kit craned her neck to look at the kitchen clock: Mark was ten minutes late. She was already anxious to see him. He'd said he had something important to tell her tonight. She had banished the feelings of foreboding that had immediately sprung to her heart; she had to learn to trust him.

She loved him; she knew that. He didn't, of course – she hadn't yet had the courage to tell him. At first she'd fought against it, terrified her defences had lost some of their power before she realised that it was too late.

The peace that now lived in her was welcome. She felt like a woman with a secret. Romantic songs on the radio were now meant just for her. The poignant words had taken on new meaning and finally made sense to her. At one time they were ridiculous lyrics lamenting emotions that didn't exist in the real world, now they were her own feelings set to haunting melodies.

She'd noticed a new tolerance within herself, a little more patience. The concept of love was no longer a joke, a notion invented by writers and directors living in another world. It was real and it felt good. And for the first time in months she had woken without the longing for a drink.

She realised that the idiotic, cheek-numbing smile was fixed to her face again. She physically forced her features to rearrange in an expression more fitting to a person with all their faculties just as his soft tapping sounded at the door.

'Umm nice,' she said of his new shorter haircut. He looked more rugged, the dark blond curls gone to reveal more of his face. A light stubble that looked fashionable but was due to a busy schedule emphasised dark circles under his eyes.

She guided him to the table. 'Here is the main course,' she said with a wild, playful glint in her eye as she placed his hand underneath her sweater. 'And this is dessert.'

He groaned. 'When I was a kid it was really weird because we always had dessert first.'

'Liar,' she teased, snaking her arms around his neck, enjoying the sensation of being totally vulnerable to his wandering hands. 'Enough,' she cried teasingly. 'It's hot enough in here already!'

They talked about work while they ate. Kit knew there was no point trying to press him – Mark did things in his own time.

Once they'd finished he guided her to the sofa where he sat contemplating as if choosing his words with care. The heat from the hot coffee did nothing to stem the cool trepidation that began to penetrate her skin. She tried desperately to think positive thoughts, and failed. A familiar panic churned with the steak she'd just eaten.

'They're closing the hostel, Kit,' he said quietly.

She sat back in shock. 'Can they just do that?'

He nodded. 'To use my boss Roy's words, "There is surplus care in the Birmingham area." Can you fucking believe that?' He rose to his feet and paced the small room agitatedly. His shoulders appeared tense, ready to explode from beneath the blue open-necked shirt. 'Surplus care, where for God's sake? If there was surplus care there'd be no fucking waiting lists!'

Kit had never seen him like this. He was always so calm and together.

'What about Mandy and the others?' Kit asked of the current occupants.

'Here's another good word: "re-distribution". That's what Roy called it. I call it uprooting people from a place where they've just begun to feel safe. They don't need this at the moment, Kit.'

'I know, Mark,' she said in a voice that assured him that she did understand. 'How long?'

'Two months before they put the property on the market.'

'What about you?' she asked softly.

He took a deep breath as he sat beside her. 'I've been approached by Leeds County Council. They're starting a two-year project aimed at reducing the increasing numbers of teenage prostitutes on the street.'

Kit heard the words but they didn't sink in. She knew only that Leeds wasn't a bus ride away. She tried to remain calm. 'Is it what you want?' Silently she prayed he would say no.

He raised his head and stared into her eyes. 'Yes, it's what I want.'

'So, you're going.' It was a statement not a question. She removed her hand from his. Her mind became busy collecting the bricks and mortar for a new wall.

He nodded.

'When did you know?'

'A few weeks…'

'And you didn't tell me?' she cried, angered by his deceit. The first course of bricks was laid. 'You've known that long and you let me think we had a future?'

'We *do* have a future. I want you to come with me.'

She stared at him aghast. 'And do what, Mark? I'm lucky to have the job I've got. Look at me! For the first time in my life I have things that are mine. And now all of a sudden you want me to throw it all away to sit in a strange place, with people I don't know, reliant on you. No, forget it, Mark! I was right, we have no future.'

Kit's rage increased. He was threatening her safe little existence. She had just started to feel normal – her own flat, a job, self-respect. Now he wanted to take it all away.

'Kit, listen to me…' His voice commanded her attention. 'We'd be going as a team, that's the whole point. They want you to go with me to help run the project. They were going to advertise but I suggested you and they agreed on a trial basis. They want someone who knows about life on the street, someone who can reach out to these girls honestly, not some fresh-faced social worker who wouldn't know a pimp if he walked up and introduced himself.'

Kit stood up and towered above him. Each word was a separate knife. 'I can't believe you're actually serious about this.'

'No one understands what those girls are going through more than you, Kit. Don't you want to do something useful with your life? Can you think of anything better than using your past to help young girls who should be at home worrying about spot creams and conditioners?'

'No… No… NO!' she repeated, with growing emphasis.

Mark stood and pulled her to him. Numbed by his words she had no control. It had to be a joke.

'Kit, we could do this, imagine—'

'Stop,' she commanded, turning hurt eyes upwards towards his, animated with hope. Her voice was little more than a tortured whisper. 'I spent years being used by pimps, beaten by punters and robbed by just about everyone. I lost everything in that time, even things that cannot physically be lost. I feel for those girls, Mark, more than you can ever imagine, but what about me? I can't believe that you of all people would be prepared to thrust me back into a world that I am still trying desperately to forget.'

'It's your past, Kit. It will always be part of you. It's made you the person you are now,' he whispered truthfully.

'I can still feel the filth in my pores. I smell those men all around me. I've left it now, I can't go back, and I hate you for thinking I could!' she cried. 'For the first time ever this morning I woke up not needing…' Her words trailed off. She wouldn't tell him, *couldn't* tell him. It revealed too much.

'But what we have, Kit, it's special. Don't dismiss it that easily.'

She had an overpowering urge to hurt him, like he was hurting her. 'Do you think so, Mark?' She saw anger flash through his eyes. 'I'm sorry you feel that way. I thought we were just having fun.'

'I know you feel more—'

'Don't flatter yourself, Mark, we had good sex, and that's all. I needed practice and thought you would be fun. But guess what, this just isn't fun any more.' The words were slapping him across the face one by one. They were leaving exit wounds as they shot from her mouth.

'Kit, don't say things you don't—'

'Why do you think I don't mean what I say? We've been seeing each other for a few weeks. It's nothing, Mark, not even a relationship. We hardly know each other.' Kit knew they had always known each other but the toothache in her heart needed anaesthetic. She wanted to punish him for his promises, for the security that she'd believed could be hers.

The tears wanted to come, but her strong will forbade them. 'I don't think you've done too badly, Mark. All the sex you could handle for three cheap meals. You had a bargain.'

Her taunts were leaving their trail across his face. He stood and faced her. 'I don't believe the words, Kit, no matter what you say. We both know we had more than that, but the fact that you can say those things confirms to me that it's over.'

The hurt in his eyes choked her. She wanted him to hold her, she wanted to say sorry, but the brick wall was about chest high and she couldn't find a way over it.

Mark looked at her once, with sadness, before he left.

Hot bitter tears of betrayal scalded Kit's cheeks as they fell. She made no effort to stop them, finding a masochistic comfort in the slow agony she knew would eventually kill her. She would continue to re-build the wall, only this time it would be thicker and stronger. It would keep her emotions in and the interlopers out. In a few months the barrier it had taken years to perfect had been broken down by Mark. She'd been weak and pathetic to allow him to crawl through the brickwork. It would not happen again.

The dinner plates on the table reminded her of the night she'd planned, the effort she'd offered so easily, the hopes she'd had before he arrived. Everything was still new to her: Mark was her first boyfriend, her first lover. She'd let herself act like a girl of sixteen and now it hurt.

She swept her arm across the dinner table, which seemed to be mocking her, and watched as everything fell to the ground. Plates smashed, cups cracked and cutlery bounced. Her legs buckled beneath her and she fell amongst the rubble. Where was the happy ending? Where was the pleasant semi and kids? That picture had once formed in her mind and remained there.

His scarf, forgotten in anger, lay folded next to the cooker. She rubbed the warm, soft length of fabric against her cheek, breathing in the aroma of him, which lingered in the fibres.

The tears stopped, suddenly. This would not happen again. During her years on the streets she had thought that nothing good in her would ever survive. The bitterness had burnt deep, scorching every inch of loving tissue. But from somewhere she'd found a morsel of living flesh on which she had built. Just one tiny part of the heart undamaged by her past and she'd used it. She'd cherished, nurtured and offered it to the first willing male who had come along.

She began to collect the scattered remains of their romantic dinner. The cuts caused by the jagged edges were unimportant. It would not happen again.

The phone on Kit's desk rang, startling her. She'd thought it was an ornament.

'Hello,' she said tentatively. She hadn't even known it was connected.

'You're in, I'll come down,' said Tyler.

The phone clicked in her ear. No greeting, no formalities.

He entered the office with a cheerful grin. 'Well, did you pass?' he asked of her IT exam the previous evening. It was a short course for which the company had paid.

'I'll know next week but I think so.'

'Great. Any more courses you're interested in? If they're ben-
eficial the company will definitely pay,' he offered magnani-
mously as though he'd be paying for them personally.

'Rocket science would be good, then I could apply for a ten
per cent wage increase.'

'I don't really think—'

'Joke, Tyler,' she stated. Christ, did no one appreciate the gift
of sarcasm any more?

He shifted uncomfortably. 'Well, if you think of any, let me
know.'

'I think I'll leave it for a while. Maybe next year. But before
you go, I have had another idea,' she offered. In an effort not to
think about Mark, Kit had been working longer hours for no
extra pay. The engineers had labelled her the company cat and
jokingly left saucers of milk on her desk. She let her mind busy
itself with ideas for improvements. Ways in which she could
actually make a difference. The inputting of the sheets did not
challenge her mentally and often her mind wandered further
than the stock numbers she typed. Her office was the only place
that didn't remind her of Mark. No matter how many times she
changed the sheets, washed the cushions or rearranged the small
rooms, she could still smell him; still hear him.

Tyler coughed as he leaned against the door frame with his
arms folded in a 'okay, let's hear it' stance.

Kit described an incident two days earlier when she'd been
listening to the engineers moan about the call-outs they had to
attend. She understood that they took it in turns to be on call.
Jack had stated that most of the time the call-outs were electrical
problems and that as a plumber he couldn't fix them so he had
to call someone else in anyway.

'Why are you moaning, you get overtime, don't you?' she'd
asked.

'Overtime is one thing, an ear-bashing from my missus when we're out is another. We can't drink the week we're on call and have to arrange a lift if we're called out other weeks.'

Kit had given it some thought and had a suggestion for Tyler.

'If you got the engineers to share some of their skills with each other there would only be a need for the on-call engineer to attend. After listening to the engineers, I've drawn up a list of some of the skills that could be shared.'

Tyler rubbed his chin and tried to pick holes in her argument. 'What about more serious problems like distribution board failure?'

Kit had no idea what that was. 'It won't work for every situation, just the little things...' She grabbed a yellow Post-it note with scribbles on. '...Out of the ten most common faults, seven could be remedied by any of the engineers if they were just shown how.'

He glanced at the list and nodded. 'Leave it with me. Anyway, more importantly, how about a meal tonight to celebrate your victory?'

'My what?'

'Passing your exam.' He smiled disarmingly. 'And I do owe you a meal.'

Kit leaned back in her chair. The thought appealed to her. It had been a month since her split with Mark and she'd spent every night alone with her books. She loved reading but it was beginning to pall in the absence of conversation. And no matter how many times she pleaded for the phone to ring, it wasn't going to.

Tyler was pleasant company and no threat to her safe little existence. He was good-looking, she had to admit, in a polished, groomed way. His dark brown hair was just a little too long, giving the impression that the impeccable suit he wore was almost a chore.

'I'll pick you up at eight,' he said.

It would have been nice if he'd waited for an answer first but she nodded her agreement anyway.

Maybe it was time to put the ice cream back in the fridge and the tracksuit back in the wardrobe and stop grieving. After staring at the wrappers of the junk food she'd recently been consuming she could recite the nutritional information of most of Cadbury's products word for word: fat, sugar and kilojoules. She knew how many scratches lived on her coffee table and when she stared at them for long enough they began to join together and form pictures. She also knew how many times she could randomly switch the channels with her remote control in one minute.

She needed to get out.

How could it hurt to have dinner with Tyler? He couldn't climb the barbed-wire fence. Nice enough, pleasant enough in a non-commanding way. He'd take her somewhere nice. She'd pretend he was someone else and her past wouldn't exist. If asked about it, she would lie. With Tyler she would have a little fun. She felt no attraction to him sexually – those feelings were dead – so why not go along for the ride? There was nothing he could do to hurt her.

CHAPTER 14

Fran

She no longer had it. She'd won the case, barely, not convincingly.

A question ran around her head like an ant on speed. Who had triumphed today? The police officer who, although the case was won, would never have the career for which he'd hoped. George Harris naively expected to return to work as if nothing had ever happened. She knew that in winning he felt vindicated for his actions. He'd even walked away convinced he'd never laid a finger on the lad. His sneering mouth had been contorted with righteous victory as he'd left the courtroom without so much as a glance at the boy who sat staring straight ahead as the court emptied, or at the mother whose tears had found their way under the rims of her thick glasses. Yes, Harris might be the victor today, she thought dismally, but surely, at some stage, he would have to face what he'd done.

As she'd intended, she swayed the jury by focusing on fights the youth had caused at school, knowing when Keith stated that it was a predominantly white school, the jury would assume Edwin Smith was crying racism even though he was completely accurate.

She had also proven that his friends, black and white, did not have jobs and this again painted a picture of young thugs on street corners, causing trouble, getting into fights and intimidating the general public, regardless of the fact that only one in four youths were in work in Birmingham.

She had totally destroyed their witness, a white shopkeeper in her late forties who was only there under duress and had been totally intimidated by the official proceedings. It had taken just one question about the last time she'd had an eye test to throw her off guard. By the time Fran finished with her she didn't even know what day it was.

Throughout the two-day trial Fran had been unable to look at the boy's mother. The woman had sat beside her son with quiet dignity even though she'd been forced to look at her battered child every day until those horrific injuries had healed. A few days ago a mother's pain might not have meant much to Fran, but today it did.

And what about me, she thought with a sickness that refused to be quelled. When will I face what I've done and what I continue to do every day? How long will the justification 'It's my job' keep the screaming banshees inside my head quiet? She'd proven reasonable doubt, she'd destroyed a witness, she'd defended her client; she'd done her job. So why did she have the urge to approach the two figures that sat staring with shared disbelief as the police officer returned to work? She watched as Keith turned, placed his hand on the woman's arm and spoke softly to them both. They nodded disinterestedly. Either they were out of strength or they knew as well as she did that this had been their last option. There was nowhere else for them to go: justice had been served.

She'd thought her next win would quench the cape of dissatisfaction that shrouded her. That another victory in the courtroom would give her back her life, her safe life. Externally she had always been able to function. She still did but the feelings inside her were becoming increasingly harder to ignore. She wanted control over that but somehow she just didn't have it any more.

She grabbed her briefcase and almost ran out of the court-room with an overwhelming urge to cry. Not a sniffle that could be demurely concealed behind a lace handkerchief but a loud, savage bawling session complete with unstifled aggression that would erode the breeze block in her stomach. She started the engine of her car in the hope that she would never see the inside of a courtroom again.

She returned to the office and half-hearted congratulatory gestures from her colleagues. But it was a game: her job was only a matter of who could win the round or produce the best party tricks. The people didn't matter, the victims or the accused. Fran wasn't sure which was which any more.

The sight of Martine waiting for her in front of the Chamber-lain Clock in the centre of the Jewellery Quarter restored a little peace inside. The previous evening they'd spoken on the phone and arranged to meet for lunch. Fran had said nothing of her father's visit. She'd mentioned it to no one. For the time being it was her secret. Her gift. A candle of warmth that had been lit inside her. She had the constant feeling that Christmas was coming tomorrow. The day she'd finally allow herself to tear off up to Selby to see her son. Her first instinct after her father left was to get in the car and drive to him immediately but for once her cool rationalisations did her a favour. At that time there was too much anger and hurt at her parents' actions, which she did not want to take with her. It had taken every ounce of self-control not to ring her mother and scream obscenities into the mouthpiece. Again her logical mind told her that the receiver would be replaced at the first sign of anger. She knew that confrontation would come later, but not before she'd seen her son. *Her son.* The words sent a delicious shiver down her spine.

Fran raised her hand to wave to Martine and then felt the breath being knocked from her body as she fell to the ground.

'I'm so sorry,' said a low deep voice from above.

It took Fran a few seconds to realise that she had been knocked backwards and was half-sitting and half-lying on the ground.

'Are you okay?' the voice asked. Fran noticed a thick ethnic tinge.

'I'm… er… I'm fine,' she stuttered.

A large black hand reached down to help her up. She accepted the assistance and was back on her feet by the time Martine came to a halt beside her.

'Are you all right?'

'It was all my fault. I'm sorry, I wasn't paying attention.'

Fran realised that the man still had her hand encased in his own. Her gaze met his and he smiled apologetically, showing two gold teeth.

'No, I was distracted also,' she said gracefully, just wishing for the encounter to be over. She stepped back from the man before her, intimidated by the sheer size of him, but there was something else. Despite the concern in his voice, amusement danced behind his eyes.

'Thank you for helping me up,' she said, taking Martine's arm and moving away. His gaze lingered on her for a moment before he turned and sauntered away.

Fran shuddered.

'Are you sure you're okay?'

Fran tore her eyes away from the retreating figure and told herself she was being silly. It had been a simple accident caused by distraction on both sides.

'I'm fine, honestly,' she said, realising how her own dark grey suit clashed with the loose cotton of Martine's trousers and cheesecloth tunic. It was a glorious day and outside of her air-conditioned office she could feel the strengthening lunchtime sun burning through her jacket.

'My, how very smart you look!' smiled Martine. 'Hmm, not exactly going to be able to sit on the grass in those, are you?' she said, raising the picnic basket.

Fran banished all other thoughts from her mind. She'd been waiting what seemed like years for Martine to return. She had an incredible urge to embrace her. To take the picnic basket from her hands and pull her close to confirm that she was really here.

They found a bench and set the picnic basket open between them. Fran peered inside. 'What?' she exclaimed. 'Chicken sandwiches with mayonnaise, cheesy puffs and fruit. Not exactly a veritable feast!' she laughed.

Martine leaned across and slapped her playfully. 'Sorry, didn't have the chance to pop down to Harrods Food Hall, you know. And don't knock it until you've tried it. My chicken sandwiches are world famous!'

Fran gave her a doubtful look as she took a bite. 'Actually you're right, that's delicious. What else is in this sandwich?' she asked, catching a small piece of chicken before it landed on her skirt.

'Well, I could tell you but then I'd have to kill you.'

Fran was relieved there was no discomfort between them, none of the awkwardness that had been present the last time they met. She wondered what passers-by thought of them. Were they just two friends sitting on a bench sharing lunch, or could they see the force that came from Martine like an electric current and touched her heart as though lighting a lamp? Could they see and what's more, she wondered, how much did she care?

'Where are you, Fran?' asked Martine, with the radar of a bat. 'I know you want to be here but there's something on your mind.'

Fran was shocked at Martine's perception. She thought she'd left the negativity in the office.

'Just work,' she replied.

'Tell me.'

'I'm not sure I know where to begin.'

'It doesn't matter as long as you do,' said Martine

Fran tried as best she could to put her emotions into words. Once she started she couldn't stop. She saw Martine glance away. 'I'm sorry, I'm boring you,' she apologised.

Martine shook her head. 'Come with me,' she ordered, closing the basket.

They walked past the Assay Office and into the old Smith and Pepper works that was now the Discovery Centre. They passed a group of craftsmen who sat around one huge bench and passed pieces of gold between them for each to undertake a different process.

'These used to be residential houses,' whispered Martine. 'They were converted into "pegs" for rent to artists.'

Martine guided her to where the lone jewellers worked with single-minded concentration as they sat at the old preserved benches of stone. Fran felt that they had entered a time warp, the only admission visible of the twenty-first century were the powerful lamps attached to the benches.

'What are we doing?' Fran asked.

'Just watch,' Martine ordered, her eyes already entranced by one jeweller in particular, who was in the process of preparing a gold ring of two separate stems, one smooth and the other already formed into a rope design.

The flame that he used to manipulate the source material danced in Fran's eyes as she barely blinked, fascinated by the demonstration. He teased the gold until he expertly brought together the two thin lengths of metal and formed them into an intertwining knot.

Beads of sweat were forming on his forehead as the ring neared completion. The jeweller, aware of his audience, did not waver from his task. He leaned over, extinguished the shooting yellow flame and smiled.

Self-consciously Fran returned the smile. The man was in his late fifties, she guessed, with a deep furrowed brow from the years of head-bent concentration.

'Hell of a job but someone has to do it!' he joked, with a pronounced Birmingham accent.

'You seem to enjoy it,' Martine observed politely.

'Wouldn't be happy doing anything else.'

'It's beautiful,' said Fran, nodding towards the ring.

'Not one of my best. Doesn't matter though. Before it was a piece of yellow metal, now it's something.'

Fran was intrigued. 'How long have you been doing this?'

He smiled good-naturedly. 'Over thirty years.'

'Do you still get satisfaction from it?'

He removed his glasses. 'Yes,' he answered. 'If I didn't, I wouldn't be here.'

'That simple?' asked Fran with a smile.

'Look, love,' he said as though talking to a child. 'I start with a raw material and I form it into something that previously only existed 'ere.' He tapped his temple. 'There ain't no greater satisfaction.'

Fran heard his words. 'Thank you,' she smiled as she moved away from the bench.

'Err... Miss...'

Fran returned to the bench. He pushed the ring towards her. 'There's a slight imperfection,' he admitted. 'You won't find it but I know it's there.'

Fran shook her head to refuse.

'Go on, love, take it! I can't sell it with a good conscience knowing of the slight fault.' He pushed it further towards her, in assurance that he was genuine. 'Go on, I want you to have it. It ain't perfect but it's still beautiful.'

Fran thanked him warmly and left the building with the ring in her hand, the warmth of the flame still evident against her fingers.

The clarity of the day as they left was only partly due to the sunshine. That man had sat in that chair for more than thirty years and was still happy to do so. She wanted that.

'Thank you,' she murmured to Martine.

'For what?' asked Martine innocently. 'All I did was get you a free ring.'

With regret, Fran realised that she would have to return to work. She wanted to give Martine some sort of sign of what she was feeling. She leaned over and stroked the soft flesh of her arm warmed by the sun. Why did almost anything seem possible on a midsummer day?

'Martine, I—'

Martine put a finger to Fran's lips to silence her. 'Don't rush anything, Fran. Just be my friend,' she said softly before walking away.

Fran knew that she was deliberately forcing her to examine and re-examine her feelings until she was sure of what she wanted. And she was glad. She also knew it was for Martine's benefit as well. She'd been hurt terribly in the past and although she was confident and at ease with her sexuality she did not want to court heartache. Fran knew that the move would have to come from her.

She re-entered the office building with Martine's face in her mind and the jeweller's words ringing in her ears.

Her first instruction to Dawn was to make an urgent appointment with Geoffrey Windsor, immediately. Her second was to get Keith Milton on the phone.

'Fran, so nice to hear from you! Thought you'd still be washing the blood off your hands,' he said with enough ice in his voice to freeze her ear to the receiver.

'Keith, I'm ringing as a friend.' She ignored his sarcastic laugh. 'Listen, I get the feeling that the force is getting a little fed up with Mr Harris. An internal inquiry and a civil case.'

'So?'

Fran took a deep breath. 'You said your clients only wanted to ensure he never got the opportunity to do this again.'

'Yes,' he replied, becoming more interested.

'Well, think about it. If he beat that lad black and blue you'd probably be safe in assuming that he didn't get his three square meals a day under the PACE guidelines.'

'Wow, if a jury wouldn't—'

'I also think, quite strongly, that the force does not want any publicity about this case, especially since the particular station Mr Harris is from has just employed a community liaison officer.'

'So you're thinking, hypothetically of course, that any press coverage would seriously damage Mr Harris's chances of keeping his job for much longer?'

'Hypothetically nothing, I know it.' She paused. 'So, should I buy a newspaper tomorrow or not?'

'Well, if you did, there might be something in there to interest you.'

'That's all I needed to know.'

'What's going on, Frances? If anyone found out about this conversation you'd be in serious trouble.'

'I'm aware of that, Keith, but I saw those people in the court-room for the first time today and it hurt,' she said honestly. 'I still had a job to do and I did it but now I have to live with what I won.'

'There's more going on here than this one case, Fran.'

She sighed long and hard as Dawn poked her head around the door to tell her that Geoffrey was ready to see her.

'Let's just say the turtle finally heard the snail,' she murmured, replacing the receiver.

She took a deep breath and tried to find some doubt within herself about what she was about to do, but it was no use. Those four walls were no longer enough; their protection now stifled her.

The walk to the top floor she made slowly, savouring the experience of complete freedom. She could do and say anything she wanted to now that she was no longer bound by the shackles of this community and that made it all look so different.

Geoffrey's expression was one of forced hospitality, which she knew was deliberate. Although he had agreed to the impromptu appointment he was less than happy about it.

He indicated for her to sit. She shook her head – she wanted to be out of this office as quickly as possible.

'I won't take much of your time, Geoffrey. I have come to tender my resignation in person with the assurance that written confirmation will follow.' She paused as she analysed his flitting expressions and registered the brief display of relief. She wasn't offended; it was too late for that. 'I'd like it to be effective imme-diately. There is nothing on my desk that can't easily be handed over to another lawyer…'

'But why, I don't understand. Please reconsider?'

Fran wondered if he realised how obviously his words did not carry the conviction they should have.

'No, Geoffrey, you can't change my mind.' Her courtroom tone brooked no argument.

'But you've always been so happy.'

Fran saw the game they were playing and decided not to play along. It didn't matter any more. This was exactly what she wanted to escape. Conversations where you had to listen just as carefully to what was not being said, conversations that should have been straightforward but operated on too many levels. It was too tiring; it was time to stop.

'No, I haven't been happy, Geoffrey. I've *survived* here. I've even used this place as a surrogate home but even parents can turn, can't they?' She couldn't help the bitterness in her voice. She no longer wanted to be a part of this charade and wished they'd had the balls to sack her, but his regretful pretence was too much.

He averted his gaze, embarrassed. Fran knew he was from her mother's camp. Bare emotions were embarrassing and should be kept locked in the family vault with the jewels and bonds and other things it was useful to have but not necessary on a daily basis.

'And what will you do?' he asked, clearing his throat.

'What I should have done years ago: study art.'

She saw the amusement behind his eyes. Art was something you took an interest in when you weren't at work. It was a mere distraction from the important, real things in life. It was a hobby. Fran had had the same argument with herself. She had defended her work. She'd struggled to find a time she'd been happy in what she did because she did it and not because she won. Unfortunately she had found that the reasons she was good at it were the reasons she was lacking in other areas. She knew there was a word, conditioning. She wondered how hospital workers, morticians, even care workers could witness such misery and sadness and not take it home with them. How was it possible that one could switch off with a timecard and forget the trauma they'd seen? Surely the steely resolution they had to acquire spilled over into other areas of their lives as it had with her?

She herself had entertained the thought of painting in her spare time, but it wasn't enough. As long as she was forced to present this other person on a daily basis she would never find the emotional freedom to see past what she'd become. There was something inside her that wanted to escape; to find its way on to canvas. An expression, a scene, a memory, or emotion, which was something she'd only just realised she possessed.

She felt lucky that she'd accumulated a little financial independence that enabled her to make this choice but when the money ran out it would be up to her to support herself. The comfort of a full-time job and good salary would not help her to attain her goal. She had to be free of comfort and control.

She wanted to struggle, for ideas, for inspiration. If she attempted this half-heartedly she would fail. It would become too easy to give in and return to the automated life she had been leading.

'What if you fail?' asked Geoffrey, as if almost reading her thoughts.

'The only way I will have failed is if I don't do this. I don't want to wake up in forty years and think "if only". My years here will never be wasted, I'll always be a lawyer. If I have no talent and enough people tell me that then I'll always have that to fall back on.'

Geoffrey nodded as though accepting her decision under duress. She shook his hand and left the office.

She collected her box of personal effects and uncharacteristically hugged Dawn, the one person in the whole place she would be sorry to leave.

Fran glanced back at the stone and concrete building with little regret. It had never given her anything back and definitely not the love and approval she'd sought.

She drove back to her flat slowly, her usual high speed of living slowing down. The burning urgency was seeping out of her. She could feel her body and mind decelerating like a gear change.

She'd come this far and Fran knew she had to find the courage to go through the doors.

The outside of the huge building was nothing like she'd expected. It was a rambling country house that consisted of four floors. There were no restrictive gates or fences, only trees and fields that seemed to stretch forever. Unknowing onlookers could innocently mistake the building for an old stately home. There were no signposts, no directions for her to follow.

She sat on a three-foot stone wall that ran in front of the entire length of the building, admiring thick marble pillars and long oval windows made up of hundreds of small panes of glass. She took three deep breaths and stood up.

The first set of double doors were open, revealing a spacious foyer that she now saw housed direction boards and a phone. Again she backed away from the entrance. It was hard to believe that she was so close to her son. He was in this building, playing, eating or sleeping. But he was here.

The anticipation of seeing him was almost too much to bear but before she went in she had to compose herself. If she was going to interrupt his life, his safety, then she had to do so devoid of selfish feelings. It was up to her to accept what had happened and see him only as he was, not as he might have been. He didn't deserve her emotional baggage, only someone who would love him unconditionally.

She braced herself and picked up the phone after checking the instructions on the wall. A pleasant, efficient voice asked for her name. Fran gave it and waited for the doors to open. They did not open automatically. The left door was opened by a middle-aged woman smartly dressed in an oversized shirt and black slacks. The shirt cleverly disguised the generous figure of its owner; the haircut was short and tidy. She stood with hands clenched before her. Behind her stood a man who towered above her by at least a foot. His casual attire did nothing to conceal the fact that he was security. He looked like a bulldog in jeans.

The woman's expression was wary. 'My name is Thelma Dunn, general manager.' She quickly appraised Fran's appearance. Feeling self-conscious, Fran did the same, hoping her loose-fitting trouser suit did not do her disservice. 'I'm sorry, we don't have your name on the visitors' list,' Thelma stated quietly. She tipped her head to one side, pursed her lips and folded her arms across her bosom.

'No, I haven't been before…' Fran paused, unsure what to say next. '…Umm, my son is here,' she blurted out.

'Your son? But then why don't we have your name?'

There was no condemnation in Thelma's tone, only a question.

'I haven't been before,' she repeated. The guilt that she'd tried to leave behind evident in her voice.

'If you'd like to come this way, I think we should talk.'

Fran followed obediently. At the moment this woman was God and if she had to jump through hoops of fire, she would.

She was led into a room that housed two sofas and a coffee table. She tried hard not to feel that she was on trial as the now officious-looking woman fetched two coffees from a vending machine.

'I'm very sorry but you're going to have to help me out here,' said Thelma, placing two plastic cups on the table. 'All the parents of the children are accounted for and on our master list.'

A feeling of terror shot through Fran. Maybe he wasn't here at all. Maybe her father had got it wrong. Maybe she'd never find him. Panic showed on her face.

'Now calm down,' Thelma ordered in a voice of granite. Fran felt twelve years old. 'It's probably some sort of misunderstanding. Just tell me the child's name.'

'Thornton... I don't know his first name,' she said apologetically.

Thelma could not hide her surprise. 'Are you sure?'

Fran nodded, her hypersensitive radar alert to the woman's discomfort.

She rose unsteadily to her feet. Fran instantly knew that something was wrong. 'Is he here? He is, isn't he? Tell me what's wrong. Is he ill?' A hundred questions darted through her mind. All of them hungry for answers.

'Please wait here a moment.'

Fran paced the room. Something was very wrong. When she had said her surname, the woman had appeared shocked. And what did she mean, all parents were accounted for?

The minutes felt like hours. Even now an unknown hurdle was waiting to send her flying to her knees, putting even more distance between her and her son.

Before Thelma was halfway through the door Fran cried, 'Please, tell me what's wrong with my son.'

'Please sit down. There is nothing wrong with the child you have named. He is safe and well.'

Thelma again sat opposite Fran, warily. 'Do you have any identification to prove who you say you are?'

Fran reached quickly in her bag for her passport and driving licence. She had expected to have to identify herself but she hadn't expected anyone to show disbelief in her existence.

She handed the passport to Thelma without words. She checked it once and then again, comparing the serious, unsmiling photograph with Fran and checking her date of birth.

Fran waited for an explanation. Thelma cleared her throat. 'I'm sorry, Miss Thornton. We have to be very careful about who we let in here. It appears that undoubtedly you are Jamie's mother.'

'Who?' she asked, dumbstruck.

'I'm sorry. His first name is Jamie.'

Fran swallowed hard. The name she had chosen for him. Thank you, Father, she thought. She fought hard to return her concentration to the woman before her.

'Is it so hard to believe that I'm his mother?'

'Well yes, I'm afraid it is, because, Miss Thornton, you are listed on our records as deceased.'

Fran's head spun out of control. 'Wh... What?'

Thelma shook her head. 'I've seen many things in my years looking after these children but never a woman raised from the dead.'

Fran slumped back in her chair. 'I assume this information came from my parents.'

Thelma nodded. For her own sanity Fran knew she had to accept what had been done and put aside the hatred that kept building and building. At the moment that was not important, only Jamie was.

'Now that you believe me, can I see him?'

'I'm afraid not.'

Fran snapped. 'Why not?' Tears of frustration threatened her composure. 'What the hell do I have to do now, jump through hoops, walk on burning coals? Just tell me and I'll do it if it means I can see my son.'

'Please don't try dramatics with me, Miss, because it won't work. I'm sure you will appreciate that my duty is to the children within my care.'

Fran nodded, rebuked. She'd hoped for nothing less.

'That being the case we have to talk about a few things first. Please don't think I am intentionally trying to keep you from your child but you have to understand that Jamie has had only one regular visitor in the eight years he's been here.'

Fran's heart reached out to the child who was playing somewhere within this huge building and put aside her bitter anger towards her father. At least he had given Jamie a little security. She could not forgive him for the lies but she was grateful for his contact.

'Reasons for that are not my business nor my concern but Jamie's welfare is,' Thelma continued. 'He has watched as many different people visited other children. Some even go out for weekends or holidays. Your son has seen this and accepts it. If your intention is—'

'I have no intention other than to be his mother,' Fran whispered.

Thelma smiled indulgently. 'Please don't interrupt me. I understand that you have good intentions but if you disrupt his life and open his heart for the sake of a couple of visits, he has that disappointment to face all over again. You see, Miss Thornton, this isn't about you at all. To be candid, your feelings matter very little here, only your actions. I appreciate at this stage you don't know what the future holds but please don't try to make yourself a necessary part of his life if you cannot make that commitment. You'll do the child no favours.'

Fran's heart ached. The harsh words made sense to her. His feelings came first. She knew that Thelma was not being deliberately hurtful but it was her job to protect the children. Fran thought she was probably a mixture of love, discipline and fierce protection.

'I want what's best for Jamie,' she whispered.

'As do I, Miss Thornton.' Thelma's voice softened. 'Have you done any reading on your son's condition? Do you have any idea what to expect when you see him?'

Fran nodded. She'd read any material she could get her eager hands on. She had an idea what to expect in his physical appearance. 'I read books from the library, sourced information on the internet, but after a while opinions and facts became blurred and began to contradict each other. I know there are different types of Down's syndrome, but I don't even know what type he has.'

Thelma smiled. 'Sometimes you can read a little too much. I'll explain it as best I can from what I know. The most severe form of the disease is called Trisomy 21. This is when three copies of the twenty-first chromosome are present instead of two. This accounts for about ninety-five per cent of all cases and is directly related to the age of the mother—'

'But—' Fran tried to interrupt. She was rewarded with a stern look.

'Jamie has another type, which is called translocation. That means that a small, extra piece of chromosome twenty-one attached itself to another chromosome.'

Fran nodded, unsure whether she was allowed to speak yet. Thelma paused for breath.

'The main problems of the condition are the associated disorders such as heart abnormalities, thyroid disorders and the risk of leukaemia. These illnesses are normally contributory factors to the cause of death.'

Fran had read that. 'What is the outlook long term?' she asked. The words came out in a strangled form but she had to know. This was another area where opinions had differed.

'Life expectancy is in the region of sixty years in some cases. There have been dramatic increases since the seventies. Doctors have learned to recognise the associated problems earlier.'

Fran felt relief flood through her body. She'd learnt more from this woman in a few moments than she had from the countless books and articles she'd studied. Her right foot, which had begun rocking to and fro, hit the leg of the table.

Thelma smiled. 'What I'd like to suggest is that we have a walk to the master playroom, where he'll be. I will point him out to you so that you may see him.' She tried to soften her next words. 'I'd appreciate it if you didn't approach him. As we've already discussed, it would draw attention to you.'

Fran nodded eagerly. She would agree to any conditions Thelma imposed. 'The children may well approach you. That is fine. You may chat and play all you like but I ask you again not to single Jamie out.'

After depositing her belongings in a cloakroom, Fran matched Thelma's surprising speed and agility stride for stride. Every step forward increased her pulse rate. She had to work hard to breathe normally.

She was led into a huge room with windows that stretched from halfway up the wall to the top and met with the high ceiling. The two walls that had no windows were covered in pictures and paintings of all descriptions. Excited squeals of delight together with unusual chatter filled her ears. Soft toys and mats littered the room. Fran was struck by the sheer brilliance of the room. Foam animal characters around two feet high were resplendent in bright, vivid colours. It was like walking into a cartoon.

Her gaze eagerly swept the room. She stopped breathing. She didn't need to be told which child was Jamie; she knew. His features, almost covered with a shock of straw-blond hair, dived straight into her heart to stay.

He was sitting on a child's red plastic chair colouring a huge picture with thick crayons in each hand. When Thelma's hand indicated where her eyes were now rooted, it only confirmed what she already knew.

She watched with undeniable pride as his small body left the seat. His red T-shirt untidily escaped out of the back of his denim dungarees as he took his picture to one of the adults sitting on a mat reading a story to five or six others.

The woman smiled, ruffling his hair, and leaned over to ask him about his picture. He dropped it to the floor and threw his arms around her neck, forcing her backward on the mat.

Fran watched as his previously inexpressive face dissolved into smiles. The other children now joined in the fun and Jamie was lost in a mass of laughing children tickling the storyteller. Fran had never envied anyone the way she did that woman who had the pleasure of holding or touching Jamie any time she wanted to. She mentally checked herself: if not for women like her, where would Jamie be? Fran chastised herself severely for the thought.

'As you can see, he is happy,' Thelma whispered.

The breathless attendant indicated that she could take no more of the merciless tickling. The children moved away, anxious to find more fun elsewhere.

Fran didn't take her eyes off Jamie. He was small for his age and his movements were slightly forced. She looked deep into his face as he sat on the rocking horse. His skull was smaller than it should have been. An extra fold of skin was obvious beneath his eyes. His nose, which was definitely hers, was flattened at the bridge. Her brain registered his physical distortions but her heart reached out to the most beautiful child she had ever seen. She felt an immediate and fierce surge of pride and love at the sight of him. Her arms longed to hold the small, frail body and protect him from all the bad things.

'He speaks quite well,' Thelma murmured kindly beside her. 'Sometimes his speech worsens when he's tired but other than particularly difficult words, he stumbles along quite well. His favourite activities are drawing and painting,' she added.

Fran nodded and fought the lump in her throat.

Definitely her son.

Her arms were becoming agitated. She linked her fingers together for something to do with them. They ached to be occupied.

Thelma passed Fran a book with buttons down the right-hand side. 'Sit down on the mat and look at it,' she suggested.

Fran cautiously did as she was told. She pressed the top button, which was decorated with a pig. A mechanical snort issued from the book. Fran chuckled. She pressed the sheep and was rewarded by a low 'Baa'.

A couple of children stopped what they were doing and glanced inquisitively in Fran's direction. Slowly, three children began moving towards her, aware that she was fresh blood.

Fran was surprised to realise she had a growing audience. She began to talk and laugh with them as she impersonated the sounds of the animals. A few more children approached, wondering at the source of the laughter. She continued to press the buttons and impersonate the sounds, to the delight of the children. Out of the corner of her eye she saw Jamie dismount the rocking horse and move slowly towards the group that surrounded her.

She tried to keep her concentration on the game she was playing but he was no more than three feet away. Her voice shook as she mooed for the audience. Jamie stood slightly away from the others and watched silently.

A couple of the children had wandered off, losing interest after hearing each animal five times. Fran knew that if she reached out she could almost touch him. Thelma's words jumped around in her head. Every ounce of effort she had was focused on holding the book. He inched a little closer. Her faltering impersonation of a duck raised a smile that lit up his face. Again he inched closer until she felt the fabric of his dungarees brushing against her bare arm. Goosebumps appeared although she wasn't cold. Another three children left the group when her noises began to lack conviction. Jamie sat next to her and laughed openly at the sound of the dog. His face creased in joyous laughter. She joined him in his merriment. Fran didn't know how much longer she could confine the arms that were eight years late in holding this little boy.

Jamie inched towards her on his bottom. She held her breath. It was just the two of them. He forced his little body sideways against her arm, leaving her no alternative but to raise it. He nudged himself inside the circle of her arm and rested comfortably against her ribs. Fran raised her eyes imploringly to Thelma.

Thelma nodded, smiling, as she watched Fran's arm snake around Jamie's body and pull him closer.

'Do you have far to go?' Thelma asked as they ate macaroni cheese in the canteen, although Fran's was barely touched.

'A long drive to Birmingham, unfortunately,' Fran replied, crestfallen. She knew she had to leave but it was hard to tear herself away. All afternoon the children had besieged her, then left her, and then besieged her again, bringing other books and toys for her to play with, but Jamie had barely left her side. Could he possibly know that she was more to him than the others? Might he sense that she wished to pick him up and run, run until she couldn't breathe, to a place where she could hold him, soothe him and make up for the last eight years? Did he know that she never wanted to let him out of her sight again?

The enforced separation had occurred at five thirty, teatime. She had hated the emptiness that his little body had left within the circle of her arm. Even now she could feel his imprint against her.

Thelma had given her a tour of the classrooms, equally vivid and bright. She'd seen the pencils with specially designed handles, seats used to facilitate movement and posture, adaptive aids for turning pages, reaching, eating. She'd even seen computers equipped with infrared cameras that determined where the eye was looking and activated accordingly. In half a day she had seen and learned so much. The thought of getting into her car and driving away choked her.

'You won't be able to see him again tonight, I'm afraid. After tea it's bath time and calming-down time, ready for sleep.'

'I understand.'

'You'd be surprised how many parents don't. Don't get me wrong, we love parental input, it takes the strain off us, but sometimes they can't comprehend the need for routine in their children's lives. They come at the weekend and want to cram a whole week's worth of loving and spoiling into two days. Most of the children don't understand the concept of weekend, they only know familiar faces are here. Then the parents have to return to their everyday lives and we're left to restore the safe routine that they know. Then the next weekend it all happens again.'

Fran observed the warmth behind the harsh words. 'I get the feeling you wouldn't swap it for anything.'

'Not a chance! This house is my life. I love these children more than anything, their openness, their trust, their individual quirks, their laughter… Please, Fran, don't think that because they're disabled they're unhappy. They don't know any other way of life. Some of them could survive outside but their parents prefer them to be here. They are taught, encouraged to grow and improve. We have some of the best knowledge in the country here.'

Fran speared a piece of macaroni. She couldn't wait for the following day, but she had questions and she felt she could ask this woman anything.

'But if the children could survive in normal daily life, isn't it wrong for them to be here?'

At this Thelma stiffened and placed her fork on the table. 'Wrong, how? In this environment they have the interaction with other children like themselves. No one stares at them, no one points. They have the freedom of a massive house with fifteen acres. They have school, play, physical and speech therapy and they have love. Our aim is to give them the best quality of life possible and we do that. I'm not saying they should stay here forever but special kids who are forced into a life outside are often pressurised by family members.'

'I don't understand.'

'If they go to school with normal children or eventually go to work with normal people it is easier for the parents of special children to believe that they are normal. The terms I use are probably not as politically correct as they should be but what I'm trying to say is that in many cases it is for the parents' benefit more than the child's.'

'So you think all disabled children should live in a place like this?'

Thelma resumed eating. 'Heavens no! But I ask you this, would you want Jamie to be the only disabled child in his school? Would you want him being pointed at and stared at and made fun of by other children? Would you like him to return at night frightened and confused because he couldn't learn at their speed?'

'No,' she replied honestly.

'Exactly. I don't think every disabled child should be institutionalised but I think young children need time to grow the confidence that is needed to live in the real world. And if they don't want to leave they shouldn't be forced to by anyone, not even family.'

'But shouldn't the parents be more actively involved?' Fran hated the thought of parents visiting and then leaving for the week.

'We have no restrictions on parental involvement. We organise day trips, short breaks away, and anyone is welcome to join us, but make no mistake, the children are always glad to come home. This is their home. Here they can be completely themselves without threat of danger, embarrassment or ridicule. The diseases of the children here differ from cerebral palsy to spina bifida to kids like Jamie but one thing they have in common is the right to happiness.'

Thelma checked her watch. 'No rest for the wicked, I'm afraid. Time to tuck the little ones in.'

'All of them?' Fran asked. There had to be two hundred children in the facility.

'That's my job.'

Fran nodded, trying not to envy the woman's task. She wanted to cry out 'Take me, I'll help' but she knew what the response would be. And she could understand. There was no way she would be here to tuck him in and kiss him goodnight every single day of the week so it would be selfish to start it.

Thelma paused at the door and studied Fran for a moment. 'I have to say there is no family resemblance at all.'

Fran smiled. 'I'm afraid my father and I would be mistaken for complete strangers.'

Confusion brought slight furrows to Thelma's forehead. 'Oh no, dear, I've never met your father! It was your mother I was talking about.'

Thelma closed the door behind her, unaware of the bewilderment she'd left behind. Fran's eyes stared unseeing at the picture-covered wall. For eight years her mother had visited Jamie without one word to her about his existence. She'd been in this very building, maybe even this room, and had easily lied to her all this time. Even during the early months when Fran's pain must have been obvious to the world; her belief that his death had somehow been caused by herself; that she had exercised too much, not enough; that she had eaten the wrong food; that during the difficult labour with no medical attention she'd done something wrong. When would it ever end? Her parents were even lying to each other.

When would the house that Jack built finally fall?

CHAPTER 15

Kit

The ringing phone held little interest for Kit any more. Not when there wasn't any chance of it being Mark. If it was Tyler ringing to cancel their date tomorrow then he could tell her at work in the morning. She smiled smugly. That would make life a little difficult for him as no one knew about the few times they'd seen each other.

'Christ, piss off!' she shouted at the ringing that was grating on her nerves. It certainly wasn't Tyler, he never rang for this long.

She lifted herself slowly from the sofa. She just hoped it was a salesperson of some description – she was just in the mood.

'Hello,' she barked into the receiver.

A small squeak sounded at the other end.

'Hello,' she repeated.

A sob.

'If this is someone trying to piss—'

'Kit—'

'Fran, is that you? What's wrong? Where are you?'

'I think it's called Macy's. It's on the—'

'Are you in Macy's wine bar?'

'Er… yes, I think I am.'

'Fran, have you had a drink?'

'I think I'm about to,' Fran said with the voice of a child.

Oh God, what can I do? Kit thought frantically. This is bad, *very* bad.

'Have you actually taken a drink yet?'

'Umm… I don't think so,' she replied vaguely.

'Listen, don't move a muscle. I mean it, Fran, stay where you are and whatever you do, don't touch that drink, okay?'

'But I want to, I need to—'

'Fran, I said no. Don't touch it.'

'But it's looking at me.'

'Fran, no!'

'Just get here quickly, Kit, please.'

Kit threw down the receiver, grabbed her coat and ran out of the door. She knew where Macy's was and if God was on her side she wouldn't have to wait too long for a taxi.

She ran down the stairs as though she was going for a gold medal. No passing taxis. She sprinted to the main road that ran along the bottom of her street. Within five minutes she was speeding towards the wine bar.

It was dark inside, and filled with a Thursday night crowd, mainly lads beginning the weekly wind-down. Kit could hear the monotonous boom-boom-boom thundering from the nightclub below. It took a few minutes for her eyes to adjust. She scanned until she found what she was looking for.

She tried to sidestep a youth whose hair looked as though it had been gelled within an inch of its life. He almost fell on her. She caught the fumes before he opened his mouth. He swayed in front of her as his eyes tried to fix on her face but seemed to be looking over her shoulder.

'Hello, gorgeous, fancy a—'

'Fuck off!' she barked, pushing him aside.

Fran sat hunched in a dark corner. Kit slid into the curved seat beside her.

'Hello Kit,' she said without taking her eyes off the glass in the middle of the table.

Kit appraised her quickly. She looked awful. Her cheeks were pale, her eyes drawn and red, but her appearance wasn't Kit's chief concern.

'Have you touched it?'

Fran shook her head. 'I was just about to when I called you.'

Thank God for that, Kit thought, letting out a sigh that had been building since she'd replaced the receiver.

'What's wrong? What's happened?'

'I've been to see him. I just got back,' she said, tipping her head slightly.

'Yes, I know, you've been to see your son,' Kit repeated, trying to ease her along slowly. She knew how excited Fran had been about going. They'd spoken the night before she went.

'He's lovely,' she continued. 'He's my son and I love him. He let me play with him,' she added sadly.

Fran raised her head and Kit tried not to panic when she saw Fran's eyes in the darkness. They were empty, like her mother's had been in The Briars all those years ago. She shuddered as she tried to understand. It sounded as though the visit had gone well. What was wrong with her?

'Fran, talk to me,' Kit ordered.

'Why did they do it, Kit?'

Kit didn't know what to say. She wasn't sure who had done what but felt sure it had to concern her parents. 'I don't know, Fran.'

'Does everyone hate me? Am I so horrible? Why did they take my son away? *Why?*'

Kit's heart ached for her. She could not imagine the pain of what Fran had been through or the facts she'd been forced to face about her parents. 'I wish I knew, but only they can tell you that.'

'But they hid my son from me for eight years. How could my mother do that when she knows how it feels to give birth?'

From what Kit had heard about Fran's mother, she suspected Fran had been grown in a test tube to avoid any inconvenience.

'It's the lies I can't stand. I'm in a maze and every way I turn the lies get worse. My father doesn't know that my mother visits Jamie. She doesn't know that he received regular progress reports about him and I didn't even know he existed.'

Kit watched as her face became more animated. 'But what I don't understand, Kit, is, if they both cared so much about him, why was he taken away in the first place?'

Kit listened as her friend talked. It was all that she could do. That and make sure Fran didn't touch the glass in the middle of the table. This figure before her bore no resemblance to the woman she'd met a few months earlier. Gone was the rigid control that decided the order of her clothes, thoughts, even her opinions. The clothes were still expensive but they didn't look it. Fran looked as if she'd just stepped out of the ironing basket and desperately needed pressing.

Kit could see that there was a difficult choice forcing itself on her friend. So far Fran had accepted everything her parents had done to her without question, but the weight of her continued acceptance was now flattening her.

'I've got this feeling inside me, Kit, and I'm scared of it. It's huge and it wants to come out and destroy them both. It's eating away at my stomach and I can't control it.'

Kit smiled. 'That's called anger, Fran. Don't fight it. You've fought it down for too many years. Don't be frightened of it. It's healthy after what you've learned.' She paused to make sure Fran understood her words. 'At some stage it will have to come out. For your own sanity you're going to have to tell them how you feel before you can move on with your life. You're no good

to anyone with "wipe your feet" tattooed across your forehead.'
Kit squeezed her arm to soften the words.

Fran nodded. 'I know, but my life has changed so much I
don't even know who I am any more. I have no job, no friends,
no family…'

'Now you just listen here, Frances Thornton, if you don't
count me as a friend then why the hell did you call me?' Kit
shouted, ignoring the curious glances.

'I didn't mean *you.*'

'I know,' Kit said, softening.

'You're my best friend. You're the best friend in the world.
Don't leave me,' she cried as the tears started to fall.

Kit moved closer and reached for Fran's hand. 'Don't be stupid. I'll always be here, Fran, but you have so much more than
just me.'

A spark of interest lit her eyes. 'You have Martine now. You
have your son, your new career. Fran, your life is beginning
over. You should be shouting from the rooftops. Everything you
have now is because of *you,* not your mother. She'd hardly have
picked me as a friend for you. She didn't introduce you to Martine and she certainly didn't force you to leave your job. Your life
is changing for the better because of *you,* not her. You're going in
the direction that's right for you. It might give her a seizure but
that's just an added bonus.'

In spite of her tears Fran chuckled.

Kit took a deep breath and pulled the offending glass closer.
'Fran, this is the hardest thing you're ever going to have to face
and it's not going to leave you. Every crisis, every drama, and
you're going to want to do this but you had the strength not to.
You have to hold on to that. You called me instead and now *I*
want to drink it,' she joked.

Fran squeezed her hand and smiled as she brushed the tears
away. 'Thank you,' she managed hoarsely.

'Come on, Fran, I think it's time I got you home,' Kit said softly as she guided her friend out of the wine bar.

Kit knew as she sat facing Tyler that the time had come. Four weeks they had been seeing each other and she knew that she needed to decide where they were going. To judge by the upmarket restaurant they were sitting in, she guessed he knew it too. Chanel suits and Hermès scarves littered the room. The smell as she'd entered had almost choked her. Kit guessed these women enjoyed wearing just a little clothing with their perfume. It was almost like a pissing contest, she thought. Who could wear the strongest, most expensive perfume with the shortest name, or even just an exclamation mark – that seemed to be the fashion at the moment. Which one would suit me? Kit wondered. Apostrophe perhaps?

There he goes, she observed, glancing at Tyler. That horrible little wave as he notices his friends. I'll sit back and peruse the menu. Hmm... peruse, now there's a good word. I'll let Tyler know that's my word of the day. He will be pleased.

What the hell is wrong with me? she chastised herself. I'm in a trendy restaurant with a fashionable man. Or should that be the other way around? I'm not sure. So why do I suddenly feel like shoving two breadsticks up my nose and impersonating a walrus?

Kit realised she had far too much time to think, as she looked across at Tyler surveying the menu. Why bother? He'd have prawns, he always had prawns. He caught her glance and smiled and she knew that tonight she would have to decide if their relationship would go any further.

At first she'd hoped that he would be the antidote to the poison that ran around her blood like a virus, called Mark. She'd wondered if this was a man who could make her forget that last night that she'd seen him and the terrible things she'd said.

The first few times she'd been out with Tyler she'd enjoyed the easy, unchallenging conversations they had. It was what she wanted. They'd discussed work, films, music and books – all the things that Kit wanted to discuss. Things that would interest her but not provoke any emotional input. But she often found herself biting her tongue, holding back opinions that he would term 'inappropriate'.

They had both agreed to keep their relationship hidden from the people at work. She guessed it wouldn't do his credibility much good and it certainly wouldn't help hers.

'Did you hear what I said?' he asked with a slight edge to his voice. Tyler wasn't used to being ignored.

'Sorry,' she murmured, shaking herself awake.

'I said Kay has handed in her notice. You could do that job.'

Kit's interest was piqued. 'What job?'

'In the accounts office.'

More number crunching, Kit thought. 'No thanks, I'll stay where I am.'

'I really think you should consider it,' he pressed.

She laughed. 'What are you, my career counsellor? I prefer to work with real people, Tyler. Not cardboard cutouts. Present company excepted, of course,' she added as an afterthought.

She saw the defensive expression that crossed his face. 'Is that what you think of us?' he asked a little sharply.

'Well, you are. On the few occasions I've been upstairs I've noticed how false everyone is. It's so transparent. The half smiles, the forced laughs. No, as I said, I like living in the real world.'

'I really think you should give it a little more thought.'

His insistence was beginning to bug her. 'Why? I've already told you I'm happy where I am. Let's face it, you're in first class complete with ballrooms and cabins and I'm in steerage. That's the way it is so why do you want me to think about it?' Her words weren't completely accurate. She was bored shitless but at least she was bored shitless and comfortable. She'd only last five minutes in that atmosphere before she bit someone's head off and earned herself an A4 envelope holding her P45.

She tried to concentrate on her chicken but she felt a restlessness that travelled to her foot, causing it to rock back and forth beneath the table. There was a word that circled in her head. Tidy. Everything was too tidy. Her appearance was now appropriate to her surroundings. Her job was tidy. Tyler was tidy. Everything was neat and tidy. It was what she'd wanted but something wasn't right.

'So what do you think, will you consider it?'

'Tyler, what's with you? I don't want to think about it. Why are you pushing me?'

'It's an improvement, that's all,' he said, shifting in his seat slightly.

'For who?' she asked, irritated.

'Whom, get it right!' he corrected.

'Don't patronise me, Tyler. Who is this about, you or me?'

The rising colour in his cheeks answered her question. She tried not to be surprised at his manipulation. It was himself he was worried about. Within the company she was the lowest of the low, she knew that. When forced to enter the management offices she received polite, puzzled smiles that told her they had no idea who she was, or where she worked. It obviously bothered Tyler more than it did her.

She watched as he sliced a prawn in half and guided the smaller portion to the edge of his plate. Kit had wondered why he did that until she read in an etiquette article that it was polite to leave something on your plate. Where she'd grown up it was good manners to polish off the whole lot. And really, if that was the extent of one's manners, half a soggy prawn, was it really worth it?

She realised now why he wanted to keep their relationship secret. It was obvious he would be more comfortable with people finding out about them if she had a more acceptable job title.

'Are you ashamed of me, Tyler?'

'No… no one knows about us, do they?' The panic that accompanied his words told her what she wanted to know.

'Oh, I see. It's okay for me to have great ideas that save the company money and I'm all right to entertain the assistant manager but preferably if I occupied more appropriate office space.' She paused to spear a broccoli floret. 'Incidentally, where's my fifty quid?'

'What fifty pounds?'

'Trevor told me that now the new call-out procedure is in place and working I should have had my fifty quid for the suggestion. Come to think of it…' she recalled with a frown '…I didn't get anything for the stock control system now in operation.'

Tyler dropped his fork, which slid from the table and stabbed him in the foot. 'I'll… umm… sort it out tomorrow, I promise.'

Kit eyed him suspiciously.

He looked around, eager for a distraction. 'Bloody hell, can't they do something about that? It's hard to stomach over a nice meal,' Tyler moaned, nodding outside.

Kit idly followed his gaze and saw a girl opposite the restaurant dressed in what was known as a 'whores' uniform' of leather and lace.

'It's a pretty sorry state that it's getting to this part of town.'

'It's a sorry state it exists anywhere!' Kit snapped, not taking her eyes away from the girl. She guessed her to be mid-teens and could just make out the grotesque make-up trowelled on in an attempt to make her look older.

'You'd think the police would move them on,' he continued, stuffing another huge prawn into his mouth. Kit held her tongue. She didn't trust herself to speak on the subject too much. Just shut up and we can move past this, her mind pleaded.

'I mean, it's a nice area. There are other places.'

Kit tried to ignore him and continued to watch the girl. The broccoli threatened to re-present itself when a blue estate car pulled up beside her. Kit held her breath. It moved along. She sighed with relief.

Tyler misunderstood her discomfort. He removed his napkin from his lap. 'I'll speak to the manager, see if he can do something about—'

'Tyler, sit down!' she snapped. He remained standing. 'Don't you feel anything other than repulsion for her?' she asked. The question was important.

He thought for a moment. It was too late. Kit could see he was searching for the appropriate response. 'Well, of course, I feel sorry for her.'

'Really, *how* sorry?' Kit asked.

'I don't know what you mean.' He sat back down, his disinterest obvious.

Kit shook her head. He couldn't understand; she shouldn't expect him to.

'Let's not fight, let's forget about it and enjoy our meal,' he mollified.

Christ, thought Kit, that wasn't even a cross word! Her idea of a good fight included spit and feathers.

She tried to do as he suggested, but every time she saw headlights reflected in the puddles outside, her breath caught as she silently prayed for the car to move along. Tyler had no such problem with his meal.

It was obvious that his previous discomfort had passed. His embarrassment, his stutters were gone. He was as relaxed as when they'd first walked in. He felt nothing for the girl standing half in the shadows of the unlit doorway. Even his anger had been fake, he didn't see her at all. Instantly she knew. He'd used that girl as a distraction only. She recalled what they'd been talking about.

She placed her fork beside her half-full plate. 'Tyler, you never passed those ideas as mine, did you?' she asked incredulously. 'That's why I've not received the money.'

'I haven't received the money, get it right!' he corrected her again.

'Fuck my grammar, Tyler! Am I right?' she demanded.

His slightly trembling hand and defiant chin confirmed her suspicion. He looked like a child who had pinched a toy and felt justified in doing so.

'They wouldn't have believed—'

'What, that I'm capable of having an original thought? My God, you people are unbelievable! How the hell do you manage to sit upright with no fucking backbone?'

He gave her a disapproving glance.

This can't work, she thought with the first ounce of honesty she'd allowed herself in weeks. The clothes, the hair, the make-up, they weren't her. She still felt like a fraud and it didn't matter how she acted, what she settled for, she'd be judged. The words 'Be careful what you wish for' sing-songed mockingly around her tidy, empty head.

'If your opinion of me is so low, why all this?' She motioned around the restaurant with its French chef, luxurious décor and five-pounds-a-glass apple juice. 'Do you think my life began when I joined your company?'

'Of course not,' he smiled indulgently.

Kit hated that smile. 'So why have you never asked me one question about my life and why haven't you yet bothered to make a move?'

His reddening face was not necessary for the answer. The fancy restaurants, a trip to the opera, the memory of which now helped her off to sleep more effectively than sheep, the constant nudges to better herself. She suddenly felt like she was on the pages of *My Fair Lady*. This was everything she'd dreamed of during the dark, lonely nights in Soho.

What was Mark doing now? she wondered, and then tried to banish the thought from her mind. She didn't want to think about Mark. He was gone now; he was in the past.

'It's not going to happen, Tyler. You've moulded me, you've shaped me and I think in your mind you've educated me. Almost to the standard that you could be happy with.' She breathed in deeply. She was tired, drained from the effort of holding on to the cape of respectability that she'd designed herself and which was now squeezing the spirit from her body.

'There's something you should know. That was me.'

He raised his head, confused. She could see he'd already forgotten the girl across the street. She felt no anger for his disregard, just a deep sadness. 'That was what I did until just before Christmas. I was lucky.' She thought again of the knife's legacy across her buttocks. She lifted her head. 'I was lucky, I got out.'

She could see remnants of half-chewed prawn in his open mouth. She would not go into detail. 'There is nothing more for you to know, except that it's over.'

She saw his struggle not to show the relief that eventually succeeded in flitting across his features. A little more disappointment would have been prudent, but he couldn't muster that.

She looked around the expensive restaurant with expensive people, with expensive clothes, and realised no matter how expensive she looked or how hard she tried to believe otherwise, she would never fit into a place like this with ease. It wasn't her. And what she was about to do would confirm that once and for all.

'I am going to leave now and I make no apologies for the fact that my actions might embarrass you.'

She didn't wait to see his expression before summoning a waiter and asking for their most expensive chicken dish to be put into a take-out box. The poor chap had no idea what she was talking about but to Tyler's acute embarrassment she pursued her request. The waiter retreated with obvious disapproval while Tyler held his head in his hands.

Upon his return she assured the waiter that her companion would settle the bill and thanked him for his assistance.

Tyler sat rigidly; only his eyes moved, darting from her to the girl outside.

'What's wrong, Tyler, feel like you've been duped?' she asked meaningfully. The terror on his face was due more to his concern of people finding out.

'I c… can't believe you were a c… call girl,' he stuttered.

'No, Tyler, the word is "whore", get it right,' she mocked, before leaving the restaurant without a backward glance.

She walked across the road. It was eleven o'clock and the traffic was slowing. An earlier storm had cooled the July heat, which was now a chilly breeze. The heat of the food warmed her hands as she approached the young girl.

'I don't do girls,' she said, rolling her eyes with the drama of a teenager.

'Neither do I,' Kit stated, sidling up beside her. 'Hungry?'

The guarded grey eyes looked at her suspiciously. 'Fuck off, lady!' she growled.

'Just left a job in customer relations, eh?'

The girl ignored her. Kit opened one of the foil cartons and popped a piece of chicken into her mouth.

'You got a name?'

'What the fuck's it to you?'

Kit nearly laughed out loud. If the hair were two shades darker, she would have been convinced she was in a time warp.

'I only asked if you got a name.'

'Terri!' she barked, glancing down at the steaming food.

'That your real name or your stage name?'

'Just piss off, will ya? I'm busy!'

Kit noted there was less defence, her concentration taken up by the food in Kit's hand.

'What you doing out here? What are you, fourteen?'

'Fifteen!' she snarled, like an angry puppy.

Kit had deliberately gone lower, knowing that in her defence and anger Terri would reveal her true age. Realising what she'd done, she stuck her chin out defiantly. 'So what you gonna do about it?'

'I could report you, you know,' Kit stated, taking a little longer than necessary to place the next piece of chicken in her mouth. She could report the girl; she could walk to the nearest police station and ensure that she would be picked up within hours. That was so nice and tidy, problem solved and a good night's sleep with a clear conscience. Except Kit knew Terri would be back on the streets tomorrow, just in a different place.

'Yeah and I could kick your ass.'

'Ooh, scary! Chicken?' Kit offered, pushing the carton towards her.

The girl knocked the food roughly out of her hands. Unperturbed, Kit fished into the paper bag. 'Voilà, here's one I made earlier but I really think this chicken does not want to fly.'

Terri's mouth twitched. 'Who the fuck are you?'

'It doesn't matter. Who are *you*?' Kit leaned against the doorway. A Peugeot 405 pulled up beside them. A balding man in his fifties wound down the window.

'How much for both?' he shouted.

'Fuck off, we're eating!' Kit shouted.

He gave her the finger and moved along.

'What the hell you do that for?'

'Because I hate eating alone.'

'You're bloody mad, you are.'

'Yep, got a certificate to prove it.' Kit watched as the hungry eyes ate the food that she was too proud to accept.

'Can you hold this a minute?' asked Kit, giving her little choice as she thrust it into the girl's stomach. She took a pencil and an old envelope out of her bag and scribbled down her address. 'Look, this is me,' she said, placing the paper in the girl's free hand.

'I don't want—'

'I know you don't, but if you do you know where to find me.'

Kit held her gaze for a few long seconds, the eyes that faced her unsure. She looked down at the tray still half full of steaming chicken and vegetables. 'I've had enough. Chuck it in that bin over there, will you?'

Kit walked away quickly. She reached the end of the road and quickly glanced back to see Terri hungrily eating the chicken.

Once around the corner she slowed slightly, enjoying the freedom of the cool night air, and tried to analyse her feelings about Tyler, which she felt should probably have been stronger.

What she hated most was the deceit. She didn't mind him putting her ideas forward as his own, it was the fact that he'd had no intention of telling her at all if he could have avoided it. She tried to feel sorry that their relationship was over but she realised he was no different to the punters in Soho, only better dressed. He still intended to use her but in a more appropriate, upmarket and definitely dishonest way. She even tried to be concerned about the fact that work would be very uncomfortable, if indeed she had a job left to go to.

Why did she feel such a fraud? She felt as though she was hiding but she didn't know why. What was left for her to overcome? She had the external forces to make her life ordinary, her little flat and her easy job. So why did she still feel like they were fragmented parts of a jigsaw? Why the hell did these things still not make her whole? She felt like a 3D object trying to force itself into a 2D picture.

What was now preventing her from mentally fading into the life of which she'd dreamed?

CHAPTER 16

Fran

'That was wonderful,' breathed Fran as they exited Symphony Hall into Centenary Square. It was the first time she had entered the huge ICC complex and the hall had taken her breath away, especially the awe-inspiring vision of the acoustic canopy and reverberation chamber.

Martine had commented, as they had taken their seats, that Symphony Hall was built on rubber cushions to prevent any disturbance from the railway tunnel underneath. It worked, thought Fran.

From the second the conductor had flexed his baton Fran had been lost. The music washed over her in waves. It had penetrated her body and soul and soothed the wounds inflicted by her parents. The melodies had aimed right for the new, warm place somewhere between her breastbone and stomach. Since the first day she'd seen Jamie she'd been walking around with a gift inside that jolted her when she thought of his fair hair or dungarees, or the imprint of his body against her own. The memory of him kept her warm.

'I can't believe you haven't visited these places in your own city.'

'I never enjoyed music like this,' Fran replied, unable to believe her own words. And it was true. Her senses seemed to have been reawakened from a deep sleep. A few months earlier the performance she'd just witnessed would have made her eyes glaze over with boredom.

'Well, I promised I'd show you the world and it looks like we don't even have to leave this city,' joked Martine.

'I'll have you know I've led an extremely sheltered life. My only liaison with music is occasionally listening to the Rolling Stones. Classy, huh?' teased Fran.

'It's not important what the music is. Any music can either lift your heart or leaden your soul. It doesn't matter if it's Michael Jackson or *Madame Butterfly*, just as long as you feel.'

Fran saw the depth of Martine's passion for music and marvelled at the diversity of her interests. 'My opinion of music was always you can't eat it, drink it or smoke it, so why bother?' she baited.

'Blasphemy,' Martine cried, covering her ears. 'Please remind me why I like you?'

Fran fluttered her long eyelashes. 'My natural warmth and charm that attracts you like an unsuspecting bug to the flypaper.'

'Will I be poisoned by arsenic, too?'

'We'll see, we'll see.'

A look passed between them that went unnoticed by the crowds leaving alongside them. It was a look meant only for them, filled with the tension of unfulfilled longing that was apparent to both.

'All ready for tomorrow?' Martine asked softly.

Fran's face sobered. 'Yes, I don't think he has long left. I want to see him before…' Her voice caught. Martine reached for her hand. Fran knew it was time to face both her parents. Too many questions swirled around her mind like debris in a tornado. It was time to question their actions. She knew it was her own reluctance to do this that had resulted in her trip to Macy's. Thank God Kit was in, she thought.

'Don't let your mother in, Fran,' Martine breathed. 'I know you're intimidated by her but you're going for your father. Be yourself, she can't threaten that which is real.'

'I just wish I knew how to feel about the whole thing. I feel sad, but do I feel sad enough? He's my father. I should be in tears. What does it say about me?' Fran asked, seriously.

'It says that you're confused. He's done a lot wrong. *They've* done a lot wrong,' Martine said softly, now aware of the whole story. 'But this might be the last chance you have.'

Fran remembered similar words she herself had spoken to Kit. She nodded uncertainly, as a black cab pulled up before them.

'Go on, you take it,' said Martine. 'I fancy a walk. Call me later.'

Fran impetuously turned and kissed her quickly, but gently, before diving into the taxi.

Martine watched with trepidation as the taxi disappeared from view. The chrysalis was emerging. The controlled, calculated movements of the caterpillar were becoming the fluttering, disjointed reflexes of a young butterfly that was unsure what to do with the new body.

They were fire and ice, she knew that. With her red hair Fran should have been the fire but it was the other way round and Martine's fire was gradually melting the ice that preserved Fran's emotions in a five-foot-eight, rock-hard ice cube.

Slowly, she had said. Spend some time together. And that's what they'd done. It was for Fran's benefit as well as her own. But it didn't matter. Martine knew she had crossed the line and she was in love with the woman with the long red hair.

Her mind was thrown back to an earlier time when a visit home had cost her the woman she loved.

She shivered with the cold that came from inside and glanced after the taxi that had turned the corner, out of sight. Was history about to repeat itself?

Foreboding consumed Fran as she pulled up outside the house.

Was it her relationship with Martine – or rather her friendship? No physical expressions of their affection had happened. Fran knew that was down to her. The thought of the physical relationship filled her with a desire and longing so deep that it reduced her to a quivering mass. She had never wanted anyone with the all-encompassing desire with which she wanted Martine, but something held her back. She was still hiding from herself and the rest of the world and she was unsure what was preventing her from taking the final step that she wanted to, needed to, take with both her body and her heart. Her life was changing almost by the minute. Layers were being peeled away to reveal a vulnerability she hadn't known was there.

Fran looked again at the exterior of the large house that had no redeeming features. No bushes or shrubs were littered to soften the edges. No attractive lamps to shine and welcome visitors. The source of her discomfort became clear. There was unfinished business in this house.

'Hello, Mother,' addressed Fran as the door was opened for her. The coolness of the large entrance hall hit her. It was the end of July but somehow this house remained the same temperature all year. 'How is Father?'

'It's not a good day today,' her mother said with just a hint of impatience.

Fran caught Alicia's disapproving look as she noted the casual jeans and V-neck T-shirt along with the mass of curls falling like a waterfall over the shoulders.

She realised that her mother's surreptitious glances were never that. They were designed to be noticed just enough to make you question yourself but not enough to provoke a confrontation.

Fran ran her hands over the denim on her hips to rid herself of the perspiration already building on her palms. Why was she peering so closely at her mother's every word or expression? What was she looking for?

'I've ordered tea to be taken in the lounge. I thought we might have a chat before you see your father.'

There was no such thing with her mother. Alicia didn't waste anything, not even syllables or syntax. They sat opposite each other in the lounge that hadn't changed at all. Two things occurred to Fran as she sat waiting for her mother's very own brand of Spanish Inquisition.

The first was her surprise that they hadn't even touched. There had been no pathetically false hug or even an attempt to kiss the air to the sides of each other's cheeks. Are the pretences falling away before my very eyes? Fran wondered. Can we not even be bothered to act as though something real exists between us? Secondly she looked around, urgently, trying to find some shred of evidence that she'd been here, lived here for the first eighteen years of her life.

There were no photographs or pictures or any little trinket she'd produced proudly at school for her parents. No chipped vases or marks on the furniture that could prove her dying conviction that she'd been a child in this house. Globe lights still shone down on to ivory wallpaper with delicate gold horizontal lines. Gold-plated picture lights illuminated limited edition prints of beautiful works of art that were wasted here. Sculptures that had been pored and sweated over that deserved respect and conversation remained unnoticed. Fran looked around sadly, wishing the house felt more like home instead of a distant memory. There had never been any children in this house. A stunted, small adult, but no child.

There were many things that she wanted to say to her mother, was desperate to scream at her, but that would inevitably be followed by her leaving the house with the intention of never returning. But she was not free to take that action yet. She had to see her father.

'You've quit your job,' Alicia stated.

'Yes,' answered Fran, feeling like a kid with her fingers caught in the cookie jar.

'Is that it?'

'What more do you want, Mother?' she asked with a show of bravery that was not mirrored in her nerves, which still jumped to attention in this woman's presence.

'You have this romantic notion of becoming an artist. You think you have the talent to produce good works and support yourself with an easel and a paintbrush. Frances, you don't have a chance.'

Fran was stung by the words. 'At this point, Mother, I have no idea what I'm capable of except the courage to try.' She tried to reason with her. 'Have you never had that urge to create something that's all you? Isn't there just one thing inside of you that you'd like to share with other people? Something that makes them laugh, cry, shiver, anything just as long as it makes them feel.'

Her passion had forced her to once more try to bridge the gap between them. If there was only one thing on which they could agree... Alicia's blank expression at the heartfelt words convinced Fran of her worst fears: there was no way back for them, ever.

'Your time would be better spent asking for your job back. Law is what you're good at, and you enjoy it.'

'That's your opinion, but just because you think it does not make it a fact. I was good at it, yes. But I wasn't happy. And I won't be going back.'

She knew by Alicia's set expression that she was not happy with the outcome of the conversation.

'I'll go up and see Father now,' said Fran, eager to be out of her mother's presence.

Alicia sighed, nodded and retrieved a book from the coffee table.

The sight of her father's fragile, ashen face shocked Fran. Only a couple of weeks had passed since she'd seen him.

She took his rough, bony hand in hers. After all their years without physical contact Fran was surprised at how easily she made that small gesture. Anger still bit deeply at her stomach, but this was not the time. It was too late. However hot the rage that boiled in her veins, she could not scald a dying man.

His face lit up slightly when he saw her. Something shifted behind his gaze as though he were disorientated. 'You look wonderful! Your hair is better like that.' Fran heard a wistful tone tinge the words that were spoken gruffly.

'You're looking well too,' she lied.

'I've made a very good living from reading people's faces. I look like shit! It won't be long now.'

'Don't—'

'It's all right, Frances. I'm not scared. There'll be someone waiting for me. I've seen her. She's unhappy with me and she's right to be, but she loves me and she's waiting.'

Fran became a little scared. She hadn't realised that he was delusional. She didn't know what to say. He was oblivious to her fear. 'I failed her and I failed you. If I could go back I would. I'd give my life to make it up to you and Bethy.'

'I think I should call—'

'I'm sick of it,' he said with more force than his body owned. 'Sick to death of never being able to mention her name. Tired of denying she ever existed and that I loved her, more than life.' He turned serious eyes on her. 'You see, Frances, I deserve my life. I courted the disappointment and disillusionment that I got. I had a chance to be happy and I blew it so I deserved what she gave me. But not you. I loved you so much and couldn't show it.'

A tear slid out of the corner of his eye. His voice was tormented. Fran was transfixed by his words. He spoke with confidence and clarity and something else, she thought it was urgency. She had the definite feeling that she'd entered the wrong room. That her father lay elsewhere in staunch silence waiting fearlessly for his final breath.

'Every day I ached to hold you and play with you. I wanted to take you places and watch you grow.' His eyes stared through her as though he were explaining his actions to someone else. 'But I didn't. I was a coward of the worst kind. I stood by and watched as she gradually picked away at your spirit because she knew. She could see that you had fire, and she knew where it had come from.'

Fran was bewildered. She still clutched the hand that lay still within hers while the other gestured with animation. She could do nothing but listen. He'd spoken more words to her in five minutes than she could remember throughout her entire life.

She wanted to understand his torment, even if it wasn't real. 'Are you talking about Mother?' she whispered.

'Don't call her that!' he roared. The effort forced artificial colour into his ashen features, which quickly faded away. Fran reared backwards. She'd never seen such deep, emotional feelings in her father. His mouth twitched. There was something hovering behind the closed lips. His eyes held fire that threatened to spill out and burn him. Fran knew something major was happening but she was fearful for his health. She pushed herself out of the chair but Patrick held fast to her hand with surprising strength. 'She'd have me go to the grave with this on my conscience just as long as it didn't open the can of worms she had nailed, locked and welded shut tighter than a Pharaoh's tomb twenty-three years ago. There is no more she can do to me now. I should have told you years ago.'

Fran felt the tight squeeze of his hand. Her bewilderment kept her silent. 'If I thought the truth would harm you I would gladly keep it inside and live with it for all eternity, but I don't think it will harm you. I think it will save you.' He took a deep breath that barely lifted his chest. 'You had a skeleton child-hood. If it can be personified as a human then you had the bare bones. You were fed, clothed and educated but you didn't get any of the flesh and muscle which is affection, encouragement and guidance.'

Fran's heartbeat began to thud against her chest wall. It felt as if the sound filled the room.

'Alicia and I were never in love. We met at college and both thought the whole concept overrated so we sort of gravitated together. To cut a long story short I met someone. She was life-blood itself. She had spirit and love and she was wise enough to see into your very soul. We had an affair – that's a horrible word for the love that we shared – but she became pregnant. Alicia found out about us at roughly the same time. It was hard to hide; you see, Fran, Beth was Alicia's sister.'

The room began to swim. Fran pushed her feet to the ground to keep from falling over. She knew what was coming.

'You're my daughter, Frances, mine and Beth's.'

Her foundations crumbled beneath her. A sickness rose up and consumed her, the full force of her father's words hitting her time after time. She's not my mother; she's not my mother. The words circled around her brain like vultures around a corpse. She wanted to pull her hand away from his but she couldn't. The familiar thudding started in her chest. A mist appeared around her father like an old photo. Oh God, not now, *please* not now, she prayed. She fought the approaching darkness with all her might. Hang on, just hang on; let me get to the truth first, she pleaded. She knew only that she gripped her father's hand with caveman strength, aware that if she let go she would fall head-first into the blackness that stalked her. She focused on his face and felt her heartbeat slow as her mind became busy. Old questions were being evicted by new ones. She was an addict; she wanted to hear it all.

'She had wild, curly hair, didn't she?' The words were barely audible but Patrick heard them. He nodded.

'Alicia hated her with as much passion as she is capable of. Beth was everything she wasn't: she was artistic and free. When she found out about us, Alicia supposedly forgave us both and asked Beth to move in so we could look after her during her pregnancy. I was ordered to stay away, and I did. The only person she saw for seven months was Alicia. During that time Alicia convinced Beth to leave you here when you were born.

'Alicia arranged for Beth to go away for a while to recuperate after the birth. By the time she returned you were legally ours and Beth had no rights to you at all.'

'But you loved her?' cried Fran. Her body was alive with a mixture of feelings that ran around her alternating between betrayal, anger and loss for something she'd never known.

'Yes, I did, but I was scared. I was weak. We were both successful. Alicia could have destroyed all that.'

'But how did you…'

'As I said, we were both successful lawyers and we knew some powerful people. The details were simple. The birth certificate was easily falsified and Doctor Treadwell had been in the family for years.'

'But why did she want me?'

'Because you were a part of something she could never understand. It gave her power to have something of Beth's.'

'How did she die?' asked Fran. She wanted to know everything.

'She was in a traffic accident on her way from a private investigator's office. She hadn't given up trying to get you back and was in the process of attempting to find a loophole in Alicia's plan.'

Fran sat silently, her whole body paralysed.

'Why couldn't you tell me sooner?' She tried to keep the accusation out of her voice but her words had an edge.

'I have no excuses to give you. I watched you as a child strive for Alicia's attention, her love. I cried inwardly every time she pushed you away. The more love you showed, the harder she pushed as she saw you become like your mother.'

Those words – 'your mother' – which now bore no relation to Alicia flew around Fran's head looking for a home.

'Even now you still try to gain her approval. I only wonder what that has cost you.'

She didn't know where they came from but one of the feelings had strayed from the others and aimed straight for her eyes. The tears scalded her cheeks. Fran didn't know whether they were for herself, her mother, father or Alicia. She only knew that they had to be released.

Everything had been built on a lie, a lie which had assured her life and the person she was only now beginning to realise was not real. She had been shaped into a product, a robot that worked by remote control. A top-of-the-range, state-of-the-art android. Alicia had wanted to make her sister's child into a carbon copy of herself and so she stripped away the soul that should have loved to sing, dance, hold a paintbrush and feel.

An image of Martine swam before Fran's blinded eyes. Yet someone had broken through. Somewhere in her battered, rejected heart remained a portion of undamaged tissue. She did have the ability to feel, and yet she still held Martine slightly away. Why was she afraid to seize what she wanted and what she knew would make her happy? Was she still trying for her approval even now? Would she, could she, break the habit of a lifetime even after what she'd just learned?

She wanted to be alone to collect her strewn emotions. Thoughts tumbled around her head like clothes in a spin dryer. She wanted someone to blame. She wanted to rage and shout at the drawn, sick figure in the bed, with whom she could have been so close.

Even now his hair held only a hint of grey but his eyes were haunted, the past running around in his head like an old, favourite movie. Her father was broken – he had been broken by a woman with a will of steel against which he'd never stood a chance. Yet Fran couldn't vent her feelings at him. He had nothing to gain by his words; he'd done it for her. She might never have known, but he was trying to set her free.

She leaned over and kissed his cheek. The moisture from her tears transferred to his cheek. 'I love you.'

Fran didn't know if Beth was waiting for him, but she hoped so. She swallowed hard. 'Dad, if you see her, tell her I'll be okay. Tell her I'm happy now.'

He nodded, eager to believe her.

They sat together for what seemed an eternity. Just holding hands and allowing the tears for a life they had lost to cleanse their hearts of the past they had endured together but separately.

After what seemed hours, and when Patrick fell into an uneasy sleep, Fran reluctantly released his hand. It was time to face the woman who called herself 'Mother'.

CHAPTER 17

Kit

It took Kit a split second to realise that something was wrong. Even in the darkness she knew that there was someone in her flat. That it had been defiled. It was too late to run as she was forced backward against the door by a five-inch shining blade pointing at her face. Her heart filled with dread and she knew, her whole body felt and knew who it was. The trembling started in her legs and quickly travelled upwards, causing her cheek to move precariously towards the steadily held knife. She closed her eyes and prayed for her life.

'You knew it wasn't over.'

The voice was the same. Soft, controlled and with a power that went straight for Kit's stomach.

She nodded. She had always known that he would find her. Her sight adjusted to the light, making his eyes visible through the darkness. A slow smile formed on his cruel mouth to reveal even white teeth punctuated by two gold ones.

'Just like old times,' he drawled.

Kit's breathing became more laboured as she recalled that same knife blade slashing through her skin to cause seven superficial wounds and the deep scar that ran the whole width of her body. Just before he'd stolen her money and dumped her in the gutter.

Concrete formed where her bones should have been and rendered her immobile.

A small cry came from her bedroom. Banda didn't flinch.

'Brought along a little insurance. Sweet little thing, you met her earlier and gave me the idea to bring her along. She's so much like you were when I arranged your first punter. I wonder if she's had that privilege yet.' He laughed at the disgust she couldn't hide. 'She'll fit in well in your old room, especially with you there to look after her.'

She breathed only with effort. She could remember her first punter and the fact that she'd been sold to him at cut price because she was inexperienced. Banda had arranged it, knowing that the punter he'd chosen enjoyed rough sex for the main course and a couple of punches for dessert. She recalled the fear, the fear that she would not live through the experience.

'I'm not going back,' she hissed.

He laughed out loud, in total control. 'Oh yes you are, Kit! Did you really think I'd let my best earner get away that easily? First you'll pay off what you owe me for your unauthorised leave and then we'll go back to the way things were. What's all this anyway? You have a shit flat, shit job. You've been gone months and this is the best you could do. Jack shit!'

He laughed out loud. 'Fancy clothes for a whore but they don't fool me.' The knife cut easily into her satin shirt. 'You're nothing, Kit. You've always been nothing and you'll always be nothing. But you're *my* nothing. I own you. You've been gone this long because I allowed it. I could have fetched you back any time I wanted. I've let you go to your fucking AA meetings. I've allowed you to make a new little friend who lives in a nice part of town. I even let you fuck that wimp for free for a couple of weeks just so you'd have a taste of the life you're going to miss, but when I saw you mixing with that prick from work I knew it was time to draw the line. Where's your reputation, whore?' he mocked, thoroughly enjoying himself.

She tried to swallow the surplus saliva that had gathered in her mouth. She knew that like a dog he could smell her fear and he thrived on it.

'Hmm, turned into quite the little homebody, haven't you, Kit? A little different to the slag that you were. I think you've developed feelings. Don't worry, my love, I'll soon cut that out of you,' he laughed, slashing her shirt again. 'And then I'll go visit your friends. I'm sure they'd love to catch up with one of your oldest mates from down south.'

Kit clenched her fists in an effort to stay calm. If he was telling the truth then he hadn't already been to see them. She didn't doubt for a moment that he knew where they were. He'd found her easily enough and obviously spied on her for months.

'The redheaded bitch looks like she could do with some loosening up.'

'You leave her alone!' she spat, struggling against his strength.

His laughter was harsh and cruel and instilled the fear of God into her breaking soul.

'Hmm... loyalty to your friend. How sweet. She reminds me a little of Val. Do you remember your old friend, whore?'

Kit said nothing. She tried to still her breathing. The fear threatened to envelop her.

'She remembered you, right up until the second she died. With every blow to her body I chanted your name. I made sure she knew that she was being punished for your sins. She died knowing that you betrayed her.'

'You killed her, you bastard.'

Banda shook his head, smiling manically. 'You sealed her fate, whore! Your actions sent her to her death. I simply arranged the meeting.'

Hot salty tears bit at Kit's eyes. A vision of Val's tortured, frightened face came into her mind and her resolve faded away. Her only friend had lost her life because she had escaped. Banda was right: she had killed Val as effectively as if she had murdered her with her own hands.

'You see, whore, it's not safe for you to have friends. You carry the kiss of death and expose them to me every minute that you resist your fate. It's you I want but if you continue to fight me…' His words trailed away as he admired the blade that was all that stood between the skin of her face and his.

'On your knees, bitch,' he ordered with an evil glint in his eye that either came from within or was a reflection of the shimmering blade.

She resisted for a second and the knife caught her beneath the chin, close to her throat. If she did what he asked then they would be safe. The only two people that she cared about were under threat; she had no choice. Again he controlled her with her weaknesses, only this time it wasn't the alcohol that he'd supplied so generously for years: it was the safety of the people that she loved. Fran and Mark need never know what had happened. Mark hated her and Fran could live without her. It didn't really matter if Fran found her disappearance suspicious. She'd be safe; they'd both be safe. Slowly she lowered herself to her knees. He'd won again.

'Now we both know I'm right, don't we?' he said.

She nodded mutely.

This was no longer her home. She was back in the flat in Soho, where she belonged. The person she'd built was seeping out of her with every laboured breath that escaped from between her lips.

He raised her head upwards so he could see her face. 'Who is in control, Kit?'

'You are,' she whispered.

'Who owns you, Kit?'

'You do.'

'And whose cock are you going to suck every night for the rest of your life for your sins?'

'Yours.'

He laughed cruelly as his face displayed a triumphant snarl, like a tiger bringing a deer to the ground.

With his free hand and one swift movement his fly was opened and his half-erect penis in her face.

She knew now that this was what she'd feared more than anything, more than her battle with the booze and more than the confrontation with Bill. It was the terror that she would have to go back.

For years Banda had controlled her mind with fear and terror. She had been forced to do things with her body that had ensured any decency would move out.

She could see herself obediently on her knees with wide, unblinking eyes. They stared at nothing and she felt nothing. She had lived like this for almost eight years and escaped it. These last eight months had been nothing more than an interlude, an intermission in what her life should be. Everything that she'd achieved meant nothing. Outwardly that wasn't much but inside, where it mattered, she was another person. And now she was being forced back. Something inside was beginning to shrivel and die.

Her heart ached for the memory of her friend; the woman who had taken her into Banda's care yet perversely taken care of her too. Val had suffered the punishment every time Kit had committed the smallest misdemeanour, and she had taken it without casting blame or accusation. Despite everything she had encouraged her to make a run for it. That last night she had desperately begged her to get away. And she had, but at what cost to her old friend?

'She knew,' Kit whispered as the realisation ran through her head leaving a blazing trail of clarity. Val had known what would happen to her and she'd wanted Kit to escape anyway. Her friend had made no attempt to avoid the certain punishment for Kit's crime. She had waited and accepted it, doing so to give Kit the chance for a better life. She had sacrificed her own life for that of the girl she had brought into her world. She had done it to give Kit a future.

She focused every ounce of hurt, betrayal and loathing into her trembling legs. She closed her mouth and rose steadily to her feet.

'No,' she said, meeting his eyes with unflinching determination.

For a second Banda's concentration wavered, surprised by her rebellion. Kit saw the opportunity to grab the knife from his hands but she resisted. To remove the physical weapon from his grasp was only a temporary solution. Removing his tool of physical pain meant that he would simply return with another. It wasn't that that she needed to show him.

'Go on, Banda, do it,' she challenged, leaning into the knife. 'Carry out your threat and do it. If my choice is the knife or a life back with you then plunge it in right now. And because she can identify you, you'd better go in there and kill Terri as well.'

'Get on your knees, bitch,' he said, touching her cheek with the end of the blade.

Kit remained still, momentarily reliving the memories that resurfaced from feeling the cold metal against her skin. Her eyes bore into his and she took courage from the confusion in his eyes.

'Is that the best you can do? Don't you get it? I'm not fucking frightened of you any more.' She flicked at the knife. 'If this is my only alternative then I'll take it. Do you hear me? I'll fucking take it but then you'll be the one running, not me.'

His face contorted into a lecherous grin. 'Be brave for your-self, whore, but your friends—'

His words stopped as her knee met with his groin. He doubled over and Kit took the opportunity to grab the knife, holding the blade instead of the handle.

'If anything happens to them, Banda, I'll always have this,' she said, waving the knife before his face, which was contorted with pain as he held on to the injured area. 'It's the knife that you used on me and I'm betting it's the one you used to murder Val, and probably others.'

'Give me that…'

Kit laughed out loud at the sight of him, clutching his dick and struggling to get to his feet. 'You're not powerful, Banda. You're just a man with the same weaknesses as everyone else, except you're deluded. You thought you could come here and control me like you did before but it's over.'

'You fucking bitch, I'll kill you for this!' he cried between sobs of pain. She was not so brave as to disregard the murderous look in his bulging eyes. 'I'll come looking—'

'No, you won't, Banda, because you don't know how to handle me any more, and if you do, I'll be ready.'

He gathered himself up and limped, half hunched, to the door. 'Watch your back, whore!' he ground out before staggering out of the room.

Kit sank to her knees and dropped the knife as though it would maim her. She had talked with more bravado than she felt. Always she would live in fear of him, that there was nowhere she could hide if he wanted to find her, but her worst fear had confronted her in the ugliest form possible and this time she had beaten it.

She would have stayed in a terrified but victorious heap by the door but another frightened cry came from behind her bedroom door. She had almost forgotten about the girl.

Banda had wedged one of the dining chairs underneath the door handle to her bedroom. She ran and opened it. Terri lay sobbing on the bed, curled up in a ball. Kit sat beside her. The tear-stained face bore no resemblance to the cocky kid she had seen earlier. She had a swollen right eye and a bruise to her neck.

'Did he do this?' she asked, softly.

Terri nodded, her bottom lip quivering. 'I thought he was a punter but as soon as I got into the car, he punched me. We drove past you and then he grabbed me by the throat, pulled me out of the car and brought me up here.' She began sobbing again.

Kit pulled her close and held her while she cried. 'It's okay, sweetheart, it's okay,' she soothed, crying inside for what could have become of both of them. 'You're safe now, he's gone.'

She wondered how long he'd been following her. She may have managed to get rid of him but she would spend the rest of her life looking over her shoulder. She suspected that she'd heard the last of him but she would never again assume.

While Terri showered Kit made a quick telephone call and then fixed the girl some warm milk. She settled her in bed and tried to find out a little more about her.

'I know you, Terri, I *was* you. That's why I tried to talk to you. Has anyone else ever tried to persuade you to go home?'

'Yeah, couple of weeks ago. Some middle-aged cow who could barely understand a fucking word I said. Kept telling me what I'd end up like. How the fuck's she gonna know?'

The face scrubbed clean of cheap make-up looked even younger than fifteen and the foul mouth didn't fit.

'I can tell you, Terri. That bloke was my pimp. I got away from him eight months ago after this.' Kit rolled up her shirt and pulled down the waistband on her skirt to reveal the deep welt across her buttocks.

'Eight months and he still had to find me to punish me, do you understand? You'll get in so deep that you'll never be free. It seems so easy, doesn't it, to sell your body and remain outside of what you're doing? It's a means to an end. You'll save the money for a place to live and then forget you ever did it.'

Kit was crying openly now, the shock and terror only just catching up with her. 'But it won't happen. It will be within you forever and it will bring you down. The streets are run by people like him, you'll be beaten if you don't work for one of them and you'll be beaten if you do.'

She tried her best to pull herself together. 'It's not for me to tell you how to live your life, but are you so sure that whatever drove you away from home is so bad that it's worse than this?'

'I want to go home,' Terri said quietly and then yawned.

Kit pulled the covers up over her and told her to get some sleep. 'I'll be right outside.'

She jumped into the shower and tried to cleanse her body. As she was slipping into her dressing gown she heard a soft tapping at the door.

'I'm sorry, I didn't know who else to call. I thought maybe you'd gone.'

'I leave tomorrow,' Mark said without emotion.

Kit noticed how pale and drawn he looked. 'I'm sorry, Mark. I know this is hard.'

'Where is she?'

'She's lying down, she's been beaten.'

He strode towards the door. 'We need to get her to a hospital.'

Kit shook her head. 'She doesn't need that. She'll just be sore for a few days.'

She wanted to cry. Having to maintain a polite conversation with the man she now knew she loved, and whom she could see hated her, caused her to fight back fresh tears.

Mark opened the bedroom door and took a quick look at the sleeping girl. 'Christ, how old?'

'Fifteen.'

'Punter or pimp?'

Kit took a deep breath. She had decided not to tell him what had happened for a few reasons. She could not stand the humiliation of telling him she'd almost had Banda's penis in her mouth and she didn't want his pity. Second, she could not bear the compassion inherent in his nature being showered on her again. The third reason was that she had to prove she was a big girl now: she couldn't go running and crying to Mark every time she had a problem. That part of their relationship had ended long ago. This would remain her secret and it would give her the strength to know she could make it on her own.

'Punter,' she said and looked away.

'May I?' Mark asked, pointing to the sofa. She wanted to hit him for being so damned polite. He had to remember what had happened on that sofa. The first time had been tender and sweet and not one word had passed between them. He had known what her body wanted and had guided her around it. The second time had been a possession. Primeval forces had locked them together in a fierce punishing act where their skins soldered together and bone hit bone in the passion that had taken them away from the sofa to a place of pain and pleasure. She remembered it clearly. Obviously he didn't.

'She should be at home worrying about spots, not turning tricks.' He slumped in the chair and ran his fingers through ruffled hair. 'I think you should tell me the whole story, don't you?'

Kit could see the dark circles beneath his eyes. 'Coffee?' she offered.

He merely nodded.

She couldn't stand it any longer. 'I'm sorry, okay. But I didn't know what else to do. I acted irrationally. I shouldn't have called you,' she said by way of an apology.

'Of course you should. Now tell me what happened.'

Kit told him everything except that it was Banda, up until the point when Terri had supposedly knocked on her door.

Mark drank his coffee during an uncomfortable silence. Kit wanted to kiss the tired lines away from around his eyes.

'I'd better go and wake her up,' he said, rising from the sofa.

'No, let her sleep.' She didn't want him to leave yet. The bitterness that existed between them made her crazy. There was a new harshness about him that didn't fit.

'Mark, I'm sorry,' she said, wringing her hands.

'You said that already.'

'Not for this, for the things I said. I was wrong.'

'Forget it,' he said dismissively. And that was when she knew that he was gone forever. Her heart plummeted. For months he had been her rock. He had been her friend, her guide and more importantly, her lover. Everything felt empty and superficial. She called this flat home but it wasn't any more because Mark wasn't here. She could see in his eyes that it was over.

'Mark, I…'

'What the hell do you want from me, Kit? There's nothing left. You've had it all. Is it my forgiveness you want now? Yeah, sure, I forgive you, Kit. Why not? It's only words after all, and that's all a relationship is to you, isn't it? Words. You can't actually get on in there and feel, can you?'

Kit was stunned. She knew it was over but she had to let him know the truth. 'The things I said. I didn't mean—'

'Do you think I give a flying shit about the things you said? Christ, Kit, an actress you're not! That's not why I left.'

'Why then?'

'Because it was our first test. The first obstacle that came our way and you failed, Kit, you failed miserably.' He spat the words at her.

'You wanted something I couldn't give,' she protested.

'You mean I asked you to go beyond the limits you'd set for yourself? Okay, that's fine. You're happy with your life, I can't argue with that, but did you have to give up on us so easily?' He lowered his voice, remembering the girl asleep.

'You're like the man who went next door to borrow the lawn-mower. By the time he gets to the end of his garden he's think-ing, "Oh, he won't lend me his lawnmower, he's a bit miserable", by the time he's in his neighbour's garden he's thinking "There's no way he'll lend me his lawnmower because I had my music on loud the other night" and by the time his neighbour answers the door he shouts, "I don't want to borrow your fucking lawn-mower anyway!" That's what you did, Kit, you had to assume that it was a foregone conclusion that it was over before you asked the question. It was easier to just turn around and run.'

She couldn't hold back the tears that his accusations brought. Stubbornly she tried to brush them away. Her actions only in-censed him further. 'Look, even now you can't do it, can you? Your body is feeling something real and you have to try and block it out. That's what I can't stand, Kit. I could never promise you that all the bad things allotted to you had already happened. I couldn't guarantee that your life would be plain sailing from now on. No one can do that. But what I could promise was that I would be there. That we would face things together, but it wasn't enough, was it? You want cast-iron guarantees of what tomorrow will bring, that's why you're happy with your safe job and safe life.'

He shook his head; the disappointment in his eyes slapped her.

She cried harder. Every word was true: she did want guar-antees. She did want assurances that she would never need to walk the streets to feed herself or her pimp again. She wanted watertight contracts that said she would never need to smell stale sweat and urine as huge grubby hands pawed her body and stole her soul. She wanted it cast in stone that when she gave her heart to someone it would not be used, battered and bruised. Yes, she wanted all that. She wanted to know what her life would be from now until the day she died, because at least then she could have control. But in order to achieve that, she had lost the most important thing in her life.

'And the funny part is you've spent this evening doing what I always knew you could. You know that girl is going home tomorrow and it's because of you. Christ, Kit, I didn't ask you to wear your past for the whole world to see and judge! I asked you to use it constructively and hopefully feel good about yourself and realise that the antidote to the virus in you is there. But again, it just wasn't worth taking the chance, was it?'

'It wasn't like that,' she protested.

His voice lowered but there was no softness there. 'What exactly has helping that girl cost you tonight? Has it weakened your resolve? Has it reduced the person that you are? Has it eroded what you've built in the last eight months, or has it made you feel something good, the fact that her body will not be for sale again?'

Kit remained silent.

Mark sighed wearily, releasing the tension that accompanied his rage. 'I can't do this, Kit. I can't have this conversation with you. It's too late.'

He walked to the door. 'Call me when she wakes and I'll send a taxi to collect her, then your tidy life can carry on.'

Kit knew he was leaving for good. She'd lost him and there was nothing she could do about it. She wouldn't see him again. For weeks she'd tried to pretend that she'd bounce back, that she could retrace her steps and bring back the old Kit but she was wrong. The Kit that was rougher than a cheese grater did not belong here and she couldn't make her fit. She was still scared, still terrified of being used or hurt, but without that tiny bit of fear there was nothing. For just ten minutes her world had been alive again.

Even the version of Mark that hated her illuminated her life and made the world feel good. And now he was leaving her.

His hand was resting on the door handle and she knew that he was waiting for one sign from her, just one act that would signal her willingness to completely leave the past behind. She ached to run to him and allow him to enfold her in his arms. Tears rolled freely down her cheeks as she stood on the precipice of complete abandonment to another person and the trust the act entailed. Her heart broke as her mouth opened to the sound of the door closing right behind him.

CHAPTER 18

Fran

Fran faced Alicia across the expensive furnishings and the perfection of a house in which no one had been young. She was afraid that the flames would leap from her eyes and melt the mask that was Alicia's face.

'I know everything,' she stated icily. Her eyes fixed on Alicia's expression as she removed her glasses and placed them on the book she'd been reading. The standard smile leapt to her face. It wasn't a smile at all, Fran realised. Only a slight movement of the lips intended purely to distract you from the searching eyes that probed your face and mind to extract your thoughts.

'I really have no idea—'

'Moth—' Fran's word trailed off. The word came so naturally to her, even in anger. 'Sorry, *Aunt* Alicia. That's what I should be calling you, isn't it?'

The name felt alien on her lips. Fran watched as the colour drained from Alicia's face. She heard the sharp intake of breath as the controlled expression that was usually glued to her features became a little shaky.

The silence infuriated her. 'For God's sake, say something!' Fran roared. How the hell could she sit there and act as if she'd just been informed that there was no pheasant for dinner? Fran leant against the door frame for support.

Alicia sat neatly forward. No emotion was evident on her face. 'What would you like me to say?' she asked calmly.

Fran felt like she'd been slapped. She didn't know what she'd expected but it wasn't this. The utter rigidity by which the woman lived her life made her want to shake some remorse into her.

'Aren't you at least sorry?' she cried.

'Please calm down, Frances. You have wealth, privilege and luxury. For what part should I be sorry?'

'The love, the affection you never gave me. You took me away from someone who loved me—'

'Be very careful, Frances.' Her voice held a note of steel. 'At this moment I am content to let you believe your father's romantic tale. Don't push me.'

'What the hell does that mean?'

'It means don't ask me questions that you really don't want answered.'

'Tell me the truth,' Fran demanded.

'You have heard the version that I'm sure suits your purpose so why do you need to hear more?'

Fran wanted to slap her. She wanted an apology; she wanted her mother to admit what she'd done wrong.

'Don't you have any inclination to defend yourself?'

Alicia nodded. 'Yes, but not at the expense of you,' she said honestly.

'I'm a big girl, I can take it.'

'Okay, Frances, you asked. You were nothing more than a toy to Beth, a doll that she wanted to dress up and squeeze to see if you cried like Tiny Tears.'

The undercurrent of rage found Fran. 'Why did you hate her?'

'That's not important. It's too far in the past. Leave it—'

'Not for me. I found out an hour ago that you're not my mother. I am entitled to answers.'

'Yes, but do you really want my truth?' Alicia asked, meaningfully.

'Of course.'

Alicia glided gracefully to the crystal decanters and poured herself a generous measure of whisky. Fran envied her that freedom of moderation as she lowered herself on to the luxurious sofa some three feet away from a grand piano she'd never played. Her shaking legs refused to hold her body any longer. Why couldn't she just leave? Why did she still want something from this woman? She could walk out of the door with a conscience as clear as a midsummer afternoon, yet she couldn't.

'You're wrong, you know. I didn't hate her. As children we were very close. Our parents were very restrictive. They were both descended from ancestors with so much blue blood there were no red pigments left. Beth was the cloud that breezed dreamily past the solid mountain that was me. I recall a distant aunt wondering how our mother could give birth to both a delicate soufflé and a hardened rock cake. I didn't mind that she got the praise for her beauty and imagination because she always came back to me. We would sit on each other's beds late at night, laughing at the idle comments of our relations. She was clever, you see. She charmed everyone as if they were her only best friend. She had a foot in every camp. Where she was dreamy, I was solid. Where she was artistic, I was—'

'Oh, but you *were*,' Fran interrupted with bitterness. 'You *were* artistic. You stripped me down to a bare canvas and then painted the picture you wanted.'

A sad smile breezed across Alicia's mouth. 'I don't expect anything from you, Frances. I'm not seeking your compassion but you asked me a question and I'm answering it. No one was concerned about Beth. It was a foregone conclusion that she would be married before she reached twenty to a rich friend of the family with wealth to keep us in the position we were accustomed to but could not afford. Only things didn't go to plan. Our parents were killed in an air crash when she was fourteen.'

Alicia drained her whisky and hastily re-filled it. Fran was aware that she was not speaking directly to her but only reliving events of which she had been a part. Fran could have left the room and Alicia would not have noticed.

'Beth acted characteristically. She ran away with some friends who had more money than sense. There was a funeral to arrange, creditors to mollify and a huge white elephant of a house to be sold. She didn't even come to the funeral. There was no one but me to do it. I was a nineteen-year-old law student.'

Fran could feel the loneliness and isolation. She summoned back the full force of her anger.

'But what you did—'

'Oh Frances, you have no idea, do you? By the time the free drinks and holidays dried up I had turned the pittance left over from the estate into enough money for a deposit on this house and married your father. I'd been out of law school for two years and was just beginning to carve a career for myself when she returned. I searched for any tiny sign of remorse for what she'd done to me. There was none. She had come back for money. I only had the deposit for this house. It was, of course, afterwards that I wished I had given it to her, because then maybe she wouldn't have taken my husband.'

Fran heard the words catch in her throat. 'Oh my God, you loved him, didn't you?'

'Yes. It didn't start out that way. We were drawn to each other because of our mutual achievements. Just as misery loves company, so does success. To us it felt right to be together. So what if the earth didn't move or the lightning strike, some things are more important.'

Alicia re-filled her glass. Fran had never seen her drink this much. She returned to the couch a little unsteadily, her eyes slightly hooded.

'During her pregnancy I kept a sharp eye on her. One never knew what Beth was going to do. When I gave her the money to go abroad it was supposed to get it out of her system, so she would return and settle down. Yes, while she was away I took certain precautions but I had every intention of relinquishing any claim on you when it was clear that she'd grown up. She returned for more money and I refused to give it to her. Patrick thinks that she was seeing a private investigator to get you back but she wasn't. She was trying to find a way to extort money from me. She wanted the PI to get something she could use.'

Fran's head was swimming. Alicia painted a very different picture to her father. She realised that Alicia didn't elaborate on her feelings about Patrick or the affair. That was too deep.

'Did you forge documents?'

There was no hesitation. 'Yes, and I'd do it again.' Alicia looked directly at her. 'What exactly do you feel I did wrong? Should I have let you be taken away into Beth's world, where you would have been a fashion accessory being dragged from place to place when things were good? But as with all things, Frances, they go out of fashion. And when she tired of you, or when her so-called friends tired of supporting her, do you think they would have given two hoots about you? You were a bundle of curly hair, Frances, innocent and unspoilt.'

Alicia drained her glass. 'What was so bad about your life?'

There it was. The question that she'd waited years to hear. Fran couldn't breathe. At last it was her turn to bare her soul. Her turn to accuse Alicia of all the things she'd done wrong; her chance to recriminate Alicia for her failings.

'The love, Mother.' The word crept in unnoticed by either. 'You took me away from my real mother and then gave me nothing. All my life I've tried to please you. I've modelled myself on you in the vain hope it would gain your affection. I would have been content with any morsel going spare, but you didn't see me. The first chance you got, I was shipped off to boarding school.' Fran's voice had raised an octave.

'Children who go to boarding schools become much more independent, Frances, that is a fact.'

Fran thought of Kit and the boarding school she'd attended. The boarding school of hard knocks, yet Kit's independence couldn't have been more obvious.

'You'll never admit it, will you? You'll never understand how lonely it was while I waited alone, terrified and pregnant.'

'Maria was a fully trained nurse,' Alicia defended hotly. 'She had impeccable references.'

'Yes, and references are everything, aren't they, Mother? Maybe when you're boarding your dogs in kennels but not when your sixteen-year-old daughter is having a baby.'

Fran was aware that she should be using words like 'Aunt', 'Niece'. But they just wouldn't come.

Before Fran's very eyes Alicia began to shrink in stature. She was deflating as she fell back against the sofa, drained, as though her shoulders had been forced to remain staunchly upright to support all the lies. She stared unseeing into the crystal glass that had not moved from her hand. Fran waited, the anger contained in the charged atmosphere palpable. She wanted to shout some more, scream some more, but the fighting spirit had left Alicia.

'I've made many mistakes. More than I care to remember, but one that I will admit to is your incarceration. I realise now that that was unforgivable. I should have helped you. Just be sure that that day was one of the saddest of my life. I have never been able to show the affection that I feel and that failing has probably hurt me in more ways than one.' Alicia imperceptibly raised her eyes to the ceiling. Fran knew she was talking about Patrick. 'I have no one to blame, no excuses to make for that. But, Frances, tell me, do you understand the difference between right and wrong?'

'Of course.'

'Are you finally beginning, in spite of your past, to find your-self in the world?'

'I think so...'

'Do you have someone that you love?'

'Yes.'

'And are you following a path that is right for you?'

'Yes...'

'Then I'm not sorry for what I did. Maybe my methods leave a lot to be desired but I see before me a beautiful, intelligent, focused woman who now appears to know her own mind. I'm not taking credit, I am merely stating the truth. You have grown into a stable, level-headed person. It's not because of me, but in spite of me. You should be proud.'

There was more, so much more that Fran could have said, but the words wouldn't come. She wanted to hate the woman sitting opposite her.

'What about Jamie?' The last seed of anger sprouted before her eyes. 'For whose benefit was it exactly that you had him sent away? Couldn't you bear to look at your own grand... great-nephew? Didn't you want your friends to know about—'

'You were sixteen, Frances,' snapped Alicia, revealing no sur-prise at Fran's knowledge of her son. 'You would not have coped with a handicapped child. I ensured that he was sent to the best facility in the country. He is well taken care of.'

Fran could not argue with that. 'But didn't I have the right to know?' she cried.

Alicia thought for a moment before answering. 'At that point, Frances, no one knew what path your life would take. If you are the person I think you are, you would have insisted on keeping the child. You would have felt the responsibility as his mother to keep him away from an institutionalised way of life and though commendable would have been wrong.'

She sounded so sure it incensed Fran further. 'How can you possibly know that?'

'Because the guilt would have made the decision for you. Come now, Frances, you've been to see him, I assume. Even in your anger at me you have to admit that he is happy and that Thelma speaks with knowledge and experience.' She paused and met Fran's eyes. They were sad and unmasked. 'I kept the name you chose. It was something for him to take from his mother.'

Fran's mind raced. She couldn't argue with the facts but the methods were wrong. Alicia had already admitted that. What more could she ask for?

'Why did you visit him?' asked Fran quietly.

'Because he's my grandson,' stated Alicia forcefully.

Fran opened her mouth to refute this. He was her great-nephew but she raised her head to see Alicia's bottom lip quivering. 'Regardless of what you might think…' her voice shook with stifled emotion, '…I'm proud of you, I love you, and you are my daughter.'

Fran gasped at the words she'd waited all her life to hear. The tears fell again. Her eyes were sore but she couldn't stop them. She craved the anger and rage that had shaped her relationship with Alicia. She searched inside herself for something solid and real to cling to as she spiralled down beneath the waters of the unknown but any negative feelings she found were cancelled out against the knowledge that, whatever mistakes had been committed, they had been made with her best intentions at heart. That although this woman had been cold and immovable, she had taken care of a child who had represented searing pain to the best of her ability. She no longer had the strength to hate her.

A lone tear escaped out of the corner of Alicia's eye and travelled slowly over the contours of her cheek. She made no attempt to brush it away.

Fran raised herself from the depth of the seat and in slow motion bridged the gap that existed between them. As if by remote control she lowered herself down on to the sofa and reached for the graceful, trembling hand of her mother.

The two-hour drive from Hampstead brought clarity to Fran's mind. The unit she had always felt excluded her actually included no one. Her parents had constructed a façade and then chosen to live behind it. It was made up of lies, misunderstanding and hostility and she didn't want to live there any more.

It was hard to take in all the information she had learned in one day. She had no feelings for the figure in the photo either way. She felt no sense of loss for the woman who should have been her mother and she didn't try to conjure any. Whatever story held the most truth, her past was her past. That Alicia was not her real mother helped and hindered her feelings. She resented the lies but she understood her distance more easily now. Many things of which she had not been aware had shaped her life before she'd even been born. It was time to stop living in the past and move on.

She knew that her relationship with Alicia, whatever that might be now, would never have a fairy-tale ending and she would never fully understand what she'd done wrong, but at least her own perception of the childhood events that had marked her could now be focused on truth and it was her choice, her decision, to move on and go forward. All the will in the world would not change the cold, sterile operating theatre that she'd grown up in, but it was now up to her to ensure it did not shape her future.

It was two in the morning when she pulled up outside her flat. Martine waited on the steps as Fran had asked her to. She made no effort to touch Martine and didn't speak until they were inside the lounge. She then chose to busy herself making a percolator of coffee.

She sat away from Martine. 'I don't want to go into the details of the day just yet, but we do need to talk.'

'You look just how you did before running away from me in London,' Martine observed sadly.

Fran smiled. The decision that she was about to make would affect her for the rest of her life. Until now their relationship had been purely platonic. She'd been forced to examine and analyse her feelings about who and what she was and what she wanted to be. This process had been hindered because she'd never questioned her sexuality and had resigned herself to the fact that her muted responses to sex were due to the reality that she'd rarely received love and didn't know how to return it. The label she'd placed on herself and would be placed by others had also caused her concern. Whether right or wrong, childish or not, she had been frightened of other people's reactions. Now she had to decide which was more important: the need for constant approval or the chance to love and be loved.

'Martine, I… umm…'

'Please don't say anything. Let me say something.'

Fran nodded. It could wait a few minutes.

Martine took in a deep breath and let it out slowly. Fran could feel the tension she'd been holding inside.

'I've been unable to concentrate all day wondering what you were doing, were you upset, were you stifled, were you coming back? Two months passed today, or so it seems.' She bowed her head. 'I wish I had the strength to save you the trouble of ending something that has never really had the chance to start, but I can't. Not while there is even the smallest chance that I can persuade you to change your mind.'

Fran nodded. She knew the decision was hers. At this point she could still go back. A highly paid, well-respected job would not be difficult to find. She had not yet committed herself to any college or university. Everything could still return to normal, her safe life and the security of knowing what every day would bring.

It was time to decide if she wanted to go back or move forward into a life littered with unknown hazards, doubts and insecurities. She'd given up a career at which she excelled for a chance at a future reliant on a talent that may not even exist: it wasn't something she could see, only feel.

She looked at Martine hard. 'My life is changing every single day. I have no idea what tomorrow is going to bring. I'm a different person to the one you met in London and even I don't know yet what it all means or what I'm going to do next. I only know that I'm sticking with it.' She saw resigned acceptance settle on Martine's pensive features.

Her voice remained calm. 'I realise now that I was not scared of loving you because you're a woman, I was just scared of loving full stop. When you meet my mother, you'll understand.'

'When I *what*?' cried Martine.

Fran became aware of her own demeanour and began to laugh. 'Oh dear, Kerry was right all those years ago! I *do* talk like her.'

She moved to sit beside Martine on the sofa. Still they did not touch.

'There's no need to treat me with kid gloves any more. I'm as whole as I'm ever going to be.'

She leaned across and caressed Martine's cheek gently. This was not something she could control. While she had been at her parents' she'd had the distinct feeling that her other half was here waiting for her. She'd never felt that before, all she'd had was herself, a solitary being that remained confined inside her and reached out to no one. But now she understood how Martine had felt once before; she knew how it felt to be missing a limb.

'What I'm trying to say is that I'm ready,' she whispered, as she placed her lips softly against Martine's.

CHAPTER 19

Kit & Fran

'Surely it has to be your turn to buy,' Fran said, rolling her eyes as they entered the dining car in which they had spent many an AA meeting. 'After all, I'm a poor struggling artist with no means to support myself and a—'

'Spare me the sob story and go grab that booth in the corner.'

Fran did as she was bid and took a moment to observe her friend. On the outside Kit had changed little. The black canvas jeans and T-shirts were occasionally replaced with a pair of stylish boot-cut trousers and a pastel coloured shirt. Her hair was still short but cut more softly around her face, framing the chocolate brown eyes that dared you to disagree.

Fran watched as a gentleman taller than Kit reached around her for a couple of packs of sugar on Kit's right. His hand accidentally caught Kit's elbow from behind. Instead of whirling around to face the threat behind her, ready for a battle, she simply turned her head and acknowledged his apology with a smile. No, it wasn't the exterior of her friend that had undergone the biggest developments. It was the person within and Fran could see that from the other side of the room. Her demeanour was no longer dogged by wariness. It was as though every muscle in her body had collaborated and decided to give her a break. Fran still wasn't sure what had provoked the peaceful composure that now shadowed her friend and she wondered if Kit would ever confide in her.

'Don't come again,' Kit said, removing the cups from the trays. 'This has cost me a packet.'

'Jeez, you buy me one coffee and then you can't stop bleating about it.'

'Come on, tell me all the gossip. How is Mommy Dearest these days? Have you told her to shove all her Ming up her bloody great—'

'Kit,' Fran warned with a laugh. 'Incidentally, at my father's funeral she asked if we could visit Jamie together one day.'

'You're joking?'

Fran shook her head. 'Apparently she knew all the time that my father had corresponded with the home.'

Eventually, one day she would let Alicia come with her but not yet. She was far too possessive of her time with her son to share him willingly. She had eight years to make up yet and because of that she never missed an opportunity to hug and kiss the eager child or tell him how much she loved him. She remembered her third visit when, unaware of their relationship, he'd asked in a quiet, tremulous voice if she was someone's mummy. His huge brown eyes had waited for an answer as she'd urgently looked around the playing fields for Thelma to seek her guidance. Unable to see her amongst the children and families playing cricket, golf and football, Fran had tried to weigh up the importance of what she was about to say with Thelma's words about his well-being ringing in her ears. But she knew, had known from the first day she laid eyes on her son, that she was not going anywhere. She would not desert him. She had only her own instincts to trust and she made her decision.

'Yes, I'm your mummy,' she had said shakily, frightened at what his reaction would be.

He had peered at her suspiciously while looking around at other families playing in the field. 'Real mummy, all mine?' he'd asked unsurely, bringing his face close to hers.

She had nodded emphatically. 'Yes,' she whispered. 'I'm your mummy.'

Satisfied that this was true he had run away to tell Luke, his best friend, that he had a real mummy. Since then she had accompanied the school on trips to the safari park, funfair and waxworks museum, enjoying every minute of it. Her mother asked every time they spoke how Jamie was and Fran knew she was itching to visit him again but was waiting to be invited. Fran knew she would soon – but not yet.

'How are things with you two?'

'As good as they'll ever be, I think. We'll never be close like mother and daughter but at least we communicate. We can talk and, believe it or not, she has a wicked sense of humour that has been buried very deep. Since my father died, she's changed. It's as if she doesn't have to keep up any type of pretence any more. She spent all those years pretending not to love him.' Fran shook her head and thought of Martine. 'I'll never understand that.'

'And what's this about a trip to France?'

'Yes, I was going to tell you. I'm going to spend some time in Paris to study. It's the next step. I have to learn everything from the beginning but I'm excited. Although I wouldn't want you to think you're going to get rid of me that easily, Kit Mason. I'll be commuting backwards and forwards, probably weekly, to see Jamie so I won't be far away, but for art, Paris is the place to be.'

'For lovers as well,' Kit offered.

'Martine is going to look into the possibility of opening a salon there. I mean, if any nationality worries about health and beauty it has to be the French…'

Martine's face wafted into Fran's mind. She'd never thought that such a connection with another person was possible. Sometimes she was sure that they spoke to each other without ever saying a word. They were spending more and more time together and had talked about living together permanently when they returned from France. They both knew it was a big step but none bigger than Martine meeting Alicia, a meeting which had taken place the previous week.

Alicia referred to and treated Martine as Fran's friend. Fran knew that was the only level at which she was able to accept their relationship and was quite happy to play along. Happy, content and fulfilled, she didn't need to ram her sexuality in Alicia's face. Martine had won her over within minutes, talking about places in France that Alicia had visited as a child. Fran had watched them talk animatedly and she remained forgotten for a while, but she hadn't minded. She loved them both.

Admitting that had been hard, especially where Alicia was concerned, but she no longer considered it a weakness. They were still learning, both of them. Fran now understood that Alicia had never received love and therefore knew not how to give it, but she was trying and that was all Fran could ask for.

'Enough about me. What about you? How's college?'

Kit groaned and shook her head, remembering enrolment day. She had found herself huddled into the corner, angered by the sight of dozens of smooth bodies running from class to class.

'They looked so young. Though I was even younger than them when I first arrived in London. It was disgusting; all youth, innocence and Colgate smiles. I could smell the excitement and anticipation that surrounded them. It choked me.'

'You'll be fine once you get to know people.'

'Yeah, I could go for sleepovers and slumber parties where we could swap stories. Sure, they'd love mine.' Kit's head fell into her hands.

'You don't have to tell everyone you meet your life story, Kit.'

'I just feel that they're all acting out Scene One. It's too late for me to do that.'

'I can lie to you if you want me to. I can try to convince you that all your bad times are over and the rest of your life will be plain sailing, but Kit, it's probably not true.' Fran's tone softened. 'These are hurdles. If they're not hard, they're not worth having.'

'Is that a message off the Shreddies box again?'

'You know that you're going back when term starts so stop feeling sorry for yourself.'

'Thanks for the pep talk. Don't give up your day job.'

'I'm trying to be honest with you. You've given up drink. You're changing, Kit. Bit by bit you're peeling off pieces of the old you and sending them back to London, where they belong.' Fran smiled, devilishly. 'Of course it's hard starting college at your age but difficult as it is you won't let it beat you.'

Kit nodded in acknowledgment of her friend's words. No matter how hard it was she would not be beaten by anything again.

'How's the new job?'

Kit suddenly felt enthused. She had left her previous job, unable to work with Tyler after their last night together. Her trip to the employment office had resulted in an interview for a family business leasing and repairing vehicles. 'It's brilliant! The guys are great and I'm learning everything about the business. Eddie, the owner, is paying for my business administration course and I'm paying for the psychology course.'

'Hmm... Not too sure that those two subjects go together.'

Kit shrugged. 'I'm interested in both, which just goes to show the versatility of my starving brain.'

Fran pretended to yawn.

Silence settled between them and Kit pre-empted Fran's next question.

'No, I haven't heard from him and it's probably for the best.'

'Are you sure about that?'

Kit thought for a moment and nodded. 'I do love him, Fran. I'm not going to lie. I miss him terribly and wish he was still around. The last time we saw each other I had a choice. I know that I could have stopped him from leaving that night with a few simple words but no matter how much I wanted to say them I just couldn't. Call it stubbornness, pig-headedness, call it anything you like, but ultimately the words wouldn't come, which means I wasn't ready to say them.

'I know how much Mark wanted me to go with him to Leeds but I have to experience my own life first. I can't just relinquish my independence so soon after the almighty fight to get it back. I'm not ready to rely on anyone but myself. I've made my life here now and this is where I want to stay for the time being.'

'Could your feelings change in time?'

Kit nodded.

'What if it's too late? Perhaps he'll meet someone else,' Fran said, gently.

'I think about that possibility all the time. Some days it makes me tremble with fear and I'm tempted to give in but that's not fair. I wouldn't do that to him. I have to do what's right for me and if that means that Mark meets someone else, then I'll have to deal with that when the time comes.'

Fran sat back in her chair and clapped her hands. 'Good grief, woman! You've come a long way from the aggressive, self-centred, demanding urchin I met six months ago.'

Kit fluttered her eyelashes in response. She chose not to tell her friend that, nestled in the side pocket of her handbag, was an address in Leeds and directions of how to get there. The knowledge of Mark's whereabouts gave her the strength to get through each day, and lay waiting for the day when she could resist temptation no more.

Kit straightened up. 'I wanted to wait until now to tell you something a little sad.' She lowered her eyes. 'Remember that night when I quoted the stages of friendship?' Fran nodded. 'Well, I'm afraid we've reached stage five. I am now officially bored rigid with you and feel it is time to move on.'

They both laughed at the memory of that night almost a lifetime ago.

'We were a mess, weren't we?' said Fran. 'I wonder how we would have fared if we hadn't met that night.'

'Probably okay but much slower. We're stronger than we gave ourselves credit for.'

'Well, as our friendship is officially over, it's probably a good time to give you this,' said Fran, reaching for the handbag placed beside her chair.

Kit remained silent as she removed a gift-wrapped box complete with a purple bow tied neatly on the top.

'But… it's… I didn't… I mean…'

'Oh shut up, Kit, and open it!'

Fran chuckled as Kit untied the bow before removing the wrapping paper carefully. The box was blank, giving her no clue as to the contents.

'Hurry up, woman! I can't believe you're normally this slow and deliberate with presents.'

Kit smiled dryly. 'I haven't had that many, you know.'

She opened the lid carefully and swallowed when she realised what it was. She pulled it tenderly out of the box and shook it softly.

'You remembered,' she almost choked.

Kit watched as the tiny flakes of transparent snow and delicate pieces of glitter swirled and then settled on the scene of a cobbled Victorian street. She held the snow scene up to the light almost shielding her eyes as the tears fell on to her cheeks.

'Look what you've done to me. I hate you, Frances Thornton,' she said tremulously.

'I know, I hate you too,' Fran replied, moving forward to hug her friend. 'Let's promise that wherever we are, whatever we're doing, we'll always be friends,' she added.

Kit nodded emotionally. Somehow their lives without each other now would be incomplete. They had travelled back from the brink together. No one else had seen them stripped down to their bare selves. No one else understood the temptation with which they would live for the rest of their lives and no one else would understand any better than they themselves that it could be overcome.

They raised their coffee cups in unison. 'To friendship,' said Fran.

'And all those who sail in her,' added Kit.

'Cheers!' they said together.

ACKNOWLEDGEMENTS

I cannot complete a book without acknowledging the support, encouragement and patience of my partner, Julie. This book was written on a rickety dressing table that she fashioned as a desk. This lady has shared my dream for thirty years without once losing the faith that one day it would happen. She is my world.

I would like to thank Bookouture for giving this book the opportunity to benefit from both their tender loving care and their expertise. Knowing that this book is important to me, the team could not have been more sensitive during the process of helping it to reach a wider audience. I remain eternally grateful to Keshini Naidoo, Oliver Rhodes, Kim Nash and the entire fabulous Bookouture team.

I remain grateful and honoured to be amongst some truly talented and inspiring authors within the Bookouture family. Every single one of them has a place in my heart.

Finally I would like to thank the fantastic readers who have taken a chance on this non-crime book and have trusted that I will still carry them on an emotional and rewarding journey.

LETTER FROM ANGELA

First of all, I want to say a huge thank you for choosing to read *The Forgotten Woman.* I hope you enjoyed the story of the friendship between Kit and Fran and the challenges they faced both separately and together.

If you did enjoy it, I would be forever grateful if you'd write a review. I'd love to hear what you think, and it can also help other readers discover one of my books for the first time. Or maybe you can recommend it to your friends and family …

This was the first book I ever wrote and it was an exploration of how a shared illness and battle can unite people from very different backgrounds.

Although there are elements of the story that are not tied off neatly at the end I felt this was a realistic ending for the journey the two women had taken.

Thank you for joining me on this emotional journey.

I'd love to hear from you – so please get in touch on my Facebook or Goodreads page, twitter or through my website. And if you'd like to keep up-to-date with all my latest releases, just sign up at this link below:

www.angelamarsons-books.com/email

Thank you so much for your support, it is hugely appreciated.

Angela Marsons

www.angelamarsons-books.com
www.facebook.com/angelamarsonsauthor
www.twitter.com/@WriteAngie